Praise for
The Dream Peddler

"Fournier Watson's tale is gorgeous and carefully paced, with subtle tensions among the townspeople and lush descriptions of the natural world. Themes of coming and going, holding on and letting go, permeate this highly engaging, captivating, and, yes, dream-infused story."   —*Kirkus Reviews*

"What an astonishing novel. *The Dream Peddler* unfolds like a gorgeous poem, leading us deep into the lives of its characters and exploring the vast underground legacy of our own desires. This is the must-read book of the year."
   —Rene Denfeld, bestselling author of *The Child Finder*

"*The Dream Peddler* is a lovely, lyrical novel. Watson's poignant and gentle storytelling and the near-poetry of her beautiful prose captivated me from the beginning. I loved every page."
   —Louisa Morgan, author of *A Secret History of Witches*

"Martine Fournier Watson's vivid writing will leave you feeling as if you are a satisfied customer of the dream peddler."
   —Mark Tompkins, author of *The Last Days of Magic*

ABOUT THE AUTHOR

Martine Fournier Watson is originally from Montreal, Canada, where she earned her master's degree in art history after a year in Chicago as a Fulbright scholar. She currently lives in Michigan with her husband and two children. *The Dream Peddler* is her first novel.

The
Dream Peddler

Martine Fournier Watson

PENGUIN BOOKS

PENGUIN BOOKS
An imprint of Penguin Random House LLC
penguinrandomhouse.com

LIBRARY OF CONGRESS CATALOGING-IN-PUBLICATION DATA
Names: Watson, Martine Fournier, author.
Title: The dream peddler / Martine Fournier Watson.
Description: New York, New York : Penguin Books, 2019.
Identifiers: LCCN 2018028423 (print) | LCCN 2018029133 (ebook) |
ISBN 9780525504955 (ebook) | ISBN 9780143133179
Classification: LCC PS3623.A8728 (ebook) |
LCC PS3623.A8728 D74 2019 (print) | DDC 813/.6--dc23
LC record available at https://lccn.loc.gov/2018028423

Printed in the United States of America
1 3 5 7 9 10 8 6 4 2

Set in Bembo
Designed by Sabrina Bowers

To my mother and father,
who gave me everything

I've dreamt in my life dreams that have stayed with me ever after, and changed my ideas: they've gone through and through me, like wine through water, and altered the colour of my mind.

—Emily Brontë, *Wuthering Heights*

What d'ye lack? What d'ye lack? A dream of success—a dream of adventure—a dream of the sea—a dream of the woodland—any kind of a dream you want at reasonable prices, including one or two unique little nightmares. What will you give me for a dream?

—L. M. Montgomery, *Emily Climbs*

Prologue

The light of the gold harvest moon woke Benjamin Dawson from his dream. He sat up in bed, and through the window he saw that moon, larger than any he had ever known before. How did it grow so close out of the black night loam? He could tell by the thickness of the quiet that he was the only one awake in his house, maybe in the whole town. The blanket his body had warmed in the night was still gathered around his legs like a dozing animal. Every moment the sky was lightening toward its dawn, and he wanted to go outside and see that moon before it set. It seemed to be hovering just beyond the winter trees, as though anyone who made it through to the other side of the woods and the edge of the bay would stumble upon some monstrous glory, like the discoverer of a continent. At nine years old, Benjamin knew he could never reach the moon, yet still he had an urge to confront this one, with nothing between the two of them but the stinging, star-speckled air.

He slipped out of bed and pulled off his nightshirt, lifting the clothes he had dropped onto his little wooden chair the night before. The clothes were cold, and he shivered into them. He crept down the stairs and tugged on the black clots of his boots, pulled his thick brown wool coat over himself, and grabbed his cap from the high shelf. The front door was stiff but silent.

Chapter 1

The dream peddler came to town at the white end of winter, before the thaw. He had no horse or motorcar, but a low wagon harnessed to himself that he pulled along. He whistled as it bumped over the road behind him, while ahead the wind sifted off the surface of snow and hissed away. His covered jars and bottles tinkled occasionally in their nests. He winced up into the brightness of the sky, where the split, frayed ends of treetops swept at the clouds, his gloved hands tucked into the harness ropes crossed over his chest. His fast breath wraithed the air before his face and vanished.

The steps of his long walk shook the past from his mind and fragmented all the faces of the place he had left. He let them be blurred by the blowing snow. As the brittle day began to soften, he stopped at the side of the road, lifted a small bottle from his coat, and imagined the kindling warmth of the drink inside. He gave it a squeeze but slipped it back into his pocket untasted. The blank spread of farmland surrounded him now, but those houses were all set too far back from the road. He was looking for the homes of the merchants, where town lives bunched together like linen gathering along a pulled seam. As the road turned away from the sun, he came to a yellow-painted house that seemed a good prospect. Two children in winter coats were eating snow off their mittens in the little front yard.

They stared him down as he turned into the gate. He looked at them and raised his eyebrows as if to ask, *May I?* But they only gazed mutely, the melting snow dripping down their reddened chins. They watched him enter their yard, openly wary while curiosity held them still.

He climbed the few steps up to the porch and gave three sharp raps on the door. Loud enough, confident, not too insistent. Then he waited.

The door swung open on a woman of medium height, whose small brown eyes shrank smaller against the light. Her clothing was old but clean, and a faded apron over her housedress told him he had interrupted the flurry of morning chores.

"I'm sorry to disturb you, ma'am—"

"Who are you?"

"Robert Owens." He touched his hat. "Do please call me Robbie."

Her lips pursed at him, as if to indicate that the word "Robbie" would never cross them. She scanned his person, and then her glance went behind him to the two frozen children staring openmouthed at their own door. Then it went beyond, to the cart he had left outside the gate.

"I'm Abigail Schumann," she told him, not in a friendly way but as though she felt obliged to trade this information.

"Very nice to meet you, Mrs. Schumann. I can see you're in the middle of some work here, so I won't take up your time. I'm new to town, today, and I wondered if I might inquire about a place to stay? An inn, perhaps a boardinghouse?"

In the gloom behind her, he discerned the outline of an elderly man sitting by a window as if he'd been placed there to catch the light, the round of his shoulders dusted white with it. The left side of the man's face hung slack from its bones, and when his eyes met Robert's, he opened only the right side of his mouth. A faint guttural sound tried to reach them at the doorway.

Mrs. Schumann waved the children back to their play, but the children stuck.

"Well, Mr. Owens, I'm not sure what to tell you. We don't get many visitors who don't already have a family to stay with. You looking for work?"

"Oh, no, ma'am, not in need of any work. I make my own living and carry it with me. It's all there in the wagon, you see."

As the wagon was covered over with a thick tarp, she folded her arms across her chest. "No, I don't see."

Robert smiled at her but said nothing. Behind her the old man's mouth was still straining, right side hauling on the deadweight of the left as if trying to save it from quicksand.

"You a salesman of some kind?"

"Of some kind, yes."

"And what would you be selling?"

"Well, ma'am"—he scratched his chin, as though there had been a beard there not long ago—"I'd rather not say just yet, if it's all the same to you. My product is very special, you see, and it needs to be presented in the right way. It's not as simple as soaps or silks or things of that nature, you see."

She huffed. If she was curious, she was not going to let him see that. Instead she pointed a cracked fingertip down the road.

"Keep going until you come to a big brown house with yellow shutters. That'll be Violet Burnley's place. She's alone there since her brother died, and sometimes she'll take in a boarder. Had as many as three last summer when the extra farm help came through. If she says no, you'll probably have to move along."

He touched the peak of his cap again. "Thank you. I greatly appreciate it."

He retreated carefully down the porch steps, as if bowing from the presence of a monarch. Only at the bottom did he turn before walking back toward the children. He knelt on the snow in front of them and wiggled a hand into one of his pockets. Like animals hoping for food, they inched closer.

"For you," he told them, and he held out two small polished stones in the leather cup of his glove. They were blackish blue as night water, flecked with mottles of gold like some people's eyes. "Put these under your pillows tonight," he whispered to the children, "and you will have marvelous dreams."

One at a time, they reached into the stiff palm and picked out their treasure. "Mine is bigger than yours," the small one said. "Stop talking big," his older brother told him, "or the old witch Whiting will come and get you." Smiling, Robert eased himself up, patted their shoulders one at a time, and continued on toward the road. They stared after him a moment before turning back to their mother. "Can't we come in now?" he heard one of them whining behind him. "I'm so hungry for dinner my tummy is rumbling. . . ."

The dream peddler passed back through the gate and bent to pick up the wagon harness. As he was fitting it over his shoulders, Mrs. Schumann clucked her tongue, handed a cookie to each of her children, and sent them away with a smack.

"Odder than a three-legged duck," she muttered to herself as she went back inside.

★ ★ ★

The dream peddler plodded on down the road. Though he had seen the sun rise, now the clouds thickened and began to slough off their silencing snow, and before long the promised brown house bobbed into view. Two bare trees had tangled their branches above the gate, rasping back and forth like a fervent pair of hands. Though the garden was smothered now, he imagined it neatly tended below, its flowers unfurling into spring, imprisoned in their gardener's careful plan of borders and stripes. He could feel the winter weakening and the ground beginning to buckle.

Only a few hours ago had Benjamin Dawson left home.

Chapter 2

Benjamin Dawson was the son of George and Evelyn. Evelyn had been a Whiting, raised in the big, broad house with the wide, deep porch on the crest of the longest road. Looking down on the other houses, it seemed to have opened its mouth and let them tumble down from it long ago like baby teeth. The Whiting house also boasted one of the few pianos in town, and in summer when Evelyn was a girl, her slow practice notes plinked out from its open windows one by one, uncertain where to land.

When the time came for beaux to call, young Evelyn had few. Like other girls her age, she had achieved a certain look—the hair curling unbridled away from her temples, a brightening in her cheeks and searching eyes—all the physical signs she would soon fall from her family tree. But her mother was weird. Her mother was given to talking aloud to their garden in a high, wheedling voice. She could be heard by passersby, but they could never make out her words; they were not sure if she was talking to her flowers or herself. They were not sure which would be worse. She lit bonfires in the evenings simply to stare at them, not even using them to burn trash or leaves. She'd never actually been caught dancing around one of them, but it was suspected she must. She refused to attend church services, although her husband dutifully took their daughter every Sunday. Sometimes, when she came down the hill into town for shopping, she did not even appear to be clean.

Any potential suitor of Evelyn had to take this mother into account. Though Evie was plump and lovely, with her glossy dark hair and her wide, dreaming smile, she was not aware of it. Evie lacked the sort of showmanship of self that might have distracted callers from a disheveled mother wandering painfully in the background. When young men came to visit, it was impossible to do anything about this. Rose Whiting was sure to say something unsettling or to take no notice of them at all, trailing through the garden beyond the swollen gloss of windows without her shoes.

None of this could be said to trouble Evie. She felt uncomfortable around any young man who came on a summer evening, expecting lemonade and a suggestive swing within the blue-ceilinged porch. The boys she saw every day at school or church activities became strangers then, somehow fumbling and awkward, their feet always crossing and uncrossing, the sweating glasses of cold drink in danger of slipping down through their hands.

★ ★ ★

George Dawson was not especially brave. That summer before he asked Evie to marry him, he was helping out for cash on the Coldbrook farm a little way out of town, and every evening if Evie was outdoors, she would see him cycling back along the side of the road. Boys and men who worked hard always had a similar slope to them at the end of the day, Evie thought, their shoulders hanging too far forward. You couldn't see the soles of their boots, but you knew they felt thinner. Evie decided she liked the look of George Dawson coasting down the road. Sometimes she watched for him from behind the curtains in her bedroom window so he wouldn't be aware of her when he pedaled by. She didn't realize, as the stifling weeks passed, that George began to know her presence, like the pollen teasing his nose.

The prospect of Evie's mother took no hold in George Dawson's mind. He did not go for Evie because he was forward-thinking or had somehow missed the hints at borning babies who would be the descendants of crazy grandmothers. George went for Evie because she came down her front walkway to the edge of the road one day. Her right hand swung by her hip, and it was rounded out from a piece of fruit she held. As he neared, she offered it to him, hanging over the fence. The skin of it was bloodred and flecked with gold. It had come straight from the orchard on the hill behind their house.

George stopped the bicycle by touching one foot to the ground. She smiled at him. "You've an awful long way to the other side of town," she said. "Have this."

He couldn't take it from her without touching her hand. When he leaned in, the bicycle had to lean with him, like a dog that wanted to scent her. Palming the fruit, he did not know what to say next.

"It's just like the Garden of Eden," he came out with at last. "You've even got the name!"

She laughed at that. He liked a girl with a ready laugh, he thought.

"I guess you'd better not eat it, then. Best to be safe on that point," and she winked at him over her shoulder as she swayed back up the drive in her blue summer dress.

George took a sniff of the fruit before he placed it in his basket and pushed on. He wondered if any trace of her could be left now on its skin. It did smell a little like he imagined a girl would, if you held her, syrupy and dark.

He took his nectarine home and set it on the windowsill in his room. His brother had married the year before and moved away, so George had the space to himself, and with no one else there to grab it down and eat it slurping, the fruit sat, unmolested, until it began to wither. The nectarine took an odd way of rotting. First it softened down, and then the quiet bruises began to mottle its surface like gathering clouds, but despite the damp summer heat it grew no mold. Its skin wrinkled in until it was puckered all over, in a corner desert complete unto itself.

★ ★ ★

The wedding of George and Evie was as grand as any the town had seen. After the marriage in the church, there was a feast for those who dared, up at the Whiting house, complete with roast pig and glistening stained-glass platters of jellied fruits. The light that day was white and hot, the bleaching kind of light. The fields rustled in tune with Evie's stiff dress, and every so often the cicadas sent up their screech of celebration. Fiddlers stomped the back-porch boards so the people could dance in the grass. Children in their Sunday best went speeding through the crowds, with Evie's mother running alongside them, laughing. George held Evie's back under his hand, wondering at the skin beneath the taffeta, proud to be her husband, looking out over the whirling party as if he had created it.

George took Evie home to live in his parents' house while he and his father built another one on the other side of the farm. Between the two houses, the rows of wheat hush-hushed. Once they were moved into their home, Evie enjoyed running down sometimes to June Dawson's kitchen when she had finished her housework. They would sit together mending or shelling peas while the men nursed the fields.

* * *

Too many years for their liking, George and Evie remained childless. George harbored a silent suspicion that he could not make a boy of his own because he was unable to take Evie's candent body for granted. The unexpected freckles on her shoulders. The damp, dense hair between her legs. There was too much to know of her; he would never have confidence in knowing, never enter there casually and thus find his way with ease. When men were among themselves, they talked of their bedroom boredom lightly, joked even, and George knew if he could not make a baby, this must be the reason. He laughed along, pretending to understand it all, how a man could grow tired of his woman, could trace her so often he dropped those seeds at the middle of the maze without even trying, but George's laughter did nothing to tamp down his terror. There was no puzzling his way out when he was with Evie. He lay on her, pulling her soft hair over his open mouth like gauze over a wound, shocked every time.

Despite his bewilderment Evie did eventually come to him with the news. It was three years since they had been married.

"My mother says it's the time," she told him, carrying two plates of supper to the long oak table. George had built it so awfully long, picturing to himself as he sanded over its knots all the generations that would someday crowd there. So far it was only ever filled by the men who tucked in, eating with quiet purpose, when they came during the season for threshing.

"Time for what?" he asked, reaching for the salt shaker, waiting for her to sit down. She remained standing behind her chair, so he could see.

She placed her right hand over her abdomen. "You know. Time. Everything in good time."

An uncertain smile skirted the corners of his mouth. "Are you saying . . . ? How far along?"

She shook her head. "I'm not pregnant, yet. But she can tell. This month it will happen."

George sighed out his disappointment, pushing his plate away and resting his forearms on the table in front of it. "For Christ's sake, Evie, why'd you have to . . . ? You'll forgive me if I don't take your mother's word for it."

"Don't worry." She was smiling still, felt she was smiling for him since he was not yet ready, and pulling her chair in across from his and raising her fork. "This is the kind of thing she always knows. I was there this afternoon for a visit, and she is *so* excited. She is just over the moon."

"Really? And how do you think she knows?"

"It doesn't matter." Evie took a big bite of chicken and hardly chewed it before she swallowed. "She just does."

Maybe George's anger was enough to work the miracle. Making love to Evie that night was different. He had never come to her with that kind of feeling before. After marrying Evie, he had soon discovered that her mother was just about as harebrained as everyone said. George never complained about her. He knew the family he was joining, so why complain? But Evie, Evie was a sensible girl. She never took up with Rose Whiting's ideas. She seemed to tolerate Rose the way one did a small child, humored her moods, steered her away from people who were unkind. It was all one could do with the woman. And now here was Evie, saddened maybe, even desperate, coming to him with the news that her batty old mother had decreed it was time for their family to begin. He pushed deeper into her, starting to sweat. Evie was lying pink beneath him the way she always did, hips rocking.

Except this time she could not keep up with him; he wouldn't let her. In the end he collapsed on her softness, his exhaustion pinning both of them to the sheet.

At the end of the month, she was able to tell him, and he was happy, and he forgot all about her mother and the way the baby was conceived.

Chapter 3

Violet Burnley was just like her house: well kept, serene, and trimmed with lace. She sat Robert Owens down in her parlor and left him there, staring at a green parrot in a cage, while she went to organize tea and cakes on a tray in the kitchen. Violet lived alone but was always ready to entertain, her pantry stocked with baked goods and her furniture polished and doilied. As she carried her tray back into the room, Robert murmured, "What a beautiful bird."

"Oh, she's a terror," said Violet, setting the tray down on a side table and lifting the plate of sweets. She held it out to Robert so he could choose a cake and, of course, a doily to hold it on. "My brother doted on her, so now I can't get rid of her. Called her Molly."

"Does she say anything interesting?"

"Not a word, actually. She chirps and squawks and beats her feathers like a storm, but I have never to this day heard that bird utter a single intelligible word. Maybe the pirates sold her off their ship because she was no good."

Robert looked into the dark, round, droplet eyes. The bird cocked her head knowingly at him. "Oh, I don't know," he said. "There's something to be said for a woman who can keep her own counsel, isn't there?"

Violet grunted. "She'd be the first one around here who can, that's for sure."

Robert laughed. The cake was good.

"Miss Burnley, I'm awfully grateful to you for opening your home to me like this. I know I'll be paying you fair room and board, and some might view such a thing as just a business transaction, but I must say I don't, no, I don't at all. It's an entirely different matter when someone invites you into their home."

Violet sipped her tea. "I've never really thought of it that way, Mr. Owens. I enjoy having people in my house, I enjoy the company. Especially since I've lost my own Robert. Too much quiet, well . . . it gives me the blues, to be honest."

The dream peddler nodded. "I've never been that way toward the quiet myself, but I gather other people don't quite like it. Maybe that's why I'm so well suited to this kind of life. I spend a lot of time on the road this way, just walking, and I never even notice how much time I pass alone."

"What do you think about when you are walking from place to place?"

Robert shrugged. "You know, no one has ever asked me that before. I'm not sure I know what I think about. Sometimes I just listen to the birds, and the squirrels chasing each other around the trees. I whistle a fair bit, to entertain myself. I'm not really much of a deep thinker, I expect." He smiled at Violet in a most disarming way.

She set her cup carefully back in its saucer, and he did the same.

The room she gave him was upstairs, clean and simply furnished. There was a small bed with a patchwork quilt, a chipped white dresser with three drawers, a washstand with a basin and mirror. The window had been clothed in striped curtains. Robert walked over to it and set his valise down before parting the stripes to take in the view of frosted fields. In the distance he noticed a dark, lumpy form against the snow, bending and bubbling. As he stood pondering what it might be, it suddenly splintered into a dozen slanted black slivers, all moving away from one another. A crowd of men, he thought. A crowd of men talking together and now going their separate ways. Yet they moved out in a perfect ring of even and deliberate growth, as if the snow were really the smooth surface of a gray lake accepting a stone.

"This sure will do nicely, Miss Burnley," he said without turning around.

"I serve breakfast at seven, Mr. Owens, and dinner at noon. Supper at six. If you aren't here around that time, I'll assume you've chosen to eat elsewhere—does that seem reasonable to you?"

"Of course, perfectly reasonable." He turned to face her again. "I thought this afternoon I might settle in by going to the store and getting myself some supplies. Would you point me in the right direction?"

"That would be the Jenkins General Store. Just keep on going the way you found me and take a right on Main Street. You can't miss it."

"And, Miss Burnley?"

She turned back from the door. Downstairs her seed catalog was waiting for her. "Yes?"

"Will you please call me Robbie?"

She smiled. "Yes I will, Robbie, if you will call me Vi."

★ ★ ★

As always, George woke before dawn to feed the animals and milk the heavy cows. When he stepped outside, he observed a golden moon, biggest he'd ever seen, buoyed up on the tops of the trees. He thought she was beautiful, but she was not the first he had seen, and he turned away from her, trying to duck his head under the chill. Inside the house Evelyn, too, was rising to dress and cook their breakfast in the lamplit kitchen, while her shadow swooped behind her like a bat.

Usually the smell of potatoes boiling and ham frying would bring Benny down from his room, but this morning he was quiet. At the last possible moment, when she had the plates ready, she went to the foot of the stairs and called him. Back in the kitchen, she began carrying loaded plates to the dining table, brought a pitcher of milk in, and set it down heavily. Still there were no sounds from upstairs. She wondered if he could have caught another cold and shook her head against the idea. Ben, he had asked her once more yesterday to please start calling him Ben instead, but she kept forgetting. On her way to the stairs again, she glanced at the coatrack and saw that his things were gone, rolled her eyes, and went back to the kitchen. As usual he was up earlier than his parents, most likely gone out to the woodpile and forgotten to bring the wood in, climbing instead on the unsteady pile and jumping off into the snow.

When George came in moments later, he was alone, and Evie frowned.

"Didn't you drag Benny back for breakfast? You know it's going to go cold on him."

"What do you mean? I never saw him out there."

Evie went to the door and threw it open. A glance at the woodpile showed it was undisturbed. The yard was a silence beaded here and there with the sounds of animals in the barn, the few brave birds tapping at the shell of the quiet with their beaks. There was the fort Benny had made a few days ago, half collapsed where he'd stomped it down in the avalanche of enemy attack. His footprints pushed everywhere in circles and crisscrossed the snow, and George's wide-spaced tread cut through that jumble in a steady straight line. But there was no jubilant boy leaping about; there was no one there.

George came to stand behind her. "He's gone off to play in the woods awhile, I expect. I guess his breakfast will keep."

Evie felt the warmth of her husband just inches behind her back, and the fresh-air smell coming at her from both before and behind. She listened a moment while the forest gave up nothing. Reluctantly she stepped back to close the door, and George gave her a quick embrace as she pressed against him.

"Come and eat," he told her. "And what are your plans for the day?"

* * *

Evie had no particular plans that day. While George went out to mend fences, she began the week's baking. She kneaded and punched down her bread dough at the kitchen counter and looked out the window into the woods. Birches veined the darker trees with white. A fine, powdery snow began to fall.

As the morning shortened toward noon, she was wondering how much she should worry. It was Saturday, so Benny knew he need not be off to school, but his chores had all gone undone. He should know they would be wondering. Was it time yet to force on boots and trudge through the snow to the neighbors' homes? She imagined herself knocking on each door until it surrendered, opening inward. Unknowingly they would allow the snow and the little wind of her nerves to whisper into the house, touching the untroubled hollows of their own warm spaces.

"George."

"Mm."

"Something isn't right. Even if he lost track of time, Benny should be back by now, because he'd be hungry." An unbidden thought ran across her mind like a stray cat. "You don't think . . . you don't think he'd have gone all the way down to the bay, do you? The ice . . ."

George looked up. "I don't think so. He knows you can't trust the ice this time of year—I've told him time and again." At the look on her face, he stood. "Let me just go out for a little walk and see if I can't hunt him down for you. I'll give him a talking-to for making his mother worry like this, you can be sure."

★ ★ ★

Evie was careful not to burn her bread. She sat by the fire in the parlor with her basket of darning and worked her needle while the fitful breath of the baking bread tried to comfort her. When George returned, she was just lifting her first two loaves from the oven with a quilted pair of oven mitts. Benny used to pull them over his arms when he was three, with her tea cozy for a hat. He'd march across the kitchen clapping the mitts together like an organ-grinder's monkey with his cymbals.

She set the pans on the counter, and her shoulders rolled forward while she listened. There were no boisterous boy sounds behind her, only George's heavy shuffling as he removed his coat and boots. So when she turned, she knew the face she would be looking at—George, smiling to convince her he was still carefree, while his eyes began to glint their little fear.

"Looked all around," he said. "Thought maybe I saw some tracks going into the woods, but it was hard to tell. The snow's beginning to cover it all, so there wasn't much to go by. I tell you what." He bent over the bread to take a smell of it, drawing its warmth up over his chin with his hand. "I think I'd better get some men together and maybe start to have a look. I don't want to wait too long, seeing as it's a cold day. He may have got himself stuck up a tree or some such caper and be needing our help."

"Let me get some dinner on the table first," said Evie, sliding the bread out from under him and turning it out of the pans to cool. "You'll need a good meal in your stomach if you're going to be traipsing through the woods all afternoon." Mindlessly she took a knife to her bread, even though it was too soft and hot to slice yet. "When you bring that boy home to me," she said, "I am going to give him a piece of my mind."

So Evie brought George the thick slices of mangled bread still steaming and a bowl of her vegetable stew. Then she bustled around him while he ate, and he knew better than to insist she eat with him. After filling himself George went out to collect his father and some of their neighbors. Evie stood by the parlor window and watched the innocent snow drift down. It knew nothing of her.

Eventually June Dawson came over from her farm to keep Evie company. Her main intent in doing this seemed the hasty erection of a protective border of thoughtless chatter, meant to distract Evie from her missing son. June was a large woman, broad-shouldered just like George, and she seemed to be bursting out of her chair as she told Evie about the udder infection of one of their cows, the new organdy ribbon she'd admired at the general store, the muffins she'd made that came out hard as hockey pucks (it was the unreliable baking powder again; she didn't know why Jenkins only stocked that one brand), and finally fell back on the weather. Evie did not try to be polite or pretend to listen, though she nodded from time to time along with the rhythm of June's deep voice. June was satisfied strewing words about the house, just as she had sprinkled the lucky salt in every corner after it was first built. She couldn't help it, and Evie didn't expect her to. The words flopped like hooked fish on the furniture and the floor, piling invisibly there until Evie thought she'd smother from them.

June was talking on about the lateness of the spring.

"I can't say as I even remember a March so cold it gets into your bones. The ice on the bay doesn't seem like to budge, and here it is almost April already."

Evie shivered, and her movement transferred something to June, who fell briefly silent.

"I know what you need, my dear. A nice hot cup of tea. I wouldn't take a bite either if I were you, but let's just have us a spot of tea and maybe a small biscuit. You could eat a small biscuit, now, couldn't you, love?"

Without waiting for an answer, she raised herself out of the rocking chair and went to the kitchen, where Evie could hear her rattling teacups and banging the kettle clumsily against the faucet over the sink. June was a noisy person, seemed to believe in noise, in its power to rumble like an oxcart over anything unpleasant and squash it flat. Evie found herself grateful for the commotion; it did seem to banish the worst possibilities. Nightmare could not intrude upon June's blithe, bumping sounds. Nightmare required stillness.

Finally Evie sat down in the chair that June had left warm and waited for her tea. Maybe she would even try a biscuit. She smoothed her palms over the arms of the chair. It was the one George would carry out to the porch for her in spring, where she could knit or mend outside. The forest breezes would find her while she rested her eyes in the undulant gold of the fields. It was still too soon to move the chair. This year the spring was suffering an unexpected shyness.

Chapter 4

The dream peddler unpacked his few belongings. His clothing did not fill half the dresser, but he found it useful for storing some of his wares. He lined the bottom drawer with straw from his cart (sneaking it in in a sack, for he had a hunch Vi might not want her dresser stuffed with musty straw of questionable cleanliness) and carefully set as many bottles as would fit upright pressed together. Like crowds in a circus tent, they kept each other from leaning or falling, their cork heads dull and uncomplaining.

Dinnertime had come and gone, so without a meal Robert decided to go ahead and take care of his errands in town. He would casually announce his presence at the store, and this would begin to spread the word of him. In winter months people clung more tightly to their homes, so news of his arrival might travel haltingly at first. If he lacked patience, though, the manner of his coming might be spoiled, like a food that was cooked too hot and unwittingly burned.

There was a way he had of introducing himself to a place. He did not set up a booth or holler out his wares, never went from door to door. He carved out the way people would think of him without their noticing. He was not to be associated with carnivals or drifting confidence men. The only way to do this was to sneak in, to leak the nature of his products, and let time and curiosity act on his behalf.

The walk to the store was brief. Small white flakes of snow dawdled down all around him, but underneath was a faint earthy warmth, as if the snow might be losing heart. He hoped it would not turn to rain—there was nothing more miserable than winter rain.

Through its big front window, the general store appeared to be empty. Robert's entrance disturbed a small bell above him, and its jangling complaint brought a red-haired young woman out from a doorway behind the counter. When she was met with the sight of someone she did not already know, a look of surprise crossed her face, and she flushed and chased it quickly away with a winsome smile.

"What a nice surprise." She beamed as if the two of them were old friends. "It's been so slow here all morning I haven't had a soul to talk to, and now here you are. You're just like a gift."

Robert removed his hat. "Please allow me to introduce myself," he said. "My name is Robert Owens, my friends call me Robbie, and I'm new to your town."

"Oh, well, of course I know *that*." She leaned forward a little over her counter, and he took a step nearer. Her skin was fair but not freckled, and her eyes were such a light brown they were almost amber. Her nose had a pinched end to it, and the teeth in her smile were white and even. Her two eyeteeth were large, which gave her a hungry look. "I'm Cora Jenkins. This is my family's store. And what can I do for you today?"

By this time Robert had reached the customer side of the counter. He placed his hands upon it not too far away from her own. Miss Cora seemed accustomed to charming the men around her, and it would not do to disappoint.

"Just a few things I need to purchase. Shaving cream, one or two handkerchiefs, some bootblacking." He turned to survey the neat shelves and all their stacks and cans of goods. He moved down the counter to the penny candy, and she followed him. "A half-pound bag of these sugar hearts, with the messages on them. And a can of those blueberries, please."

She raised her eyebrows at this list that had begun so typically for a bachelor and yet ended so strangely. "A half pound of sweets! My goodness, you men sure are fortunate you don't have to watch your figures." She turned toward the hearts, and it gave him a view of her own shape in her brown wool dress, narrow but full through the bosom. Coming around to his side of the counter, she brandished a metal scoop, opened the container he'd pointed to, and began to fill a paper bag with his purchase. The hearts fell together with a beady sound like a threatened rattlesnake. When she went to weigh the bag on the scale, it was exactly one half pound.

"Well, miss, you sure do know your business."

"Just takes practice, that's all! I've been measuring out candy since before I could spell, so I guess I'm a pretty good hand at it by now."

She walked around the store, plucking down the other things he had asked for and fitting them all carefully into a larger paper bag. Back behind the counter, she began to do her sums on a pad of paper. She looked so much like a schoolgirl, biting her lip in concentration, that he found himself smiling at her.

"By the way, the candies are not all for me." He winked as he took a heart from the packet and slid it across the wood toward her.

"Thank you," she said, looking down at it. "But you know it's a bit silly to treat me. I can help myself whenever I want."

"Even so," he said, "now you've one as a gift from me.

Not the same as helping yourself. I like to think a gift is an important thing."

"Do you, now?" She left off from her pad of paper to look up at him. "Are you going to be expecting some kind of gift from me in return, then?"

He held his hands apart. "Not a thing. Not a thing, to be sure. I just meant that . . . now we can be friends."

"Friends! I don't know you at all, I'm sure."

"You can ask me anything you like, to remedy that."

She tilted her head to one side. "All right." She put the candy heart into her pretty mouth and took a small bite. With the sugar still on her tongue, she asked, "Why are you here?"

Satisfied, the dream peddler carried his paper sack of purchases back to Violet's house. From the front hall, he saw her sitting on the davenport with her hands clasped together in her lap. He paused there in the doorway, uncertain what it was that made him sure she was upset. She was simply staring out the window at the occasional drifting snowflake, parted from the storm like a stray bird left behind by a migrating flock. Then he realized that the caps of her knuckles had all gone white.

As he shifted his weight, the paper bag crinkled inquiringly, and Violet turned to see him. He crossed the room and set his parcel on the low table in front of her like an offering. "Vi? Is something the matter?"

She shook her head, and Molly the bird puffed herself up and squawked. Violet stood up and tossed the tea towel over the top of her cage to silence her. "Nighttime will be here soon, Molly," she lied, and pulled her arms across her chest.

"I'm afraid you've come here on an unfortunate day," she said at last. "I've had a visitor while you were out. My . . .

my friend Esther Coldbrook. Her husband has gone to join the search party. . . ."

Robert remembered the stone of men thrown into the snow of the field, the men who had been both stone and its ensuing ripple.

"There's a little boy gone missing since this morning. The Dawsons' boy, Benny. Can't think what might have come to him. They've been assuming he'd just turn up, but it seems George decided not to wait anymore and get some help looking for him. All the available men are scouring the woods, and the shore. . . . If he went down shore, that could be an awful thing. The ice is like to break under you this time of year."

"Well, surely . . ."

She turned from the window.

"I don't suppose you saw anything this morning, as you were coming to us? They say he hasn't been seen since before breakfast. I'm sure you'd have taken note of a small boy wandering off by himself so early in the morning, on a winter's morning, wouldn't you?"

Her eyes had gone wide around her questions, and Robert rubbed his hands against his coat. He patted his pockets as if feeling for cigarettes he had stowed there, then let them drop.

"Well, I'm sure I would have, Vi. But I think I was still a good distance away from here, if it wasn't even breakfast yet. It would have been quite dark, and I guess I wouldn't have seen him, even if he went by me on the other side of the road. When I woke up this morning, I was in a barn a number of miles west of town. I'm sorry I can't say as I saw anything."

"You came from the west?"

"That's right."

Violet nodded to herself. "No, I don't suppose you could be of any help to us, then. The Dawsons live out on the eastern side—the sun rises over their place. Theirs and the parents, George's parents. They must all be beside themselves with worry. I am going to get busy after supper and make a corn bread I can take over tomorrow, with maybe some cold ham."

Robert and Violet shared a thoughtful supper. Vi had a pretty dining room off her kitchen with pink patterned wallpaper and lace curtains. Under the oil lamp, the room was rosy, but it did not have its own fireplace. Instead it relied on the warmth from the kitchen, and the food went cold quickly.

After a roast pork and potatoes, there came the peach pie and a cup of tea. Robert leaned back in his chair and patted his stomach. "That was delicious, Vi. I must say I feel I've had some very good luck today."

She smiled absently. "The peaches were wonderful last year. I've got jars and jars of them. Every time I open one and eat them, I feel like I'm standing outside in the yard again, picking them from the trees." Robert had a sudden image of Violet in a pale summer dress, the tree light shifting across her floury skin, surrounded by peaches hanging heavy and blushed like her own dreams.

"I used to know his mother well," she said. "The boy. Since she was a little girl. I used to go up to the big house and give her piano lessons." She looked at Robert. "That was her mother's piano, sent out with her from the city—a wedding gift, I think. But you couldn't expect her to teach her own daughter. No. She'd be too busy wandering the fields or talking to the flowers in her garden. I used to hear her sometimes, mumbling under the lesson."

"Really?"

"Well, she's a bit touched, to tell you the truth. Just not quite right. No harm to anyone, but a bit hard on poor Evie,

I expect. She was always on the outside, with a mother like that. A bit left out of things. Sweet girl, though, from what I could tell of trying to teach her." She could hear her own voice struggling to get at the cold corners of the room, scrabbling like a trapped moth, but she couldn't seem to stop talking. "Though not very musical, mind you. Plunking fingers, she had, no sense of the light touch. Everyone thought George Dawson must be off himself, marrying into that lot. But it all seemed to work out just fine, and now he's their only child. It's just not right. He must be found."

She stood up, brushed her skirt, and began to clear the plates. Robert stood up quickly, too, saying, "Let me help you," but she waved him away.

"Certainly not. You pay good room and board. You'll not help me with any of this." She stacked his plate with her own and nested his empty teacup in hers. "I must get in there now and start on my bread. Evie will have enough to deal with without spending all day in her kitchen making food." Little did she imagine that a few miles away Evie was spending all her time cleaning house and punching down her own bread. She could have made enough bread to feed the whole town.

"I wish I could do something," Robert told her, leaning in the doorway of the kitchen he was not supposed to enter. But he was no longer talking about the housework. "D'you think they'd object to me? Maybe I could search with the men."

She turned now from the sink to look back at him over her shoulder.

"Well, now, I don't know," she said. "I'm sure they would think it's very kind of you. But it's a bit strange, is all. Because nobody knows you. And you don't know the boy you'd be looking for."

He tucked his taskless hands into his pockets. "I just can't help feeling I should be helping in some way, even so." He stared at her.

Vi considered. "You're a kind man, I think, Robert Owens. Since I'll be going down tomorrow with this food for them, why don't you let me ask. Hopefully by then there will be nothing for you to do."

Robert nodded and shuffled back out to the hall, found his way to the stairs and up to his tidy room. He sat on the bed, looking at the window whose curtains he'd left open. There was nothing beyond them now but the pitch.

★ ★ ★

Evie, too, was looking out the window of her house, in the direction of the trees she could no longer see. If someone opened the door, then a rectangle of light passed over the ground, and the boot prints all jumped out like dark rabbits from holes.

George had returned alone. The other men he'd gathered together had gone back to their homes for supper with their own wives and children, promising to assemble again the next day at Jenkins's store. Evie could picture all the families around their tables, everyone enjoying their meal and feeling sorry for the Dawsons. Food would still have flavor for them, and fire would still have heat.

"I'm going to keep it up myself, Evie, don't worry. I'll take a lantern with me. Maybe he's gotten into a barn and fallen asleep."

The night would be very cold, Evie thought. Benny needed to have been brought in before now, or he could freeze. In a neighbor's barn, the animal heat might keep him warm enough, but what would he be doing there? She had some idea that she was supposed to know. She was his mother, she should have some feeling about whether he was alive or dead. But she found there was nothing of sense inside her, only the fear whose tentacles had seized every vein in her body, so there was no more warm blood but only thick blindness sludging through her. She found herself still able to move, but she was slower, winding down like a neglected clock toward some dreaded stillness. She hoped she would never run out of methodical household tasks.

"You mustn't stay out there all night, George," she said without looking at him. "You must be able to go on still to-morrow."

"I won't stay out all night. But I'm not ready to quit yet, I still need a little more time."

There was a scuffling just outside the door. Evie's head snapped to the sound. "Benny?" At once her sluggish veins quickened, as every drop of her went rushing toward that little noise. She ran and pulled the door open and looked out into the snow. Her lantern light glanced off the beady eyes of a startled raccoon. She heard herself screaming at it.

★ ★ ★

It was morning again. Mornings were still going to keep coming, she thought. Not just for everyone else but for her as well.

Evie had not changed her clothes, as she had not gone to bed. She had sat in her rocking chair moving slightly back and forth, watching the fire and rising to stoke it from time to time. Her eyelids dried like corn sheaves, as if they had some-how been separated from her. George had come in, gone wordlessly upstairs, and lay on their bed. She knew he was awake, and she could hear the movement overhead as he rolled one way and then the other. He was like the dream in the sleeping mind of the house.

Evie realized when her eyes opened to the sound of George

plodding downstairs again that she had slept in flickers after all. Her fire was low and tired. She did not rise to offer George breakfast as she normally would have. She heard him moving around in the kitchen, probably taking bread and cheese from the cupboard and cutting off slices to eat. The pump squeaked as he worked the water from it. He would stand by the sink with crumbs falling down all around him, a thing that would have made her crazy at him before. After a moment of silence, she turned her head to see him looking in from the hall.

"I'll be going in to the store today," he said. "I thought you might want me to call down to your folks."

Evie nodded. She'd forgotten all about them. She heard George's bulk move to the front doorway and the clumping sound of boots being donned, a swish of moving coat and another of door.

It was early. The world was just beginning to blue. Evie stood and mechanically went to the door and put on her own things. She needed more wood from the pile, so she went out and hefted as many logs as she could into her arms. Inside she brought them over to the black log cradle, then looked behind at the snow she had tracked mindlessly over the floor. She went back then to the front entry to remove her coat and boots and walked to the kitchen for a rag to wipe the dirty water. It took a bit of time to build her fire back up again— paper, then kindling, then wood. How many times she had knelt at her hearth, feeding in paper, then kindling, then wood. All she could think was that they must not let the house go cold.

★ ★ ★

Later in the morning, while the rising sun was fanning the shadows of bare trees across the snow in full blue feathers, a knock came at the door. Evie's heart quickened. It might be

George, she thought, then knew it could not be George; he wouldn't knock at his own door. It might be some other searcher who had found Benny, some neighbor bringing him home. She might open the door to see him flopping slack in someone's arms. She went to it anyway.

It was only Violet Burnley in her winter coat and hat, holding two wrapped parcels in her scrawny woolen arms.

"Oh, Violet, hello," she said dully.

"I hope I'm not bothering you, but I just wanted to do something for you and thought I might bring down this dinner for you and George . . . or supper, whatever you need."

"Thank you," said Evie, taking the bundles. "Please come inside," she added automatically.

Violet stepped in and looked around, uncertain whether she should remove her things. She had intended to stay for a while and warm up, but she'd had no idea what the house would be like. For some reason she hadn't pictured Evie all alone here like this. She had imagined something more like a wake already in progress, crowds of purposeful women bustling about, other people she could talk to. This was different, this was just the two of them, with the shadow of a boy in between.

"I won't ask how you are holding up," Violet began.

"Thank you," Evie said again.

Violet made as if to move toward the parlor, then stopped self-consciously. Seeing her hesitate, Evie offered, "Oh, won't you sit down?"

"Thank you, thank you." She sat on the sofa while Evie stood in the doorway, still holding the ham in its paper packaging and the tin of corn bread cut carefully into squares. "Why don't you set those down in the kitchen?" Violet suggested gently.

"Yes, of course." Puzzled, as if her hands had forgotten

their contents, Evie went into the kitchen and put her gifts on the counter. She filled the kettle.

She came back and sat down across from Violet. "It will be nice to have that food for George when he gets back," she murmured.

"I have some news, Evie. Would you like to hear it?"

"Of course." The way Evie stared at Violet made her wish there were someone, anyone else, in the room with them.

"A man has come into town," she said, her voice tripping into the quickness of gossip. It sounded wrong in her ears, in the hush of Evie's stricken house. "He's some kind of traveling salesman, I believe, although for some reason he's being a bit secretive about what it is he sells. He seems all right, I think. I've agreed to let him board with me for a while."

Evie nodded.

"He seems an all right sort of fellow," she said again. "His name is Robert Owens. And he . . . well, he's heard about your trouble, and he wanted to know if he might be of any help. Maybe he could go out with the other men who are searching?"

Still Evie said nothing, and Violet rushed on.

"I did not intend to tell him. It's just I was upset when I heard, and he asked me why. I told him without even thinking."

Evie seemed to wake up to what was being said.

"Oh, no. That doesn't matter. It doesn't matter at all." She looked down at her own hands for a moment, the ones that had forgotten the ham and corn-bread packages. "He sounds a nice man. He doesn't even know us." She lifted her head. "If he wants to help look for Benny, I don't see why he shouldn't. But the group has already organized this morning, and I don't know what places they've checked and what they haven't." She sighed. "I guess if they're still looking tomorrow, I can make sure George gets word to you about where he should be in the morning, when they all meet."

Violet bounced her head vigorously. "Yes, that sounds a plan. I'll let him know. It's very good of you, Evie."

Evie said nothing. It was not good of her at all, but there was no need to argue.

For a while they sat with the silence holding its leaden breath around them.

"Should we have some tea?" Evie asked.

Violet sighed outward, wondering how long politeness would require her to stay.

"That would be lovely. I can warm up before I head back."

Evie rose to return to her kitchen. Violet would not realize she had only offered, had only thought of the tea because as she sat there, her mind had been racing over the ways to escape from Violet, from her staring white face with the huge blue eyes and spinster hair pulled back so tightly from her temples.

Chapter 5

The Whitings' phone rarely rang, since so few others in town even owned a phone. Messages were usually sent through the trusted bodies of children, coursing through back lots and parting the tall, golden grass of the fields like wind. They would arrive wherever they had been sent and gasp out their important words, waiting for a response and a payment in cookies, in lemonade to dampen down the dust coating their lips.

Once in a while, the phone would ring because someone had gone into Jenkins's and asked to use theirs. Normally Rose would not have answered the phone. There was something about its smug insistence on braying into the silence, interrupting her thoughts, that made her hate it. She preferred generally not to acknowledge its existence. If Sam chose to pick it up, that was fine with her. But today Sam was lying on the sofa in his office with another headache. She'd been waiting, ready to turn away any patient not in danger of dying, but the house had been quiet. From time to time, she nudged open the office door and peered at him. The last few years had deepened those curving lines across his brow and silvered the tips of his hair like a sly frost. For these hard hours of headache, he would appear older even than he was, and she did not want the noise to disturb him.

When it rang this time, Rose walked into the hall where the phone resided stylishly upon a polished mahogany side table and lifted the earpiece. By the time she set it down again, her face had changed, and she went to the wardrobe for her coat. Her hand was on the doorknob when she remembered, went back for the pencil and paper on the phone table, and scribbled a note for Sam. She left him sleeping still, turning over in his pain from time to time like game on a spit.

★ ★ ★

Robert was not expecting any customers yet. After he told Cora what he was selling, he assumed she would whisper to anyone who shopped in the general store. He must wait quietly while news of him spread through the town, testing each home like a spring virus. He sat in Violet's living room reading a book the afternoon she took her gift of food down to the family of the missing boy. If you had asked him what book he was reading, he could not have told you. He crossed one leg over the other and back again, felt the cloth binding shift under his fingertips.

In fact, the first client of the dream peddler was already outside. His name was Tobias Jenkins, the younger brother of Cora. He stood with his hands in his pockets on the porch of Violet's house, shifting his weight from foot to foot. He stared at the door a full minute, until it swung open and startled him backward.

"Come on," Robert's voice boomed jovially out at him. "I seen you come down the road, heard you come on up the steps, but I haven't heard a knock yet. I can't stand it any longer. A man can't think, you know, with someone just hovering outside on the porch in the cold, can't think at all. I had to put down my book." He jerked his head backward, indicating that Tobias should step inside.

The young man didn't seem inclined to speak. He glanced around the room, from doily to doily.

"Come on, now, don't be shy," said Robert. He sat down on the big rocker by the birdcage, folding his hands on his lap. He did not rock. The young man looked like he was still thinking of bolting, and Robert did not want to risk making him dizzy. "It's all right, boy. Miss Burnley's not even home. It's just the two of us men." He looked over at the sofa, and Toby slunk toward it, and his tall frame came down and dented it deeply. The sofa sighed as if pleased.

"You could start off by telling me your name. If you like."

Toby's face grew hot, which meant his skin was beginning to blush, and he inwardly cursed his red hair. "Tobias Jenkins, sir. I'm Cora's brother. Everyone calls me Toby."

Now Robert began to rock slowly, gently, as if by this movement he might hypnotize his prey.

He leaned forward conspiratorially.

"Well, son," he said. Low, even though there was no one else in the house. "Listen to me now. I'm going to go ahead and guess, since you've come to me, there is something you want in your dreams. I can make that happen, I promise you. And there's no need to be embarrassed. I've made dreams for all kinds of people, some of 'em kind of common, some of 'em downright strange. And I think I can just about guarantee that whatever you're hoping for, it's not something I haven't heard before. What are you, about sixteen?"

Toby nodded. "Seventeen next month, sir." His voice sounded too high to himself, and he cleared his throat trying to work it down.

"Young man, I can probably take a few guesses as to what

you might be after, but it'll be easier if you just go on ahead and tell me. If it's a dream I can give you, it's yours."

Toby thought about this. "So there are some you can't do?" he asked. This had never occurred to him.

Robert smiled. "Well, sure. I'm not going to pretend with you. Some things just can't be conjured, not with any certainty. Let's say a man comes to me and says he wants to dream of . . . heaven. So he can know what it'll be like, so he can find out if his mama is there waiting for him and all that kind of thing. I can maybe make a dream of heaven, but how do I know it will be a true likeness? I can make heaven for him, or for you, but would they be the same? Some things I have to refuse to make guarantees on. Most of the time, I can deliver. But there is the rare case when it is just something that's out of my hands."

Toby thought about this. "Sir," he said, "I think my request will be simple enough."

Robert's hands folded over his suspenders. "Go ahead, then."

Toby leaned in as the rocker came forward and halted, tilting against the floor. "I would like a dream of a girl. A good one."

"Go on."

"You need more . . . details?"

"I need a bit more than that."

Toby shrugged his big shoulders. "Sir, I dream about girls all the time. I'm sure most of my friends do, too. But here's the thing." He lowered his voice almost to a whisper. "I've never really been with a girl, see." Toby paused, as if waiting for some surprise to register on Robert's face. "A lot of my dreams, they just turn out bad. She doesn't like me, or she lets me kiss her and then she just runs away, and even though my legs are much longer than hers, I can never catch up. I'm tired of dreaming of running. I just want to catch her for once. I just want to know what it's like, and"—he was almost rose-colored now with earnestness—"I want her to like me, to . . . want me."

Robert thought about this for a while. The breeze outside bent the wash freezing on the line. "Tell me, is there a particular girl you would like in this dream? Someone you know, perhaps?"

"Oh, no, sir, I mean . . . I'm not particular, any girl would do, I think. I guess I'd like it if she were pretty."

Robert smiled again and let the rocker ease back to its center. "Toby," he said, "I'm quite sure I can help you. Give me just a moment."

Toby listened to the receding creaks as Robert went upstairs to his room. When he returned, he was carrying a case, just as gently and carefully as you would an infant. He set the case on its side on the coffee table and unlatched it and lifted the lid. He studied the rows of bottles carefully, selected one, and held it up to the light. Its contents were purple as jelly. He shook it gently, then opened a smaller, empty vial and poured a modest amount into it. He stoppered it with a cork and held it out gingerly, as if rough handling might damage it.

"Take this just before you plan to sleep," he instructed. "Take it all, leave none behind in the vial."

Toby held the glass tube carefully. "And what do I owe you, sir?" he asked.

Robert shook his head. "You know what, Toby? That's all right, that's on me. You're the first customer I've had so far, and I'll be satisfied if you just take that product and see how it works. If you're happy, feel free to come back for some more, and we'll arrange a price. See"—he lowered his voice confidentially—"not everyone is like you. Not everyone is willing to take a chance. Too afraid of looking like fools, I guess. But you will see, what I have does work, and if you would spread the word for me, why, that's payment enough for now. I'd be much obliged to you, actually."

"Well, gosh, Mr. Owens, that sure seems like a fair deal to me. I'll try this out for you." Toby stood up. Robert Owens stood as well, and the youth towered over him shyly. Robert grinned, and after a moment Toby mirrored him.

After seeing his customer out, the dream peddler returned to his rocking chair and listened to the young man whistling as he went back down the path. The little bottle churned in the darkness of Toby's pocket. The smudged warmth of their hands upon it faded quickly in the winter chill.

★ ★ ★

When Samuel Whiting finally awoke, he listened, wondering just how long he had been asleep. The roiling waters of migraine had tossed him on the shores of silence, and he knew that Rose had gone. He sat up slowly into his own stiffness, tilting his head this way and that, stretching his neck. At his age the sofa was no place to sleep, but he kept on doing it. He'd lie down with the intention of spending ten minutes waiting for the throbbing behind his eyes to subside, and come to hours later, blinking at he knew not what time or light.

Samuel didn't like it when Rose left him alone. Her presence made everything work: made the curtains breathe at their windows, the gold in the wallpaper brighten and preen. Without her, Sam was clumsy, splashing water over the sides of the basin, forcing the tight windows up too high until they shrieked. He stumbled over footstools that had not moved in twenty years.

Most people assumed Rose had bewitched Sam into the

marriage by her beauty, but Sam knew that Rose understood it was not the case. He only ever loved Rose because she was herself. He had never known anyone before who cared so little for public opinion, who was immune to prejudice and criticism. To him it indicated some kind of strength of personality, of dignity, which he could never himself hope to have.

Sam Whiting was unusually rich for a country doctor, who was often paid in chickens and jars of vegetables by his farming patients. Samuel's father had come from money and invested wisely himself, but his wife's fondest dream was to have a physician for a son. Sam never gave much thought to what he most wanted for himself. There was no need to think of money, so he could do whatever he chose. Pleasing his mother seemed like the best thing to do. Everyone he knew enjoyed pleasing their parents. Until he met Rose.

She was visiting her cousins in the city, and they brought her to a ball. Rose was wearing a yellow dress with her namesake flower tucked a few times into the coil of her hair. As she danced, the hair would make its way loose from its pinnings, a few black strands that stuck in the sheen on her neck. Eventually a golden rose fell down to the floor, and it was squashed and kicked around until it skittered off to the side of the room, where Samuel rescued it.

That night Rose laughed too loudly for her aunt's taste, ate too much to be ladylike, and danced until she went over on her ankle and had to be helped to a chaise to lie down. Never having asked her to dance, Samuel was just thinking how careless he'd been to miss that chance when he was prevailed upon to look at her ankle. As he bent over Rose and nervously probed the flesh above her foot with his stammering fingers, his coat fell open slightly and Rose could see into it, could see the crushed little flower hanging out of his inner pocket. Samuel never noticed; he was intent on keeping his features still, so his face would not betray how much he enjoyed the silk of the stockings between his skin and hers.

For Rose he abandoned his city practice and moved to a small farming town, because she did not want to leave the place where she had grown up. Their pantry was always stocked with gifts from grateful neighbors, and Samuel bought Rose fine-quality fabrics for dresses and a baby grand piano for music, and rugs and lamps with rose-colored shades, all with the money his family had and very little with money he actually earned. Sam spent his time peering into inflamed red throats and between women's opened laboring legs, and sometimes even into the orifices of farm animals, while Rose tended her garden and wandered the forests and eventually gave birth to the miracle of Evie.

He had no idea now how long Rose had been gone. He wandered through the rooms, and his gaze fell on the phone table. Had Rose written something on the paper there? He went over and picked it up, and then he found out where his wife had gone. He was stroking the hair of his beard with his free hand as he read, and he went on rubbing for a while as though polishing his chin, as though the motion would push the news into him through his skin.

Sam went to the front hall to put on his things. It was too late to join the party that was now looking for Ben, but he could go on his own. He would go out right away and start his own search. Outdoors he'd be able to breathe. The idea of it would shrink, surely, just like everything else in the cold, and he'd be able to see around it. As Sam stepped out his front door, though, a black horse trotted up to his gate and a flustered rider dismounted and floundered up the snowy lawn.

"Dr. Whiting, sir," he gasped out, and as Sam could see who it was, he knew exactly why he was here.

"It's Mary's time, sir. She's awful bad. I've come to fetch you back for her."

With a sigh Sam put on his hat and followed Billy Thomson down the steps. His own trouble seemed to dissipate on the air, spreading out into vagueness around this sharper pinpoint of birth. He went to saddle his own bay mare. The horses both knew their way, and the men leaned over them silently. Sam was cursing the timing of this arrival of Billy's child, all those months of waiting whittled down now unluckily into this day. This was their fifth, and every time Bill panicked just as he had with the first. Sam had no heart to tell him he doubted they would get there in time. Most likely the women would catch Mary's baby as it slipped out, its path already forged by the four that came before it.

In his head Sam tried to calculate the distance of the roads between the Thomson farm and the Dawsons'. He thought he might be able to check on the baby and the health of the mother and still arrive before dark. If the birth had been uneventful. If everyone was well.

★ ★ ★

The next morning the Dawson house's occupants rose heavy and slow from their beds. There was an unfamiliar weight now to their limbs and hanging hands. The beds themselves were swirled like eddies from the roll of sleepless bodies. Evie mechanically made the coffee in the kitchen. Rose came down looking rumpled, having lain in her clothes. She had forgotten to brush her hair.

"You didn't need to stay the night," Evie told her tiredly.

"Evie, I am not leaving this house again until we find that boy."

Evie pressed her lips together. "I hope you didn't find his bed too small. I know it's quite small."

"I am also small. It was just fine." She went to the window and looked out. "Your father still on the sofa?"

"I think so. It was late when he came in."

"I'll go wake him. He'll want to be ready when George is."

They ate their breakfast in silence.

★ ★ ★

Robert Owens awoke to the smell of frying bacon. He splashed his face at the washbasin and looked in the spotted mirror hanging over it. His beard was starting to come in again. Tomorrow he would shave it.

Knowing better now than to poke his head into Violet's kitchen to say good morning, he waited for her instead in the stiff pink dining room. When she came in, they smiled uneasily at each other.

"I made extra of the corn bread the other day," she said. "Mind you take a big slice, and plenty of bacon. You'll need a good breakfast if you are going out with the men this morning."

"I hope to, but I still have no idea how to go about it."

"I told Evie about you yesterday." She reached for the butter dish. "I expect they'll find you somehow."

"How did she seem?"

Vi forked a pile of bacon onto his plate. "Just about as you'd expect. She looks like a ghost, pretty much. No color left in her."

"I'm very sorry for her. I can't imagine anything worse than losing a child."

"Well, I guess that's one thing you and me won't ever have to worry about. Maybe we are lucky in a way."

Robert spent some time pulling his corn bread apart. "Maybe we are," he agreed.

As they were finishing, they heard a pounding at the door. Molly squawked a greeting while Robert followed Vi into the hallway. A big, bearded man stood on the doorstep, peering in, shuffling one uncertain foot.

"I'm heading to the store to meet the men," he said. "I've come to collect him."

Violet turned over her shoulder, and they both looked at Robert.

★ ★ ★

Up at the general store, there was a small knot of men, steadily growing. Men dark against the snow rode their cutters in from the farms or they walked from the houses nearby and the damp snow clung to their boots. Robert was aware of seeing the same thing he had the other day but in reverse, and instead of breaking apart they were drawing together. It gave him a strange sense of moving backward in time.

Two men arrived on horseback and dismounted. While the older one began tethering their horses to the rail outside the store, the younger one climbed the steps and faced the crowd. All the men twisted toward him like army privates awaiting their orders. This must be George Dawson. Robert studied him, figuring him to be quite a bit younger than himself, maybe as much as ten years. Only the burden he carried had stooped him a little, and sleeplessness hollowed his eyes, making it hard to tell. George surveyed the group, and when his gaze fell on the dream peddler, he seemed to know him as the only stranger among them. He came down the wooden steps toward him and held out his hand, and Robert took it.

"You must be our newcomer," he said quietly. His voice had a hoarseness, and Robert wondered if it was always there.

"Robert Owens."

George gave him a look he did not know how to interpret, then turned away sharply.

"All right," he called out, facing the group of men he had known since childhood. Most of them were shifting their weight from foot to foot in an effort to keep warm, but no one wanted to make any noise. It was as though they were already in attendance at the boy's funeral. Robert noticed young Toby among them, holding his hands tightly in his own pockets and whistling slightly through his nose as he breathed. When Toby saw Robert looking at him, he glanced away, embarrassed.

"As you know, we have gone through the woods around my property and my closest neighbors' and up behind the schoolhouse and the skating pond where Benny would go to play." He took a breath, and Robert felt it, too, the morning air entering his chest, sharp as pain. "We will go farther today, up by the Jameson and Lowell farms and Black Ridge, where the children like to go sledding." He paused. "Thank you all again for your help. May God be in our eyes today, because he sees everything."

The men all nodded soberly. Robert remembered a time when he would have said something similar. And maybe even would have believed it. George began the business of dividing them into groups and sending them out to the different areas he had named. Robert he ignored until he was done, and then he motioned to him. "Come with me," he said.

The two men walked along the road, heading eastward into the struggle of a rising sun.

After what seemed about a half mile of walking with no sound but the bite of their boots in the snow, Robert could stand it no longer.

"I was very sorry to hear about your boy," he told George. "Very sorry indeed."

George was looking straight ahead. "Yes, of course," he said. "Everyone is very sorry for us. And everyone is very glad it is not their own child. This is how I would feel, in their shoes."

Robert imagined the fathers in the search party going home in the evening to their warm homes. Would they feel their own good fortune? Would they grab their children and rasp the young soft faces with their beards?

They walked on a little longer, and George without warning turned off the road onto a narrow path heading into the woods.

"I'm pretty sure at this point that what we are all looking for . . . is no longer my son."

Robert was silent, not knowing what to say. Agreeing didn't feel like the right thing to do. The boy's body came into his mind, a lump as cold as the ground, then gradually warming, a sunrise of pink coming into the cheeks as if the days could somehow be wheeled backward. He sighed the useless wish into the wool of his scarf.

"Surely there must still be some hope? If he were injured and took shelter somewhere out of the cold but was unable to come home . . . we may yet find him."

George nodded. "That's what I said to my wife. But I don't really believe it."

As soon as they came into the shelter of trees, George stopped and spun so quickly that Robert wondered for a shocked second if George were going to strike him. But Ben's father only looked out over Robert's shoulder.

"Now, see here," said George. He humphed. "I went into Jenkins's store yesterday. I had to phone down to Evie's

father." He frowned down into the shadowed snow, drawing
a ridge through it with his boot. He swallowed and forced
himself to look Robert in the eye. "Cora tells me you have
something to sell. Something to do with dreams, she says."

"Yes, that's right. If you tell me what you want to dream,
I mix a drink for you to give you that dream."

"And this really works?"

The sun burned beyond the forest. It had escaped the
clouds and tossed down the pick-up-sticks shadows of hun-
dreds of trees.

"Most of the time. Not every single time. If you are not
satisfied after taking the mixture, I refund your money."

George appeared to be thinking this over. The doubles
of the trees on the ground were such a tangle it was as if the
two men stood snared in an endless blue web upon the snow.

"Was there something I could do for you, Mr. Dawson?
Is there a dream you'd like to have?"

"My wife is not doing too well. We need to find our boy,
whether it's for good or . . . the other. Have you ever heard
of those people, you know, who sometimes . . . they can dream
the future and things like this?"

"You mean a clairvoyant?"

"Well, I guess. I don't know the word for it."

"Mr. Dawson—"

George stood up straighter. "Look, you don't need to tell
me what a ridiculous idea that is. I think the whole notion
of selling dreams is nonsense, and normally I wouldn't have
any part of it. But this is a chance, something I can do, and I
am running out of things to do. I've prayed two nights, I've
racked my brain. And I have nothing. We wake in the morning, and we are in the same place." He took a deep breath.
"I don't have much hope, but if you would just try. Maybe

you could mix me up a dream of where he is, or where he might be, someplace more where I could look."

Robert watched a deer come into view, swivel its head to their breathing, and stare at them, terrified. "It is not possible," he said finally. "I can't make a dream tell you anything you don't already know."

George didn't even look especially discouraged. He sighed and began to trudge again through the woods. Trees came into his path, and he stepped around them slowly, sometimes to the left, sometimes to the right, weaving through the motionless crowd. Robert followed along until they came to a clearing, and there before them was the ridge, crisscrossed with the sled marks of the children's fun and then abandoned.

"I wish I could be more help to you."

George was beginning to circle the bottom of the hill, peering into the scrubby trees where the forest began. There was something in his figure, something that reminded Robert of childhood. As if George were the unwanted playmate who'd been deemed seeker in an elaborate game of hide-and-seek, and while he'd been counting to one hundred, the other children had all gone home. Robert ran after him, lifting his boots heavily out and out again of the deep snow. He reached George's side with little breath left.

"I will try to make you a dream," he gasped. "After all. Maybe there is something you do know, deep down, but just can't remember. I suppose it can't hurt to try."

Robert went back to Vi's for his midday meal, and while she was busy with her clearing away, he slipped up to his room. He pulled the drawer open gently, but the bottles still trembled. He ran his fingertips uncertainly over the corks, then plucked a few out. With a dropper he drew precise amounts from each one and mixed them in a new vial, stoppering it and then shaking it slightly. Then he waited, until the sun began to go down on its day and he thought the searchers would be heading home.

★ ★ ★

This time it was not Cora but Toby Jenkins behind the counter. No one else was in the store when Robert entered, and Toby smiled at him shyly. He leaned over the counter.

"I just wanted to say thank you," he said quietly, "for the dream." He turned his face slightly away as he spoke, as if he were really addressing some invisible person off to the side. "It was just what I asked for, I couldn't believe it. Anyone who wants to know, I can vouch for 'em your product really works, it really does."

Robert smiled slightly. "That's fine, Toby. I'm glad to hear it was to your satisfaction."

"I'd love to have another one, you know, whenever you have the time. . . . If you just mix me up one, I can come out and pay you, or you can bring it here with you next time you come."

Robert nodded, looking back toward the door. "That's fine, Toby," he said again.

"I expect the rest of the men will be quitting soon, won't they? For today, I mean. As it's getting dark out and all."

"Yes, I think they will."

A sigh of cold came over the two of them as the door opened, reproaching first Robert and then the boy. George Dawson stood there stamping his boots in the doorway. He wafted in the silver smell of snows and pine, the distant smoke of burning leaves. He stood and let himself soften in the warmth of the stove.

"Evening, Mr. Dawson," said Toby. Robert turned to face George and removed a small bottle from his coat. With his back turned to Toby, he blocked the silent transaction from view as he held the bottle out to George, who pocketed it in turn, saying, "Evening, Toby. Thanks for all your help this morning."

Robert left the store like any other puff of warmth escaping and walked back to Violet's house, and as he entered, she was still humming and clinking in the kitchen. He was satisfied she had not even known of his absence.

Chapter 6

When George and Sam returned once again without Ben, George noticed a difference in Evie's eyes. Now the hope that flickered out from under her lids retreated just as quickly into the depths. As the women went to the kitchen to get supper onto the table, he and Sam stood in the parlor in front of the fire.

"I was surprised we didn't have some luck today," Sam said. "I tell you I really thought, when we were heading out . . . that group you put me with, they were determined. I really did think we would find him." Sam was pacing the room, stopping now and then at the fire, rubbing his hands together, not looking George in the eye.

George watched his blustering and mimicked Sam's big hairy head with his own submissive nods. He understood this enthusiasm, almost felt it himself at times, dragging under his watery fatigue like the tide. This was what it was to be men, putting shoulders to the problem and shoving, waiting for it to collapse. It was how they farmed, it was how they lived: they did not know any other ways.

The four sat down to their supper at the long oak table and passed the dishes of vegetables and rolls around in a circle. They all took heaps of food they did not intend to eat. The silence gathered itself in tight around them. It grew so thick they hesitated to speak, as if poking at it with a voice might hurt, like punching a wall. Only Evie didn't notice the density of it, couldn't gauge the tastes and touch outside herself.

"Did you meet our newcomer this morning?" she asked her father.

"Can't say as I did."

George shot Evie a look she did not see.

"We have a traveling salesman staying at Violet Burnley's place."

She was tearing her roll into little pieces and dropping them on her supper plate. None of them made it into her mouth, but they formed a crusty little snowfall over her meat and carrots. "He was out this morning, too, to volunteer, to . . ."

Sam took a bite and chewed viciously. He was determined to eat, no matter what the situation. "Well, that sounds all right to me," he said thoughtfully. "Sounds like he must be an all right sort of fellow. What kinds of things is he selling?"

This time Evie's gray eyes met George's blue ones, and he thought for one second that maybe she knew what he had done, but all she did was look down at her plate and talk to her food.

"I don't even know. Hocus-pocus, I imagine."

Rose was watching George all through the evening. Her dark eyes reflected him picking up a book and setting it down again, staring at the window while it flickered the room's lamplit interior, turning and taking a cup of hot tea from his wife. She almost followed him when he pulled on his coat and boots to tramp through the snow to the outhouse. Sam, uneasy in the quiet, went to the Victrola to turn some music. When Rose saw George come back into the house and head upstairs, she left her chair and went after him.

Rose stood on the landing outside the door of George

and Evie's bedroom and listened to the quiet. There were no sounds of George puttering around the room or getting himself ready for bed, only this waxy stillness. As carefully as she could, Rose turned the doorknob. As if it understood her, it made just a whisper of noise, and then she was nudging the door open and exposing George as he uncorked a small vial and threw its contents down his throat. He had a grimace on as though he were taking some bitter medicine.

"George," she hissed, "George!" and she came into the room and closed the door firmly behind her. "What is the matter with you?"

He merely looked at her, like a child who'd been caught at something he never realized was wrong, the questioning bright in his eyes.

"I know this is a bad time," she began, then shook her head. "Not a bad time—what am I saying? unimaginable— but this—" She gestured at the glass still clutched in his hand. "This is not going to happen. I am not going to allow it, do you understand? I will not stand by and watch you let down my girl. Evie has been let down by the universe, don't you see? You can't fall apart, George. You have to hold her up for me."

George's shoulders rounded under her words as he pushed the cork back gently into the mouth of the empty vial and laid it down on a bedside table.

"I'm sorry," he told her.

"Don't be sorry, just don't fall apart. I won't have you drinking and . . . going down that road. I will not have it."

For a moment they stood facing each other in their different attitudes, Rose with her feet planted wide and her fists denting her skirts, George with his hands held loose and defenseless, head dipping downward.

"Rose," George whispered, "now, Rose, it's not what you think."

★ ★ ★

"You said you knew about this visitor, this Robert Owens?"

Sam and Evie were startled out of their silent stone positions, Evie looking up at Rose with her eyes like gray dawn snow.

"Yes," she said, "yes, of course we know about him." She pushed her palms along her skirt to the edge of her knees. "I told you he went with the men today."

Evie's mother stared her down for a moment. "What I mean is, do you understand what he is trying to sell here?"

Evie looked away again, as if her eyes had no strength left in them to hold still. Rose took a long breath, long enough to draw warmth out of the room, to leave less air for the rest of them.

"Are you aware of why he has come here?"

Evie's shoulders shrugged.

"He claims to be selling dreams, Evie. That's what George tells me. Little bottles of liquid dreams, any dream you might desire." Her breath flew out. "It's ridiculous," she said finally.

Evie shook her head. "I don't understand. Bottles of dreams? There is no such thing."

"That is apparently no matter. You take the potion he has mixed for you and dream of whatever you like. He's a charlatan. I don't want him anywhere near this family. He will find a way—he will prey on our situation."

Evie's face, which had been tautened by her mother's anger, settled back now into its folds of worry. "I don't care," she said. "He could not possibly make things worse."

"Toby Jenkins has vouched for him." George had come down the stairs behind Rose so quietly that no one had noticed him. "He took a potion, and it worked. He had his dream. Robert gave it to him to try, for free."

"I'll just bet he did."

"That's what he said, Rose. How do you know it couldn't work? How do you know?"

They faced each other.

"It's not possible, George," said Rose. "It's piffle."

"I'm a little surprised by you, Rose, I must say."

He was of course thinking about Rose's gardens and their hot blooms of bonfires, her strange ability to sometimes heal pain in patients her husband could not cure. No one ever called Rose a witch in front of George, but people would mention she was peculiar and then look at the ground.

"And I'm surprised by you."

George held his tongue. He knew she would forbear from telling them what she'd seen in the bedroom. But it puzzled him, that his revealing the true contents of the vial had made her more angry with him, not less.

★ ★ ★

That night George went into his dream languidly while Evie seemed to drift away from his side. The evenness of her sleeping breath took him down a road like careful footsteps. In his dream it is the high summer, a warm night with a large moon sifting its light over the landscape in a shimmering talc. He walks by fields where the tips of grass blades lean and quaver, and it seems he must continue walking here until something happens. In time a golden-gowned woman emerges from the dim horizon like a ghost, and he knows he must follow her. Pain distends his chest if he thinks of turning away, though he cannot even see who she is. He believes she is a stranger, but she's also familiar, like someone who has passed him many times in the street although they've never met. She leads him down to the water, where he watches her push a canoe away from the shore. There's a soft tearing noise as the boat slides off the bank, as if the land begrudges giving her to the water. George watches the lady dropping her paddle into the ripples on one side of her canoe, the cadence of paddling, then pulling it across herself to the other side. He looks around, but there are no other boats for him to take. If he can't follow her, he knows his heart will cease to beat in his chest and a cave of ash will be hollowed out within him. She is the spirit animating his heart, he realizes; without her he cannot live. He steps into the water. The ice of it shocks him. It shouldn't be this cold in summer, and instead of caressing his legs it bites them. As he wanders into the river up to his waist, he can feel the current straining against him, and he is not going fast enough to chase her. Petaled with moonlight, the black-white water needles the warmth of sensation away from his limbs. He feels himself dissolve like a doll of mud, the sand of him drifting down to the river bottom. His head remains above the surface, but his breath departs him anyway, seeking its home in her distant silver canoe.

Charles Bachmeier sat up into the darkness before his wife had woken. It was a strange thing not to hear Laura moving about below, making the coffee and breakfast by lamplight in the kitchen. As his weight left the bed, she rolled slightly and coughed but never opened her eyes. Charles dressed quietly and took his lamp downstairs. He began to make up the fire in the kitchen stove, raking out the ash before adding new coal. He watched the dark lumps take the heat into themselves and begin to glow, like a group of girls reddening at whispered compliments. Then he filled a pot with water for his coffee. He did not know how to make pancakes, so instead he laid some slices of bacon in a pan and waited for them to melt. As he was making the coffee, he listened for the hiss of the bacon beginning to fry.

He had stayed close to the house this past week, worried over the increasing depth of Laura's sunken cough. Today Charles could stay no longer at home, and he knew it was wasteful to worry over Laura anymore. If he did not go out on the bay to get ice for the icehouse, it might soon be impossible, and if Laura had no ice all summer, he would not hear the end of it. He jumped when he burned his thumb on the edge of the pan as he was lifting out his meat. He sat thoughtfully with his breakfast and a second cup of coffee. Once the animals were fed and their stalls sprinkled with clean hay, he should see the Banks boys coming into the yard to meet him, and he would harness Martha and take the sled down for their ice.

He clumped up the stairs to check on his wife once more. Cutting ice would make a long day of it, and he would not be back until nightfall. As he peered into the room, he saw that her eyes were open, like the blue places where water wells up in spring. He stepped over the creak of the threshold, came by the bed, and laid a hand against her cheek, which was fuzzy and cool.

"Good morning, sleeper," he said.

"I think I'm feeling better today." She smiled at him. "That was bad," she went on, trying to sit up. "It sure was."

Charles placed a hand on her shoulder.

"Don't get up. I've taken care of my breakfast, and I just wanted to see you before I go out for the ice."

"Oh, the ice, the ice, my goodness, I'd forgotten all about it. Yes, we must have that. But you be careful, Charles. Has it been warming this week?"

"Don't worry yourself. No, it hasn't been warm at all. It's bitter cold again today, so perfect weather for it."

Laura leaned back again, folded her hands over the blanket. She turned her head and gazed out the window, as if from there she could keep watch.

He waited with Martha as the sunlight settled downward from the tips of the trees to their thickened trunks planted in snow, but the Banks boys never showed. Shiftless, that's what Jackson Banks was, he thought. The boy would never make a farmer. It would be the city for him, no doubt, and a job in a factory. Just enough money left over at the end of a week to swing the girls across the scuffed floors of the dance hall. Never a penny saved. Charles would have to go without them.

There was a path through the forest down to the bay, and Charles rode Martha and the sleigh out of the yard toward the opening in the trees. The rising sun drew ribbons of shadow across the smooth snow, and Martha's hooves pocked into them, the sleigh runners whispering behind. He touched the horse's back lightly with the reins, not to urge her faster but to remind her of him, behind her, watching her effort. Her head bobbed up and down in its usual way, and from time to time she tossed it to one side or the other, steam from her muzzle straying up over the swiveling alertness of her ears.

The sun was brightening but the day refusing to warm as Charles came into that familiar thinning of the trees, and then the vastness of the ice spread out before him. Far away it was uncertain, rippled in places from the water's unseen movement, but here where he stood closer to shore it was still thick and faithful. Martha walked onto it without fear, nostrils quivering in the cold. Charles dismounted and unhitched the sleigh so he could fasten the long scraper to the ties instead. He would walk Martha up and down a few times to clear the snow from his work surface. Ice cutting was hard work, but Charles enjoyed it. He was always enthralled by the white precision of the blocks as he lifted them from their hold, like marble destined for the walls of some exotic palace in a land he would never see.

Responding to his gentle shake of the reins, Martha willingly dragged the scraper over the ice. Charles walked along beside her while the snow furled slowly onto itself like bedclothes pushing back. As he breathed, the air pinched the hairs in his nose together, and his chest took in the ache of it. His scarf that Laura had knit for him last winter began to chafe; he could feel the moisture of his own breath caught in the weave and the unhappy wetted wool rasping his skin in turn.

Once more around for Martha. She turned, and as her horse's eye stared at him, he felt that her obedience, bought with oats and apples, was also somehow the product of this shared discomfort. As he stopped her near the edge of their snow clearing and unhitched the scraper, it dawned on him that he hadn't brought any sandwiches for lunch. He'd forgotten that Laura was not up to do it for him. Now he would not eat until he had packed at least one load of ice into the icehouse, with the sawdust to keep it from melting.

From the sleigh he pulled down his pick and worked on chopping a large wedge out of the bay's deep crust. Every year when he did this, he would imagine the lives of the miners out east, the heft of the pick arcing through the air and catching in the niveous rock surface of the ice, lift again, arc again, the burning dazzle of the winter sun on sifting snow as blinding as the darkness of underground.

With his ax, too, he scraped and whacked in the ice until he had chipped away a good-size triangle through to the black water wiggling below. The ice was quick to reappear, like a cataract clouding an eye. It was at least a foot thick still, and he wedged his long saw against one point of the triangle and forced the blade up and down. He looked away to the hidden shore where the young trees spindled up from the water's edge, then back down to his work. Patient Martha pawed the ice and snorted, watching him.

Down one long line of the ice he worked, then back to the hole and sawed another parallel line beside the first, until he had one long, squared-off log of ice to saw into blocks. When this was done, he brought the two great picks from the sleigh and dug them into a block, hefting it first out of the water and then onto his abdomen, and staggering under its weight to the sleigh. He did this with block after block, Martha observing disinterestedly while her load back grew heavier and heavier. As he was nearing the end of this first pile of ice blocks, he looked up to see a figure coming through the trees at the edge of the bay.

He thought, at first, something about the gait and shape of the coat, that it might be Laura. Lifting his hand to his temple, unsure what to do, he finally stopped work and started toward the trees. From the hazy, distant figure he could eventually carve his wife's outline, sharpening her edges out of the cold as he had with the ice. He quickened his pace; something must be terribly wrong if she had dressed to come down and get him when she was not yet well.

The end of the braid she slept with still hung twisting down below her hood, but she smiled at him, a squinted smile defending her blue eyes from the glare, and she held up a bundle in her hand.

"What on earth are you doing, my dear?" Charles gasped out, stomping across the ice. It was goose-bumpy under his boots, here, like a skin.

"I brought you some lunch, silly!" she said, shaking her parcel of sandwiches. "I just knew you'd forget. I was feeling so much better, and then I thought of you maybe out here hungry and working away, and I knew you wouldn't come back in the middle just to eat."

"You foolish girl," he said, pleased, taking the sandwiches and folding her into his free arm. "You should never have strained yourself, feeling better or not. You'll end up back in your bed from getting up too soon."

"Nonsense." She patted his back—thumping, really—so he'd feel her hand through all his layers of winter clothing. "I haven't strained myself. I took Charlie with me." And a few yards away he could see the pony, whom Laura had named after him as a joke, standing perfectly still with his legs planted as though he had somehow grown there, not needing to be tethered.

Though he scolded her, Charles was grateful for the bundle. The hard work had emptied his stomach just as if he'd been digging inside himself all morning.

"Thank you," he told her, and as he turned to take the lunch back with him, he slipped in the powdery snow and went down. Scrambling to pull himself up again, his gloved hands swam against the snow until he found a wobbly purchase and lurched to a standing position. Laura sucked her breath in with a suddenness that alarmed him, and he turned to her, searching her face for signs of resurfaced pain. He frowned. She needed to get back to the house now, and he needed to return to his work.

"Oh, my God, Charles, oh, my God," she said, one mittened hand going up to her face and the other out to him as she stared down, down into the ice.

He looked back again to where he had just been lying, where his floundering had swiped away the snow the way children do, making angels. At first all he saw was a splotch of red welling up through the waxy layers, but, like a murmur he couldn't quite hear, it compelled him to move closer in. And there inside the ice was the missing boy, who must somehow have broken into the water and drifted down toward the shore, caught here by the tree roots two miles from his home.

Charles could remember coming across young Ben in the summer, playing with a birchbark boat he'd made, following it along the swirling current and leaping through the trees. He could hear Laura's breath shuddering behind him, but he stood in silence, looking down at the little gray face so perfectly preserved. It was like something out of a fairy tale, a sleeping spell that might be sundered with the right words, the right kindness, if the best tools could be brought to the task. He wasn't so far, really, from his house and his own little piece of the shore. His winter hat was gone, but a red knitted scarf still hooped his neck, the work of his mother's hands. Charles bent to the ice that lay over the boy in a brittle veil, touched it with his gloved hand.

"I must go and get the sled. I must bring the ice pick," he said.

"Don't forget the blanket," Laura whispered over his shoulder. "To wrap him in."

★ ★ ★

All that morning Evie and her mother moved through the household chores without talking. George and her father had left early again that morning, and Evie decided to bake some cookies for the men from the search. Every day she imagined there would be a man or two fewer, as each was drawn back eventually into his own orbit of family and work, but she wanted to make something to thank them with, and she needed something more to do. If her hands weren't always busy with some task, she would come unmoored, just waiting for news.

There was a low tap at the front of the house as she was
bending over to slide her first sheets into the oven. Her stomach clenched inward, her only warning against standing up
again. Outwardly calm, she was pulling off her oven mitts
and placing them neatly on the counter while her mother
went to the door. She stepped into the hallway, brushing invisible flour from her palms. The door opened, and a man's
silhouette came into the entry, the outline of Charles Bachmeier from the neighboring farm. In Charles's bulky arms
there was a bundle, a heavy gray blanket. As her eyes adjusted
to the light coming in around him, she was able to make it
out better, the thing he was cradling. She was warding off the
answer in his face as she held her gaze down and studied the
form. . . . There were two icy boots falling out at one end . . .
and near the center a mottled hand dangled from the folds. A
flood of saliva rushed into her mouth, and she heaved, throwing up onto the floor.

Chapter 7

It was a pitiless cold day to be crunching outside in the brittle-topped snow. The men were gathering again at Jenkins's store after the day's search, and they were a little earlier than the day before without meaning to be. It was bitter enough to kill the hope of finding Benjamin Dawson safe. So they drained back into town, the skin on their cheeks burned pink, limbs stiffening. Icicles along the eaves of the store flashed in the setting sun, like bared fangs.

In twos and threes they came in, clapping their gloves together trying to bring the thaw into their hands, pulling their scarves down to let the warmer air tingle their lips. They stood around looking at one another, expecting news to break between them, then silently turning out to consider the shelves in case there was something their wives had wanted, something they'd forgotten.

George arrived with Sam, both of them stamping their boots against the floorboards, George blowing on his palms even though they could no longer feel his breath. He looked at the faces circling him and saw his friends, and even the men he did not like so well. They all stood like dogs at attention, gazes shifting up at him and then away, as if they'd failed to learn some new trick but were hoping for kindness anyway. He was thinking he wouldn't ask them to continue on, not much longer, even though he couldn't stop looking himself. Maybe when spring arrived, when it was time to plow the fields and drop the little seeds into their secret places and he had work to do again, real work, or if Evie asked him to. Until then he didn't know how to return to her again empty-handed, without their boy. He stood there dumbly with his frozen brain dawdling, trying to thaw, trying to figure out how he had lost him.

When Cora Jenkins entered from the storage room, he saw. She kept her head down while she walked through the room of men, and he was thinking how Cora never did that. She always looked up and around so she could show off her pretty neck and eyes. She liked to take in the admiration of all who saw her, the way water would take the sunlight and glint it giddily back at the sky. Now she scuttled, pulling the end of her long copper braid forward over her shoulder. The men all turned instinctively toward her. They all knew that braid so well and had followed the woven trail of it many times with their eyes, down to where it ended at her waist. Now she was stroking it like a stray animal she'd picked up and must protect from them.

When Cora looked up, they could see that her eyes were outlined with pink, and the flirtation that usually flashed inside them was flattened now and dead. George walked over to the counter and placed his hand on hers. He meant to be helpful, but the cold of it made her start.

"Mr. Dawson," she rasped, cleared her throat. "Mr. Bachmeier was here."

He nodded. He clutched her hand and petted it.

"That's all right, Cora," he told her. "That's all right."

No other word made it into the air through the tightly closing silence, but they all understood that the search had been called off now, and they could go home and they would have to tell their wives to take out their black suits and brush them off, check for the small moth holes and mend them. They let their heads fall prayerfully forward because that's what you did, and you kept your eyes down. This was out of respect, but also because no one wished to look George Dawson in the face.

As George shuffled home with Sam through the stubborn whiteness, he was surprised to feel some tears trying to slither out from his eyes, but they froze in his lashes. It was too cold even to snow, too sharp for that kind of softening, and part of him was relieved to know now that Ben did not suffer this cold. And part of him could not even grasp that Ben was beyond the winter, beyond the world, would never feel it tugging at his body ever again. He was able to freeze and thaw and be immune, could be eaten, even, by pale, patient grubs curling underground and would nevermore feel a thing.

★ ★ ★

The men arrived home, and George found himself looking at his own door in a way he never had before. He had painted it green because that was Evie's favorite color, but when he entered there, his mind's eye always leaped forward to what was inside, the beautiful form of his wife turning toward him and the impish laugh of his son.

Now he could not cross over. For the first time in his life, he did not want to enter here, and he noticed how the rain and the damp of the bay had slunk under the paint and blistered, lifting it up in places from the underside. He pressed the handle and went in. The first eyes he saw there were Rose's, dark and dry.

"Upstairs," she told him.

He lifted each knee steadily over the risers of the stairs, hearing the thud of his foot dropping onto each one.

He looked into his own bedroom, where Evie was lying on the bed, curled onto her side. She seemed unaware of him, though her eyes were open and staring out the window where the snow was trying to emerge again, its white thoughts skimming out of the night's dark mind and wheeling back. He paused in the doorway, watching her, then went to the next door, which was his son's. Ben, too, was lying in his bed, and someone had covered him up to his chin with the blanket. George went over to him and looked down at the closed face. The skin was no longer a natural color, but the features were the same, the round bump of nose, the curved seams of mouth and eyes. He touched the cold hair, and it was still damp. He sat on the edge of the bed and drew back the blanket enough to take the small hand in his own. When he was done holding the hand, he replaced it gently by the hip where it had lain and pulled the blanket up carefully. It was only the stillness that was strange. He had visited Ben many times before like this, brushing the hair away from his eyebrows and sometimes bending to the peaceful forehead with his own lips, but always there had been that breath, the measured rise of the belly under its covers, the whispered release of air as it went down again, more of a warmth of life in the room than a fully formed sound.

After he tucked Ben back in, he went to his own bed. He sat on it to remove his boots but did not bother to undress. He opened his side of the bedclothes and jostled in next to his wife. He wasn't sure if she would want him to put his arms around her, but he did it anyway, pressing his face into the hair at the nape of her neck. It smelled familiar, like baking and smoke. She said nothing but covered his hand with her own, her sign of welcome. With his arms around her, he cried into her back, tears and tears until her hair was wet like their son's.

Evie lay awake listening. The house flexed its joints one by one, and George shuddered the bed around her with his soundless sobs. When the tremors subsided, she knew he slept, and eventually she heard his soft snore behind her. That snore had made her crazy with rage many nights. It was such a small noise, so unassuming, as if even in his sleep he would not have disturbed her, would do anything, in fact, for her comfort. Yet it didn't matter how small it was; it could keep her own sleep at bay for hours, as if sleep were a timid animal circling, giving a wide berth to the slightest sounds. She had seethed, wanting to clamp her hand over his face. Whenever she shoved him and rolled him over, the sound would cease, but it was only a matter of time until it resumed. It was like pushing a bar of Ivory soap underwater again and again only to watch it resurface, unsinkable.

Tonight she was grateful for the snuffle at her back, this familiar something to listen to. The darkness stroked her for hours, the snoring sucked at her thoughts until she was hollowed out, and she stretched into senselessness. She felt a prayer welling up from her heart that the night would go on, and the sounds of George breathing be the only thing she would ever hear, and the light never come again to her eyes and make them see. But at the edge of the bare, blackened trees, the sky began to flush, its first low streak spreading upward slow and sneaking, until the waking face of the world was a reddened sadness burning. She sat up.

Yes, she thought to it. *That is the way of you. This is your shame.*

Chapter 8

Robert skulked across the street from the church and watched them come. After that diamond-hard day of cold when Benjamin Dawson was found, the weather had loosened and the ice had given up its hold. Warmth came creeping in, abashed, and things began to drip. Melting icicles pocked the snow below them, and the sleepy surface of the bay broke up so it moved and lived again.

Outside the church the mourners hitched their horses and drifted together. They stood talking in low voices or turning their solemn faces toward the sun that tried halfheartedly to warm them from its field of clouds. Eventually the street quieted, and he knew the funeral was beginning when he heard the organ halt in its prelude, pause as if uncertain what to do next, and drizzle out the opening bars of "Nearer My God to Thee." There was the frayed sound of voices staggering upward into song. Up and down the singing wandered while Robert listened, thinking that to raise one's voice in mourning should be a wail and a tuneless keening, and hymnals had no business here.

It was Violet playing the organ. She had left the house well before him, expecting him to follow her later, but now that he was here, he couldn't go in. He'd been no use to Benjamin's parents, had only floundered after George Dawson that day in the snow like a child pretending to help, and even his little hopeful vial had done nothing. He stood outside waiting for Violet, thankful the cold had eased.

When the wood doors opened, he took an instinctive step back and watched a shrunken casket ride out on the shoulders of four stooped men. The people who had faltered into the church now spilled out of it fast, like pumped water. Robert saw the casket floating along on this dark river, past him into the cemetery's moored fleet of stones. Following behind was the family—Robert recognized George, so the dark-haired woman beside him must be Ben's mother. Close on their heels was an older couple he thought would be her parents, clasping each other's hand. The father kept reaching forward to try to place his free hand on his daughter's shoulder, until it seemed to dawn on him they could not walk like that.

Robert found himself staring at Mrs. Dawson's face. His chest seized at its familiarity. It wasn't her features so much as her expression. He had known it, he felt, once before, in the last look he'd seen on another beautiful face, a face he had loved. He remembered the surprise of seeing no more pain in her eyes, only blank disbelief.

He could see that the tears had been shocked out of the boy's family; wetness had left their bodies, just as breath does after a certain kind of fall. Weepers trailed after them as the rest of the mourners proceeded across the road, leaving a little fearful distance between themselves and the clump of stricken family. Men held the backs of their women steady with their work-worn palms, the rough, red shell of their knuckles turned toward the air. It was a parade of adults and only the oldest children, as though the Pied Piper had passed through town the night before. All the littlest children were at home eating Evie's cookies under the watchful eyes of their grand-mothers.

Sturdy laced winter boots shuffled through the melting snow beneath the dark funereal finery. They seemed to say that this was all that might be done; there was no such thing here as fancy boots, and working farm life would resume as soon as it could to turn the earth over this interlude of help-lessness. In the graveyard they gathered around the pine cof-fin and the minister's murmuring as they might have around a fire. The ground was still frozen. A small pile of ceremo-nial earth was mounded nearby for the mourners to sift from their fists over the boy's wooden roof. When this ritual was over, the casket was left politely in the graveyard. Only in private would it be removed to the shed where it must be stored until the earth had softened.

Robert shrank back as the people again filed past. They would go to Dr. Whiting's home now for some cakes and a muffled tea service. Robert thought he would wait there to take Violet home, but really it was Evelyn Dawson he wanted to see again. The damage done. Like a truant he slipped be-hind a big tree and hid there. He stood at an angle so the tree was between himself and the people as they spread out from the cemetery gate, and then he came forward.

The only person who turned and saw him was Evie. His stare had spun her around like a tug. She did it quickly, as George was guiding her toward their sleigh, and fixed her gray eyes on Robert's face. Did she know who he was? Or did she wonder? He couldn't tell from her expression, and she did not look at him very long. As fast as it flashed away, though, Robert felt it lingering on him like a touch. He never even saw Violet pass on the other side of the road, and as all the horses were untied and all the people climbed into buggies and rolled away, Robert stood alone, the snow shadows creep-ing toward him. He stood so deep in his own silence that he was unaware even of the much larger silence around him.

Until it was disturbed by something shuffling in the snow behind him, muffling its own breath, stopping now and again as if to measure a safe distance from him. Robert stepped back to where he could look along the blue edge of snow behind the graveyard wall. A hatted, mittened creature dented the drift, its rough tracks dotting and dragging away behind it, a little patch of wetness under its nose, which it wiped away on the sleeve of its coat.

"Hello," said Robert.

The boy shifted. He seemed undecided about bolting away or coming still closer. Robert smiled, and the boy took one step nearer. "Who are you?"

"I'm Robert Owens."

Another step. "I don't know you."

"No, you wouldn't. I've just come to town."

"Did we get a new schoolmaster?"

"No, you've got a new dream peddler."

"A dream peddler? What's that?"

Robert stooped down and scooped up some snow. He shaped it between his gloves while he spoke. "A dream peddler is a person who can make magic potions. Stir up any kind of a dream you want, and after you drink it, you have your best-ever dream."

The boy looked up at him. Mixed with the wonder in his eyes was a twinkling suspicion, common to little brothers who had often been teased. "Gosh. I've never heard of that."

"It might be I'm the only one."

"Oh." He rubbed at his freckles. He seemed to be thinking. "I don't see why they had to keep us away. We all know he's dead."

"Yes."

"And we're not allowed to go skating on the bay anymore. Not till next year."

"I imagine not." Robert studied him. Now that he'd made up his mind to acquaintance, the boy did not seem to be shy.

"Did you see his dead body?"

"No. I've been waiting out here, but I didn't go in."

"Wouldn't they let you in either?"

"Didn't seem right. Strangers don't go to funerals."

"But then why are you standing out here in the cold?"

"I don't know." Robert pulled up his collar. "And yourself? Why are *you* here in the cold?"

The boy pointed to a distant spot beyond the gravestones, where a lumped-up, lopsided snowman leaned into the trees. "I'm not supposed to be here. They wouldn't let me come. It's not fair. I wanted to, but everyone said I was too young." He squared his shoulders. "I'm eight, you know."

"I see."

"I'm Alistair McBryde, and I sat close to Ben in school, only we called him Dawson, and we even played baseball together, too. Sometimes." He kicked at the snow. "He was our fastest runner. Faster even than Richie Smith Elk. His daddy's an Indian."

"Ah." Robert eyed the sky, where the light was beginning to give, to yellow away from white like aging cloth. "Won't someone soon be looking for you?"

Alistair sniffled. "I don't care."

"Well, I should be getting inside where it's warm. So I can have my supper. I expect you'll want to do the same."

He touched his hat and turned away. He heard no more sounds from the boy behind, and he knew that Alistair must be watching him walk down the road beyond the low wall, until he would turn the corner. He and the stump of snowman staring where Robert had tracked through the snow.

When he arrived back at Violet's, she jumped from her chair in the parlor and headed out to the kitchen, as if she'd been waiting on him to start supper. He poked his head in to see her shifting pots around, lifting lids and clanging them down, her corseted back to him rigid under her dress.

"Everything all right?" he asked.

She turned. "Of course it's all right." She walked to her pantry, and while she scanned its shelves, she said, "You weren't at the service, were you? I thought you said you intended to come."

"I realized I didn't belong there. How could I say goodbye to someone I never knew?"

"I see." She stalked out of the pantry empty-handed, then walked back in and took out the day's bread. She lifted the lid on her butter dish to check the contents.

"It was a lovely service. Instead of flowers they had . . . Evie or someone had put spruce boughs down, mounds and mounds of them, and the whole church smelled like Christmas. I suppose flowers would have been impossible, and this was so much finer and fresher. . . . Just like a forest . . . for a little boy . . ."

She put the bread down. Robert broke her rule about crossing into the kitchen. He reached into his pocket and unfurled a white handkerchief like a magician, and Violet took it.

* * *

The moon had risen early, almost full like a white face turning away. The dream peddler put on his coat and went out into the sunset. Each house he passed exhaled a warm food smell into the road—a puff of bread baking, smoke. All the townspeople had gone in for supper, and he felt as if the houses themselves were now watching him, the flickers of light at their windows following him down Main Street and out of town. He walked away from them all, from the church and the store, and the distance between the buildings stretched like blankness between snowflakes at the end of a storm. The snow funneled the quiet toward his bootsteps and past, his movements swallowed like sound.

He left his tracks across the snow of a farmer he did not yet know. The bay tried to hide herself behind the trees, and as he snaked his way through the sparse fringe of saplings that leaned over the edge of the ice, his boots slipped under him. He thrust out his arms to grab at stunted trunks and steady himself. From then on he took each step on its own, pausing between them to stay upright, listening as he went farther out for the deep shock of sound, a first crack crazing away from him into its surface. Behind him the sunset flared, and the sky glittered with the gold underbellies of birds as they wheeled through it.

He remembered Evelyn Dawson, with the same feeling of a hand pressing into his chest, over the cave of his heart. If she had not been outside the town life before, she would be now. And he remembered her mother behind her, looking so like her that it was as if Evelyn's shadow were cast not by light then but time.

Over the back of the bay, the gray shadows rose. Out there in the thickest darkness, where the white ice turned black, a person might break through and be lost. Even here, he thought, if the burden were heavy enough, it might smash its way under and be carried away by the brackish current. He lifted a feeling of relief from that thought, pictured the dark, heavy water dense as tar. He imagined bending in supplication and tapping a small hole into the surface, putting his face to the hole like an egg painter blowing out an egg. Every secret of the past could be breathed down into it, and he could replace that water with all his breath.

Afterward Evie would think it was strange she'd been able to rise and dress herself to attend Ben's funeral.

She had never noticed so many buttons down the front of her black dress before. It was almost impossible to focus on them and fasten them. Her fingers fumbled as if they were nervous, and that was crazy because there was nothing left in this life for her to fear. There was nothing but the black dress and the dark, fancy buttons, too fancy, with the carved edges of roses digging into the pads of her fingers as she tried to force them through their holes. While she struggled, she thought about how she had made this dress herself, and she made perfect buttonholes, never too small. So why wouldn't the darn buttons go through?

Ben's she used to make a little looser for him, when he was three years old and learning to dress himself. She remembered the working of his chubby apricot fingers, so patient for such a young boy. When he grasped a big button and pulled it through and glanced up at her in triumph, there was the prize for her of the flash of a smile before he bent his head to the next one.

On the brown sweater she had knit for him, the neckhole had come out a bit snug. Talk about popping a button through a hole. Sometimes his head, which was golden blond back then, would get stuck in there, and like a brown bear he would shuffle across the room at her growling, wool sleeves flapping down at his sides while his real arms rose up clawing, and she would scream and laugh and run from him. That was the challenge, how long he could be this bear before the game collapsed, before the giggles came up through the growls and gave him away.

Afterward she remembered the funeral, but then only days in bed. Day days and night days, George coming and going and pretending to ignore her, George unsure what to do. She tried to imagine it hurting if she lost him, too, but she didn't think it would. That hole from Ben was big enough for everything else to pass through easily now, and she would feel nothing because nothing else could ever graze its sides.

The funeral itself was night. All attended in their darkest clothes. Even the church clothes of the younger people were inked in the pot just for this, little bud flowers and pinstripes of once-cheerful fabric still ghosting through. Hands touched her, and she hated it. To be grasped in sympathy by people who were suddenly strangers, as they were strangers to her grief. She moved through what was required of her, and then at the end came that moment when she was lifted out for one instant. It felt like a reward, the peppermint she was given as a little girl whenever she'd been still and silent long enough. She didn't know what had compelled her to turn around and see him there, the one true stranger beyond the crowd, but to look at his new, unfamiliar eyes as he stood against that tree was a shock that woke her. It shook her loose from the darkness, briefly, before she lost her hold and slipped back. He must have been the dream peddler.

Chapter 9

In the rooms of Violet's boardinghouse, Robert passed the waiting time. He waited in his bedroom, checking vials and polishing flasks, holding them up to the light and jiggling them into sparkle for his own amusement. He waited in Violet's doily-and-velvet parlor, tapping his foot. He waited in the dining room while they spooned hot foods into themselves, searching for talk. She knew he was waiting but did not know how long it would last, and she wished if all he would do was wait that he would go and do it somewhere else. She might remark on the sudden warm turn the weather had taken. Then he would suggest after a pause that he could help her put in her garden when the time came.

The funeral of Benjamin Dawson had brought everything to a halt, but that did not necessarily mean the dream peddler would have to move on. Some things had stopped for despair, not the daily needs of eating and sleeping and work, but the wants, the wants had quit. It did not seem fair, Robert knew, in the aftermath of loss, to want anything. Pleasure disappeared, went underground, bided its time. Sometimes, though, the waiting only gave the wanting time to grow, until it broke from its cage a bigger monster. What people tried to ignore at night would bubble over into their days anyway. If this was one of those times, he might have a good run here. Perhaps an exceptional one.

Robert sat with the volumes of Vi's modest library, leafing through books and wondering who would come to him next. He took it for granted he would one day soon be greeted by the teetering embarrassment of another teenage boy, most likely one of Toby Jenkins's friends, looking for the same kind of dream. He was caught off guard, then, when a young woman appeared at Violet's door one day, shifting her shyness from one foot to the other. While his surprise ebbed away he smiled at her.

"Are you here for Violet?"

She seemed so nervous that he tried to smile wider, as if that might settle her down. It didn't appear to, so he stood there feeling foolish behind his lavish smile, like the canny smile the wolf would have made at Little Red Riding Hood.

"She's just in the kitchen. I can get her for you."

There was the slightest shake of her head. She was a tiny thing, with dark hair swept back into a felt hat, a high white forehead.

"Would you like to come in?"

He leaned, trying to let the smile fall slowly and naturally and finding it tricky to do. Then the girl stepped in through the doorway so quickly that her head touched his chest and she bobbled back, mortified, her gloved hand flying up to her temple. Robert backed away from her so fast he stumbled as well, on the rag carpet, and then began to laugh low at the ridiculousness of it. To his surprise, the girl smiled a little, too, as if she got the joke, and she pulled her hat off, since her hand was already up there.

"Please tell me your name, miss. I'm Robert Owens, and I'm boarding here with Miss Burnley, as you can see." He drew her into the parlor by retreating slowly while he spoke. "I'm the dream peddler."

She nodded and sat down without being invited.

"I've heard of you, sir," she said finally. She balled her hands together in her lap.

"May I take your coat, Miss . . . ?"

"Blackwell. Christina." She seemed to be getting by on as few words as possible, and they all came out hushed, like secrets.

"Miss Blackwell. If you don't mind my leaving you for a moment, I can just pop into the kitchen and let Violet know you're here."

"No thank you," she said quickly. They looked at each other. "I came to see you."

"Me?" He sat down across from her, and one rogue eyebrow went up before he could stop it. "I must say I'm delighted. And what can I do for you?"

"They say you sell dreams. That's what I've heard from . . . from some of my friends."

She looked up over his head as though telling the ceiling.

"Well, yes, miss, yes I do. I'll tell you how it works. If you describe what you would like to dream about, I will mix a special elixir just for you that should bring about your dream. Once in a while, of course, it doesn't work as I intended. But I stand by my product, and I issue a full refund or replacement to anyone who's dissatisfied."

She stared at him. "So you'd have to trust people, then, wouldn't you? To be honest about their satisfaction?"

He smiled. "That's true. But then they also have to trust me."

Miss Blackwell swallowed and thought for a moment. "Are you a magician, then? Or some kind of a . . . wizard?"

Robert smiled again. "I don't think so. It's hard to explain exactly how it works. A little bit of magic and a little bit of medicine, I suppose. I feel a strong connection to the people who come to me. . . . Perhaps that helps."

Miss Blackwell looked embarrassed. "I will tell you what I want," she began. She tugged the ends of her glove fingers one at a time, as if she were planning to take them off, then pulled at the wrists until her fingers wriggled into their tips again. She continued to do this the entire time she was speaking.

"I've always wondered about . . . well, who I am going to marry," she told him. "It's really the most important question in life for any girl, I think. And there is this particular boy. . . . Well, you know, I've been to the field to pull petals off daisies, and I threw an apple peel over my shoulder last Halloween, but I couldn't make heads or tails of it, and I know those are just silly games. I think it might be possible to marry the boy I like, though he's never really paid much attention to me—" She halted here, swallowed again, and forced her hands to clasp. "I just wondered, would it be possible to have a dream about the future? Could I dream of my future husband?"

Robert's face became grave, and he tapped his fingers together thoughtfully.

"Well," he said, "I always feel it's only fair to warn anyone who wants that kind of a dream. It's a little bit tricky to arrange. Dreaming of the future, you see, can be done, but the future is not set in stone. I will give you a dream of your future husband as he is right now, let's say, but when you are ready to marry in real life, the dream may not come true. Do you understand what that means?"

Miss Blackwell concentrated on him. "I'm not sure I do."

Robert considered her for a minute. "I guess what I'm saying is, all we can do is try. Are you willing?" She nodded yes. "That's settled, then. Let me mix a dream of a husband for you and we'll see how we do, shall we?"

She smiled, glad the transaction was almost over.

"I'll just go upstairs real quick to create your product, my dear, and then we can discuss the matter of my fee."

The sound of his feet thumping the old wooden stairs rose upward, and for a while the young girl heard only the faint clinking of Miss Burnley washing dishes in the kitchen. She wondered if she might be so lucky as to escape without being seen. If it worked, she would tell all her friends about it, but if not . . . well, she did not want to seem a fool for trying such a far-fetched thing. There was the matter of Toby Jenkins, of course, but still . . . A boy was not a boy if he was not stupid from time to time. Her mother and father expected better of her.

She did not have to wait long before Mr. Owens returned, and she let out her breath as he held up a pale pink liquid glowing in a vial. From her pocket she pulled a knotted handkerchief and fought to work it loose while he watched her. As the white cloth fell open, he saw the coins she had saved, and he put out his free hand to exact his price from the pile. She stuffed away what was left while he offered the potion to her between his thumb and forefinger and gave her instructions for taking it. Between them his mind let out this pleasant image like a cobweb, of Christina Blackwell standing in her nightgown pondering the mysteries of the vial before swallowing its contents. When she tipped her head back, that whiter, barely creased skin of her neck would expose itself and his creation would slip down and pool within her. He hoped she would dream of her heart's desire.

She stood up, and Robert held the door open for her.

"Oh, I almost forgot," he said, reaching into his vest and pulling out a small paper bag. He unfolded the crinkled mouth of it and held it out to her. "Please take a sweet. A sugar heart comes free with every purchase, for the ladies."

Christina popped the candy into her mouth. "Thank you," she said around it as she turned away. Violet came out from the kitchen just in time to see him pat Miss Blackwell's shoulder lightly in farewell and both of them breathe in the smell of distant spring, chests uplifting to it.

★ ★ ★

Christina Blackwell had never known anything beyond the edges of her town, and she did not care to. She did well at her school lessons, because she had little else to do with her time but devote it to them. Her childhood had been spent in school and learning from her mother the ways of their women's world—she could darn stockings with fine stitching like a spider, and her bread rose puffed and golden from the pan. She worked white lace on a little row of pins and used it to trim nightgowns and tablecloths for her hope chest. Her piecrust fell apart in your mouth and dissolved like snowflakes, and her knitting needles quivered like a hummingbird's wings. All she needed now was the man to please with her skills. There was really nothing left for her to learn.

Her only ambition was to fall in love with a choice boy who also knew nothing outside their town and to live her life on a farm and populate the land with more hearty children. She would care for her husband so expertly he'd be known as the happiest man in town, with his stomach full of her good cooking, his Sunday-shirt collar perfectly starched, the back of his neck just barely wet with her kiss when he stepped out their door. What else in life could there be?

For all her growing years, she had imagined this, living her life as her mother did, while the man in her father's spot was only a blurred, faceless man. However, for some months now Christina had had her eye on a particular boy for the role. She thought it strange that he could not feel her covering him over with admiration, casting her vision of their future over him like a silver net, but he didn't seem to. The boy of her dreams was Jackson Banks, and he was boisterous and funny and liked to wink at the girls when he spoke to them. Christina had been on the receiving end of these winks. She found they did something to her, as though when he closed one eye, he snapped a lid on her breath, then released it again. Her parents didn't like him because he was so lighthearted; there didn't seem to be anything solid to him at all. Her father said he was a "smart aleck," and that was the end of the discussion.

Christina carried her pink potion rolling in her coat pocket as she walked home. She stopped just outside her own door and lifted the hem of her skirt, working a small hole into the even stitching she'd made. When it was big enough, she poked the tiny vial into it, concealing it inside her dress. She entered the house and hung up her things and smoothed her bodice, then helped her mother prepare and serve the supper, all with her secret close around her ankles like a hungry cat.

The family ate in near-perfect silence together. Christina was an only child, whose mother had given birth to her later in life, after several miscarriages had led her to believe she might never have children. Christina was such a blessing that she was tightly wrapped and overwarmed and carried her whole life like a piece of glass.

At the end of the day, Robert Owens's vision did come to pass in her bedroom, except she was not wearing her nightgown when she took his potion. She sat on her bed and pulled her skirt up over her knees to retrieve the vial, then cupped it awhile in her palms. She rolled it back and forth, letting it warm to her. A foolish waste of money, her parents would have said. But she found she did not care that it was a waste, or foolish. It was the first thing she had ever done that would have caused their disapproval, and she found herself both ashamed and thrilled by it. This thing, this little liquid, was hers in a way the lace and nightgowns would never be.

She uncorked her vial carefully and drank quickly. She found it tasted of sweetness and not much else. She had expected it to be bitter like medicine, as though having what she wanted must be paid for with unpleasantness. Sitting still for a moment, she tried to discover if she felt any different, but she didn't; she felt only full from supper. So she stood and began to undress in the chilly room and shrugged herself into an old nightgown, untrimmed. She had brought a jar of hot water for her bed, and she tucked it into the foot and slid in after, pulling the covers over her chest and staring at the ceiling. She should have blown out her candle then, but she let it burn on. The flame wobbled and sent beckoning, cloudlike shadows across the plaster above, and they drew her into a trance. She did not feel sleepy. She was so anxious to discover what would happen when she fell asleep that she could not conjure it. Dreamland, they called it. But it had nothing to do with land; it was only air.

Chapter 10

Once Evie made up her mind to rise, she could not go down again, could not sit still. All she could do was clean and bake and mend and straighten and scrub. How familiar it seemed, just like before, when Ben was missing and she did not know what to do so she did everything she knew. Just like, but without fear, a feeling that had abandoned her.

She must decide about Ben's belongings, which had been lying unused and seeming to thicken with stillness—she would put them in a trunk. There was one upstairs where they kept extra blankets for cold nights, and she took those out and began layering in some of his things. There were balls, and jacks to go with them, and puzzles and ice skates, a few extra sweaters and a few tin toys he would have considered himself too old for, trains and cars, which he kept on a high shelf anyway. They had watched him while he did the things of an older boy. Evie wasn't ready yet to throw or give them away, these castoffs that had been with him so long and had witnessed even his solitude. She placed them in the trunk, where they could remember in darkness, and she would not have to see them.

One afternoon she was finally sitting in front of the fire drinking a cup of tea, at George's insistence. His worried look had pressed down on her as hard as if he'd put his big hands on her shoulders, so she took the offered cup from him and sat. It was a bright day, that aching brightness possible only when there are no leaves on the trees to temper it. The sun flashed in through the windows and showed all her work and all the dust she had just chased off already finding its way back to the polished furniture. In a flash it made visible something she had missed. There on one of the windowpanes behind their good chesterfield was the print of a hand. Not quite a hand, but the four perfect fingers and then an arced streaking downward, as Ben had pressed it grimy to the glass and turned quickly away. What had he seen? A bird outside to follow, maybe, or a squirrel to feed. Or perhaps she herself had called him away, to his dinner or to help his father, something more important than daydreaming out the window. If he were here now, she would be scolding him for forgetting and touching the window when she'd asked him not to, for not keeping his hands cleaner in the first place.

The tea had scalded her tongue, which she held thick and furry in her mouth like a wet mouse. She blew, dimpling its surface. Her rag was nearby in the kitchen, but she found she could not make herself move to fetch it. The rag would wipe away that ghost of his hand, and though she had put all his things aside today, she still could not do it. He had been there, had left this pale, greasy wave, streaked his boyhood there for her, clear as a photograph. If she left it suspended for the sun to find with its searing cyclops eye, then just once a day she would have that, and only on very bright days.

★ ★ ★

When Christina Blackwell awoke, she was right away panicked, because she could not remember her dream. She placed her fingers lightly on her temples like a fortune-teller, concentrating. Her heart beat through, whispering the blood along, and then the dream fluttered in and lifted her eyelids.

This was unexpected. The face of the man in the dream was not the twisting comic face of Jackson Banks but a smooth, expressionless one with ginger freckles clustering under two light blue eyes. She wasn't sure she could grasp the dream's details through the haze of sleep. They seemed to be floating just beyond her, as trees and houses appear to drift across a morning fog. She remembered dancing in a white satin wedding dress, encircled in arms, and the freckled cheek close to her own, reflecting her own flush back at her.

The face was not unfamiliar to her. In fact, she knew it well. She'd caught it shyly turning to her sometimes at school and church, but she did not like the face and hadn't paid it much mind. His name was Rolf Baer, and his parents were immigrants, although he'd been born in the north and spoke perfect English himself. He might as well have spoken only a foreign tongue, she thought, since he never had anything interesting to say. He only *looked*.

Rolf. Christina sat in her nightgown with the chilly air nosing its way under to her skin and considered him. Her first impulse was to reject him, because he was, after all, Rolf and not Jackson Banks. Had the dream been wrong? Was the potion faulty? She did not think she could go to the dream peddler and complain when she had in fact dreamed of a wedding day and a husband, just as promised. Then she remembered, too, what the dream peddler had said about the future changing, and all of a sudden the problem became clear to her. At the time she had not understood him, but as she stared in her mind's eye at Rolf's pale, spotted features, it made sense. Rolf preferred her above all others. He must, if he had earned this place in her dream. But she loved Jackson.

Her dream had been a warning. If she wanted to change the future, she would have to take action.

★ ★ ★

The buds were beginning now on the trees, the tight yellow knots of them mossing the branches and belying how quickly they would spring out into the big, flopping leaves. Though thick mud was bubbling on the roads, the people began walking, taking the sun, young couples strolling side by side and letting their hands swing close enough to touch. And girls, girls in twos and threes could always be seen ambling, talking in low voices together, a sound that hovered around them in a midgey cloud. They clasped arms around each other's slender waist, and from time to time their bright laughter flew up like a flock of birds and settled again. Sitting outside the general store on a bench, one could admire the flutter of their spring dresses and the gentle sway of their figures as they left their sloppy wake in the clotting mud.

Everything was slither and slime, the spinning of cocoons and the rain running roads to slick and shine, and the leaves uncurling idly as they would. Robert spent a good deal of his time reposing there outside the store, that townspeople might see him and stop quietly if they wished to pass the time of day or make a private appointment with him. The girls all knew who he was and would slide him shy glances and then giggle to each other as they looked away. Most of them had no money to buy a dream and would hesitate to engage him even if they had. He didn't mind them; they were pleasant to look at, and he also counted on them to take the memory of him home to their families. He would have a place, then, at the supper table, the shadow of him cast there even as he ate his own supper with Violet far away. As talk of him circulated, he hoped the blood of the town would quicken with his presence.

There were often children playing about the store as well, coming in with their pennies for candy and using the wide porch boards to shoot their marbles. When wayward marbles rolled under his feet, he would tap them gently back out. If any of the children came crawling under the bench after a lost marble or ball, they'd be scooped up with a growl and tickled; he became a great favorite with them.

One afternoon Cora Jenkins came by arm in arm with her friend Christina Blackwell. They smirked at him, and he tapped his hat brim gallantly, murmuring, "Ladies." He gave no sign of knowing Miss Blackwell except to see her. He never hinted at having customers, ever, even as weeks went by and it became obvious, simply by his still being there, that he must. He kept his counsel as a priest would among them.

"He's a handsome man, isn't he?" Cora observed, casually as she could, when she decided they were out of earshot.

"Yes, I suppose he is."

"I wonder why he's not married? So unusual."

"Well, you can't be married and do what he does, dragging a wife and children along behind you, can you, now?"

"I don't see why not. The circus people all live like that. He could land himself a fine bearded wife, I expect." Cora laughed at her own idea.

Christina's voice went down low, like it was trying to hide itself.

"If you want to know what I think . . . maybe he has a gift. And he has had to make sacrifices for his gift. Maybe he wouldn't have anything left over, you know, for making his wife happy and playing with babies at the end of the day. Maybe he has to use it all up on his magic."

"Magic!" Cora considered this as she gazed down the road at the long muck and the wide-open pale blue sky rippled with clouds whose tide had gone out. "I don't know about that."

"Well, your own brother said his dream worked. He said it was *exactly* what he was hoping for."

Cora frowned. "Toby says a lot of things, you know. He'd be just as likely to brag about that dream if he couldn't remember it at all. Just to have a story to tell, I mean. Just to have something to say."

Christina was quiet for a while. She tired of walking along arm in arm. Because Cora was so much taller than she was, they could never really match their strides, and their hips jostled together uncomfortably. She slipped her arm away and stooped to check the laces on her boot. When she stood again, they walked on with a little space between them.

"He has magic, Cora. I know because I went to see him."

Cora stopped still in the street. "Christina Blackwell, you never did!"

Christina didn't bother to insist.

"Where would you even get the money to see such a man?"

Christina sniffed. "It's not so expensive as all that, really. I have some put away. . . . You know I used to help Winnie Macon with her sewing business sometimes in the summers, and she always paid me a little something."

"Did he sell you a potion? Did you take it yet?"

Christina glanced around, but they were almost out of town now and there was no one within a mile except old Mr. Hollister driving his horse and cart down the road in the distance. The houses were all quiet, with their dark windows reflecting the sunlit world like squares of motionless pond.

Christina said, as meekly as if she were confessing a crime, "He did sell me a potion. And I did take it."

Cora drew in her breath, then squealed it out like a swollen window forced open. "Oh, Chrissy! This is the most exciting thing I've heard about in a month." They both inadvertently thought back to the disappearance of Benjamin Dawson, and their conversation tripped over it, because you couldn't help but think of it but it was not supposed to be exciting—that was not the right feeling at all. Then Cora gathered herself back into her delight. She was good at that.

"You must tell me everything—absolutely everything. First you have to tell me how you ever got the gumption to go over to Violet Burnley's house to see him. Was she there? Do you suppose he gives her dreams, too? And what was he like to talk to? He's such a fine-looking man. I don't think I could talk to him at all if I went there, if I got the courage. I'd be hypnotized."

She didn't ask about the dream itself yet. Christina was like a butterfly—you couldn't blow on her, or she'd wobble away. Christina for her part was thinking she need hardly bother telling Cora a thing—just let her imagine it all for herself, and that would be easier. She shrugged her shoulders.

"I don't know how to describe it exactly. Miss Burnley was at home, I think, but she was cleaning in the kitchen, and he was the one answered the door. I'm glad. I don't think she ever knew I was there."

"And what about him? What was he like?"

"You know, I was so nervous I don't remember. He was kind, he was very warm and kind, like talking to your own father. You don't think about what he looks like when you talk to him."

Cora clapped her hands together. "That could be the hypnotizing effect!"

"Maybe. I don't think so. I didn't feel hypnotized, just sick to my stomach." She looked past her friend at a mob of birds in a nearby tree. They were so obvious now in the bare branches. By summertime those same birds would be invisible in the leaves and she'd hear them without ever knowing exactly where they were.

"I have to tell you about the dream I had, Cora. It wasn't at all what I expected."

"Maybe it didn't work? Do you think he gave you the wrong one, then?"

"No, it's not that. He makes up your dream while you wait for him, I don't think he could ever mix them up. It's just . . . Do you ever think about getting married someday?"

"Well, of course I do! What else is there to think about in this sleepy old town?"

"Do you ever think about who you want it to be?"

Cora turned her face away. "I don't know. Seems like we don't have a whole lot of choice in the matter, living out here. Sometimes I do imagine how great it would be if we could leave and go to a city where there would be all kinds of people to meet. Or if someone different came—" She stopped short.

"I know what you mean. But"—Christina dropped her voice low again—"lately I've been thinking about someone."

"Oh, I know." Cora began to nod, and her lips curved smug into her cheeks. Christina noticed they were still chapped from the winter cold, and small white disks of skin curled like salt flakes away from the pink. Christina wanted to reach out and scratch them off with her fingernail. "I can see that, Chrissy. I've seen the way you look at—"

"You don't need to say his name." Christina sighed. "He doesn't know, does he?"

"No, he doesn't know." Cora pulled at her lips as if she had read her friend's mind. "There's something about Jackson and the way he talks, the way he winks and flirts. . . . I don't know if he's ever been sweet on anyone, really. That's just something he does for himself."

"I asked Mr. Owens to give me a dream of the man I'm going to marry."

Cora looked sideways at her with a new admiration. "Christina Blackwell!" she exclaimed again. "You do surprise me. Who would have thought you had all this in you?"

"Not me, that's one thing. But somehow, I don't know, this feeling came over me and I just had to find out. I thought there was a chance he might be able to help me. But it wasn't at all what I thought."

"What did you dream about, then?"

"Well, I did dream about my wedding, and I could see my husband plain as day—but it wasn't Jackson. It was Rolf Baer."

Cora cackled at that. "Oh, my goodness. Well, I can't say as I'm surprised. That boy is definitely crazy about you. He stares when he's around you like he thinks you're going to disappear if he takes his eyes off you."

"But don't you see? I don't want to marry him."

"Oh, I don't know," Cora said thoughtfully. "That might not be so bad."

Christina could not tell if she was being teased.

"What on earth can you mean, 'not so bad'?"

"I just meant . . . to be married to someone who adores you like that."

Christina thought for a minute. "Maybe," she said. "But . . . but I want to adore him back."

Cora sighed. "Well, that's a tall order, now, isn't it? Kind of hard to picture anyone worshipping that long, freckly mug."

"Oh, I know!" Christina burst out. "I don't want to! I don't want to marry him. I wonder what you think about . . . the possibility that the dream was wrong."

"Of course it could be wrong," said Cora immediately, comfortingly. "Dreams are just dreams. Did he tell you about his guarantee? I think you can get your money back."

"Sure he did. I don't want my money back. But I have this idea that my dream was . . . just one possible future. There could be others. Don't you think? If Rolf came to me in my dream because he wants to be my husband and maybe he's my only choice right at this moment. But maybe I could change that, too."

Cora was thoughtful for a while. She lifted her arms up to the sun and spun around, and her red hair blazed and seemed also to kindle everything around her. Christina admired her friend. If anyone could have Jackson Banks's attention, it would be her, this living doll with her skin so white it was almost like frosted glass. Frosted glass with a red wine poured into it.

"We will just have to do something about this," Cora said finally. "Let's put our heads together and think how we can shift old Jackson's attention off his jokes and onto you. It won't be so hard, I don't think. He just needs to be put off his balance, you know? Then we can tip him in your direction."

Chapter 11

Evie was going into town today. She did not like to see people since the funeral, their glassy, pitying eyes, so she'd had George going in for sugar and tea, little things as she missed them. Today she changed her mind. It was doing no good to hide. Even though she didn't really care whether she was doing herself any good, she did care about George. She could still see him vaguely, moving through the murky house around her, as though she were encountering him underwater. It even felt like her limbs were weighted down with it, propelling her sluggishly through the depths. She felt George's worry as it drifted and ensnared her like seaweed, and she thought she could try to be normal, for him. Even if she could only recover a surface of herself, she thought it could work; she could help him have a life.

So she put on the spring dress she would usually wear if she were visiting, a blue dress not so shabby as her housedress but maybe not good enough anymore for church. She pulled it down over her head, and she felt pale and soft, vulnerable like a grub turned up by the plow. As the dress hung loosely around her, she noticed for the first time how her body had shrunk, how she'd lost the fat of herself and the curves somewhere. She was more like a young girl now. She'd gone back in time to when she was still growing and the flinty bones inside her used to show through the skin.

She went to the mirror over their old brown dresser and studied herself. She smoothed her hair back from her temples out of habit—the curls there would not be put down. Her chest before had been plump and smooth, with white hitched creases just beginning to show around her neck. Now her collarbones had emerged, and there was a hollow between them that she had not known would be there. It looked as if a finger had pressed down on her, trying to close her throat, as if she were made of dough.

She stepped out of her house and into the sunlight she no longer loved. The breeze had become unfamiliar, the way it grew bolder when it found her and gusted to lift the hair off the back of her neck, like George going to plant a kiss. She rubbed her own arms, trying to slough this pleasure off them.

George had taken Bess, her favorite horse, to go and pull her father's motorcar out of the mud again, so she would walk. There was not enough to do at home these days, and walking would wear out the time. She moved her boots forward doggedly, feeling them sometimes sucking in the mud, sometimes finding purchase on a patch of spongy brown grass or slushing through a lingering plate of snow. She thought of the earth like a hide, a surfacing creature whose back she was riding.

Once the ground was that warm, as warm as an animal, then they would go back and bury her son.

She turned and looked at the trail she had made behind her, tracks like tooth marks biting a long, dark wound around the world. She walked an hour toward town and passed no one, but as she came nearer to Main Street, she began to see them drifting, like stray snowflakes, all around her. It was hard to make out their faces, as if they could come only so close before they whirled away again. Evie looked down and watched her boots instead. Strange to feel the cotton dress push between her legs like an exploring hand, where once her thighs would have rubbed against each other as she walked. Now she understood what the lack of appetite meant for her body, that the heft of her might actually start to lift, the layers of her evaporating into the air.

Eventually she sensed the storefront quivering into view at the edge of her vision. As always, a few men enjoyed their pipes on the bench outside. Two of them she knew, older farmers whose sons and sons-in-law now tended their land while they rested, recuperating from forty years of forcing the dirt. Now they were stretching their legs before them like long, stiff oars on a boat left to drift.

The third man she had never met, but she knew who he was: the one she had seen staring at her from under his hat brim when they left the funeral. He was much closer now, and she could see the cloudless blue of his eyes. Out of politeness he nodded her way, but she noticed today he would not take the hook of her; his eyes merely skimmed her surface and slid away. The two old farmers noticed nothing, and she went wordlessly into the store. She was not the first bereaved woman they had seen and would not be the last. Their sympathy came out naturally and easy, like a sweat, and would dry just as swiftly with the next cool breeze.

Inside the store there were other customers, and she tried to skirt them unnoticed. Once they saw her, the unease would thicken around them all like a plaster, taking the mold of their shapes. There was Mr. Jenkins behind the counter adding up a purchase, and Mrs. Jones, who had not seen her yet, fingering the cotton percale she was considering to make some new sheets. Mrs. Edison and Mrs. Winters turned toward her, in

the midst of some harmless gossiping giggle, and it died away
there behind the canned goods in their witless rows of tin.
Evie smiled at them, looked away from the strain of their own
answering smiles, and went up behind Mrs. Jones to place her
order. Mrs. Jones was normally a hale, loud woman who was
always laughing and sighing over her nine grandchildren, and
she was a very hard worker in the church and a beloved
woman in the town.

"Oh, Evie," she started when she turned around. "I'm
sorry, dear, I didn't even hear you come in."

"I didn't mean to startle you," murmured Evie.

Mrs. Jones laid her plump brown hand on Evie's arm.
"You must come around for tea and cake," she told her. "You
are wasting away now. We can't have this." She frowned up
and down Evie's figure.

Evie let the warm pressure of well-meaning Mrs. Jones
sink into her skin. "Thank you. Maybe I will do that."

"Of course you will. You will come tomorrow at three
o'clock."

Unable to think of any excuse, Evie nodded helplessly as
Mr. Jenkins wrapped the cotton in paper and tied the pack-
age. "All right. All right, I will."

With her goods nestled safely in her basket, Mrs. Jones
plumped her way out of the store, pleased with herself.

Now it was Evie's turn.

"Hello there, Evie Dawson. It's very nice to see you. I
hope you're well."

Evie's throat constricted around her answer as if it were
an egg. She realized she had lost the control over her body
she was supposed to have, used to have, that still she might
frighten people by crying or screaming when she was only
supposed to exchange pleasantries. They were already frightened of her enough.

In the end she swallowed down the egg while Mr. Jenkins stared patiently at her forehead.

"I need two pounds of sugar, Tom," she said. "And five pounds of flour."

"Certainly, coming right up."

She knew he was grateful to turn away from her, fill the paper bags from the bins with his dark tin scoop. The sugar hissed as it slid into the hill of itself. The flour was almost soundless in its turn, like falling snow.

The ladies in the corner had resumed their conversation, but more quietly, as if Evie were a sleepwalker and they did not wish to wake her. Mr. Jenkins had finished sealing the paper bags and was watching her while he clutched them. She wished he would not speak of it, but she understood people needed to give her sympathy; it was all they had to give. They tucked it into her like crumpled paper into mouse holes, until she was nothing but cracks and flutters.

"Evie," said Mr. Jenkins, and he rumbled down in his throat as if he were turning cement in there, as if the speech would harden and set without constant movement. "I never had a chance to speak to you . . . at the funeral . . . and to tell you how sorry Mary and I are. And if there's anything we could do for you and George during this time, you must be sure to ask us, if you think of anything."

He looked away then into the far corner of the store, so she had a chance to observe his face up close, in a way she never had before. Toby and Cora got their red heads and freckles from their mother, while Mr. Jenkins was brown in hair and eyes. But she had never noticed before that he had long eyelashes. He was not as rough as the farmers who spent all their days being scoured by the wind and blistered in the sun, but still he had creases as fine as hairs around his eyes and mouth corners. She had never thought of him as a handsome man, but she noticed it now, and she wanted to laugh out loud at the strangeness of noticing such a thing, in such a moment. What would he think of her?

"Mary wanted to be sure you knew that," he was saying. How like him his son Toby was, awkward and kind.

"I know it, Tom," she told him. "There really isn't anything, but of course I will. If I think of something."

"Mary sent down that basket of muffins for you when George stopped in the other day. Did you get those?"

"Yes, of course. They were very good," she lied, for she had not tasted them. George had eaten them.

"Oh, good, that's good." He reached across the counter around the big paper sacks, tapped her wrist stiffly, then drew back and shoved the bags toward her.

"I think you will be all right, Evie," he said, turning his profile to her and tucking his chin into his neck, as if it sealed the thing. "You and George, you'll be all right. It just takes time."

"Thank you," she said. She would say this in response to every stupid thing she was told.

She took the bags into her arms like two brown, wrinkled babies. They did not seem heavy now, but she knew they would on the long walk home, and her arms would burn with them. She thought about time and taking time, and what did that really mean? Would giving up enough of it, passing enough time in sadness, entitle her to something else? Was there time in the swaying wheat fields of late summer—did time even exist in them? Time for Benny with his last breath freezing in his chest, burst under the ice with the shock of having gone down, and being mortal after all? Was the agony over in an instant, or did it go on forever? She would never know.

She had made up her mind she would seek out Robert Owens, make an appointment to buy from him. There was something from him she needed, and she thought if she could have it, maybe it would be possible. To leave behind the Evie that was, for this was the only way she could go on into the rest of her time. There had been an Evie before, who had a child, and his name was Ben. But this was a different woman now, with the weight in her arms and none on her legs, the woman with the dwindling frame and ugly dress like a big blue sack. She noticed her own heartbeat below that new hollow in her neck. It picked up speed as she pushed out the door with her tight-folded arms, the bell jingling overhead to signal her passage. And Robert Owens's place on the bench was empty, as if he'd been spooked back to that other world he came from by the pealing sound of her coming.

★ ★ ★

The next morning Evie took her blue dress over to the sewing machine and stood considering it with her cup of coffee in hand. She wore her nightgown and an old fuzzy sweater of George's, and she had pinned the dress the night before down the new inward curve of her waist before taking it off. The slivers of metal pins darted the light down its sides where they pinched the fabric. She drained her cup, felt the coffee roll acrid back to her throat, and swallowed. With the empty mug to watch her from its ring on the nearby table, she sat at the sewing machine and worked her dress under the needle. Her foot began to pump the treadle below, like rocking a cradle, as if some little creature might be comforted by the motion.

Dressed later in her newly tailored blue, she considered herself in the mirror. In her mind the transformation of her body had a meaning: that if she tried, she could become this unfamiliar person, this childless woman. She was again reminded of her youth, before she had even begun to bleed, before her hips had widened and her chest swelled. Until that happened, she had been lithe, her limbs light like hay. Now she encountered this forgotten girl-figure again. If she ignored the few gray hairs and wavy tidelines across the forehead, this was her, the very same, insides untouched and never lived in.

She passed the rest of the morning in her usual way. She dusted the furniture carefully, moving her cloth over the knobs and legs she knew so well. She watched George through the window, out in the fields cultivating, for it was the warm time and long working days had begun. Part of her missed him, but deeper down was a gladness for his absence, that wanted no witness to her pain. She knew that it was something they shared, but still she preferred to keep it to herself, curl into it and smother it with her back turned to him.

Her arms were sore enough today that they reminded her with every movement. At first she wondered why, then remembered that long walk home with the bundles of sugar and flour. They had felt light until she left the town behind and entered the fields, and then like any burden they'd grown heavier as she walked. It was as if they were expanding in her arms, like they were living things and time was passing faster than usual. By the time she turned in to her own lane, they were fifty pounds apiece, and she was afraid to set them down in case she could not pick them up again, and the ground moisture would seep through the paper and ruin them while she ran to get George. She didn't have his strength for these kinds of things, although she used to have those thick, round limbs, and people thought she should, thought she could probably bale the hay and pull up the stumps right alongside him. How George would have laughed at the lightness of the weights that had defeated her. She had always hated to be laughed at.

She would never let George know now how she had struggled with them. She kept quiet and fried pancakes this morning for his breakfast and kissed his syrupy lips the way she used to. In the early days of their marriage, she used to kiss him whenever he ate something sweet and tell him he tasted like candy. And he would squeeze his hands on her breasts and tell her there was more where that came from, and she would laugh in the way that was part panting. They wouldn't bother to finish eating, in their hurry to make love before the cows lowed heavy and miserable.

"Me first," she would whisper toward his ear while she held his hands on her waist. "Take care of me first." And he always did.

Watching the distant blur of George bending now down to the fields, she was suddenly shy of herself in the old blue dress she'd taken in. She suspected that George wouldn't like her being so thin, that he would worry. But knowing now it wouldn't change, she simply had to alter the dress or she wouldn't look in her right mind. People would say it was her mother all over again, floating around in a dress too big and looking downright unkempt and not even caring. She penciled George a note about her invitation to the Jones house and left it by his plate. She went out and into the woods by the back way, so he wouldn't see her running from him as he pulled his big boots through the fields, his knees lifting unnaturally over the damp ground places, squinting ahead toward his home as though he'd been gone for years and was no longer certain he recognized it.

★ ★ ★

Evie took her time walking into town again. She passed the tall grove of maple trees, their heights swaying a bloodred mist of buds. The forsythia had burst their yellow blooms along the roadsides. There was still little shade, as the trees held back their soft leaves from the eager sun, and she felt a narrow tickle of sweat finding its way down her back between her shoulder blades.

In her chest was that ache she brought everywhere with her, like a loyal dog who can't be left behind. Sometimes it struck her how odd it was that others couldn't see it. As she neared the town and began to encounter more people, she had the feeling there was a knife sticking out of her chest. But everyone passed her by in spite of it, ignored her as if she were part of a street-fair magic act they did not want to stop for. She was the woman being sawed in half, her head and feet parting swiftly in their two painted boxes, her audience watching quietly and without surprise.

There was a broad, empty berth around her now, but there had always been something like it. A lapping space, a drift. Her mother had this thing, this turning-away effect on people as if she embarrassed them, and now Evie had caught it, too, through her own misfortune. Now she thought back on her girlhood and realized she'd had so few close friends. She had rarely brought anyone to her house, and only because of her father's standing had anyone invited her to theirs. When Evie married a farmer, the other farmers' wives did not know what to make of her. They imagined that a decent man had crooked his finger and Evie had jumped, and now she must billow her fancy skirts out to sit on their plain wooden chairs. George never noticed. Dutifully Evie went to the quilting bees and the church suppers, and the other young wives were cordial with her.

Now that she had lost her son, that space around her only widened a little. Tragedy was a catching thing, like disease. The bereaved must carry on with their lives in a kind of quarantine. Irma Jones was a well-meaning woman, but Evie had made up her mind about where she must go, and it was not to the Jones house.

Chapter 12

Whenever Robert Owens passed a quiet afternoon at Violet Burnley's, his thoughts were stitched with her sounds like a needlework sampler—her whispery sweeping of the floors, the satisfied bang of oven and cupboard doors. It didn't bother him; rather he enjoyed how they worked their way through whatever book he was reading, the scrapes and thumps in the background, a coverlet of sounds if he lay down to nap.

Today he listened to the sibilant sounds of Violet wetting and starching clothes while she ironed them. There was the frustrated hiss of the hot iron searing damp cloth, the thunk as her hand set it upright while she shook out a shirt and changed its drape across the table. She had offered to do Robert's laundry with her own as part of his board, had noticed the yellow soil creeping along the back of his collars when they went too long between halfhearted scrubbings with a washboard and pail in his room.

Robert was at his leisure while Violet worked, and most days he read one of her books, but today he wandered, unable to settle. He peered into the kitchen, looking for talk. When he saw the way she frowned to herself, brow taking on furrows as if it lifted them straight from his shirts, he went away silently. He was drawn then from window to window but did not go out, as if the house were a cage. Watching to see if any new customer might come, this was how he happened to see Evelyn Dawson walking down the street toward him. He stepped quickly back from the glass, then darted again to the kitchen.

"Vi," he said, "do something for me."

Violet looked up from the pillowcase she was ironing. "What's that, now?"

"It's Mrs. Dawson—Evelyn—she's coming up the lane."

"Oh, I wonder how she's been. I wonder if she will stop in? I wish I hadn't given all those scones away to the Andersons."

"No, no," he said. "You can't let her in."

Violet was folding up the case, pressing it flat. "Of course she must come in."

"But I don't want her to know I'm here."

"For pity's sake. Even if this *is* where she's stopping. Why not?"

He waited for her to look up at him. "It's me. I think she's coming to me, for a dream. And I don't want to sell her one."

Violet clucked her tongue. "You can make her up a dream as easy as for anyone else, can't you? If that's what she wants. Weren't none of you could give her that boy back, so it's the least you could do for the poor soul." She turned back to her work.

"No," he said again. He looked down at the iron dithering over the board. "I won't take her money," he said.

"There's no law says you have to take money," she told him. "Why don't you just give it to her, then? If that woman wants to dream about something, if she wants a bit of escape, I think you should give it to her."

"If she knocks here, I want you to tell her I'm not in."

She wet her finger impatiently and tapped the iron's dull face, then tipped it back onto the stove to warm.

"Fine. I'll do it for you. If she comes to this door, I'll tell her you're not in. But if you'll take my two cents"—they smiled at each other because they both knew he had no choice in this—"if you're never going to mix her a dream and that's what she wants, you may as well tell her that now and get it over and done."

He kissed her on the cheek. "I won't have anything to do with her."

Surprised, Violet had no answer. In a moment she heard him jumping the stairs two at a time, like a boy, and then the knock he had predicted. She went to the door, fixing her face against lying. In the kitchen the black iron waited, losing heat quickly.

Evelyn Dawson looked as if she'd left half of herself behind somewhere. Grief should be a private thing, thought Violet. Let it scour away at your insides if it must, but what Evie was missing now had taken its piece of her in no uncertain terms, and the shape of her showed the loss.

She looked at Violet steadily with her dark-rimmed gray irises. Under her lower lashes, there were shadowed hollows now, as if she'd given up sleeping.

"Well, what a surprise," said Violet.

"I've come—I was invited to Irma Jones's place." Evie twisted her wedding band around on her finger and looked past Violet into the dimness of the hall and the gleam of the polished stairs leading in dark-light stripes up to the landing.

"Were you, now? Wonderful. Such a lovely woman. And the whole family, really, fine people, and the children always underfoot . . . well . . . It's such a cheerful place. . . . " Violet trailed off, unsure if she should be talking about having children or feeling cheerful. "Will you come inside?"

Evie shook her head. "I have to be getting back home, and it's a bit of a walk—"

"Have you walked all that way? You really should ride, you know. You'll wear out your constitution."

"But I'm not tired."

Violet would have liked to show her a mirror and ask her to repeat herself, but she let Evie go on.

"I like the walk. I only stopped in . . . I was just wondering if your boarder was here? I was thinking I might speak with him about . . . something."

Upstairs in his room, Robert twisted his head toward the crack of the just-open door. He stopped breathing in the golden stillness, so he would not really be there. If he was not there, she could not draw him to her. His hands clenched in the lap of nothing. The more he itched to see her face again, to study that lost familiar gaze, the more he resisted. He held on to the bedpost, and he thought of Odysseus lashing himself to the mast of his ship.

Violet hesitated. Then she spoke unnaturally loudly.

"I'm sorry to tell you he's not in. I do expect him for supper, but I don't imagine you'd want to wait that long."

Evie turned slightly toward the road she would be taking to her home fields. The softening sun was beginning to pick out the blades of grass and gild them fleetingly.

"No, no, I can't wait. I have to be getting supper for George as well."

For one second, Violet thought of herself and Evie as two wives, busied with the daily tasks that having husbands demanded.

"Maybe you'll run into him one of these times," she said. "He enjoys wandering about, too. Never in much of a hurry to get anywhere."

Evie smiled without much confidence at that.

"I guess I might. Would you please let him know I would like to speak with him? I don't expect him to come out to the farm or anything, but maybe if he knows . . . I imagine he's a little afraid of me. Because of what happened. But I think maybe . . . maybe he came here because I need him."

She pulled a loose curl of hair and tucked it back into the dark knot at the nape of her neck while Violet stared at her. It slid forward again anyway. "That sounds strange, now that I've said it out loud."

Violet thought Evie was talking a bit like her mother.

"But I do want to see him. Tell him . . . well, tell him he'll have bad luck if he denies an audience to the woman who lost her son."

Violet nodded gravely instead of smiling at Evie's humor.

"I will tell him. When he comes in for supper. I hope . . . he can give you what you want."

"Thank you for that."

Evie turned and left, blue dress blowing back behind her, winking in and out of the long evening rails of shadow. When she was far enough away, thought Violet, you could still make out the blue, but you could no longer see just how much she had changed.

Violet turned back to the stairs and glowered at Robert, who had come down silently as a cat when he was sure she was closing the door. "Shame on you," she spit, but he only shrugged at her.

When George came in that evening from the milking, he leaned, and Evie brought him supper without speaking much. Whenever George was tired, his voice seemed to leave him. Words became heavy like thick metal chain, the links of sentences rusted. He didn't seem to take in how much smaller she and her dress had become. He did not ask about her visit to the Jones house.

After supper she washed the dishes and made the pot of tea, and they sat looking out the window in the front room. There was a rise in the land off in the distance, and behind it the sun was going down, letting its weight take it below the horizon as if it could understand their exhaustion. The sky was a bleed of seeping pink, and all along the ridge stood a strange row of single cloud puffs darkening gray against the light, like a row of the sheep you were supposed to count to send yourself to sleep.

Chapter 13

If one did not attend church regularly, one was not to be trusted. So every Sunday Robert Owens would put on his cleanest shirt, brush his coat and pants, and head down the street like everyone else. His first Sunday there, the Reverend Arnold had made a point to welcome him and shake his hand, but while he pumped, Robert had had the distinct impression he was being sized up. As if a dream peddler's wares, being intangible, were just a bit too much like his own.

Robert walked alone because Violet went over early to warm up her organ. As he joined the crowd outside, the organ's heavy breath would blanket them, and it seemed to bend their bodies toward their worship as the wind would bow the tall grass. Sometimes he would fall in with a family on the steps. The father would ask him how business went, his daughter giggling and his wife digging him hard in the ribs.

"Can't complain, can't complain," Robert would always say, and compliment the ladies on their attire.

This week, though, he entered alone, and there, not steps away from him in the vestibule, was Evelyn Dawson. He stood aside, hoping she might not notice, and watched her back as it went up the aisle beside her husband's. He continued to stare at her as he made his way into the sanctuary, and he walked right into the side of a pew and stumbled, hat tumbling onto the floor. As he picked it up and tried to sneak quietly into the pew he had assaulted, the heads turned anyway, lighter faces after darker hair like the undersides of leaves. He fumbled with the hat still in his hand as he tried to open his hymnal to the first hymn. He could not find the page and keep hold of the hat at the same time. Finally he set the hat down on the pew beside him. He tried to still his fluster.

All around, the church was dotted with his customers, their dreams of the night before unfolding silently and secretly inside them. Young Jenna Coldbrook had finally won the blue ribbon for quilting at the county fair, and Ansen Smith had worked up the courage to ask if he might see her home. Arthur Jones had climbed to the peak of Mount Everest and looked out over the blue-white world. And Elsbeth Maynard had spent one more perfect golden childhood day with her long dead grandmother. Pastor Arnold, looking gravely down at this flock, had the distinct impression their hearts were not beating entirely in rhythm with the solemnity of his church service. And some of them, he suspected, might not even have been listening to him at all.

There were Billy and Mary Thomson taking turns jiggling their new baby, who appeared to have arrived in the world in the form of a big bundle of crocheted yarn. Every so often the voice of the bundle would shudder out, that goatlike bleating of the uncomfortable newborn. Evie Dawson stared ahead as if she took no notice, but George Dawson watched them intently. He watched the couple whisper an argument during the hymn over whether the blanket was necessary in the warmer air of the church, and he watched while the baby was worked out of it and the bobbling head appeared over her mother's shoulder. He was remembering the feel of that strange spot on a baby's skull, where the bones did not quite meet and the pulse showed through.

Christina Blackwell sat with her parents, and Cora Jenkins across the aisle from them. Toby sat next to Cora with an unwitting grin on his face, staring up at the front of the church. He was so light of step he had almost developed a swagger. Several pews behind Christina was the freckle-faced Rolf, watching how the coils of her dark hair ribboned the light, how they rolled it back and forth when she moved her head. He was wishing he could put his finger on the curve of her cheek, the line of her jaw. While he watched, a darkness of flush moved up her skin, because Jackson Banks had just snuck in late to join his family. Christina made an effort not to look at him—let his winks waste themselves on someone else, she thought.

Robert followed along, standing when everyone stood to sing and then sitting back down again and standing once more. As if they could not make up their minds. Evelyn Dawson was not far enough from him for his comfort, and he felt her turning toward him every so often as the service went on. He kept his eyes on his hymnal. He tried hard not to see her there, and because of that she was the only thing he could see, inside his mind.

The entire service he was only wondering when he might slip out unnoticed. If he didn't get away before the others, he risked being cornered by her, so when they took up the offering, he did it. He dropped his coins into the brass plate and passed it to the man next to him, excused himself under his breath, and squeezed out to the aisle. No one paid any attention to him, as they were all occupied finding their money in pockets and purses, and he escaped into the street and the buzzing spring air.

He wandered down the road to wait for Violet, leaning against a cherry tree about to bloom. He remembered standing just like this when the funeral darkness had washed across the road, and still it felt like the right place to be, away from grieving eyes and out where he could breathe. As Vi went past his tree, Robert came out and stepped into stride beside her, and she gasped at him, then laughed. She pulled up the hat he'd left behind and slanted it over his head.

"I thought you'd gone home," she said.

"Didn't go home yet. You know I walk you back every week. I just decided to leave early."

"I see," said Violet, and pressed her lips together. She'd noticed Evie Dawson back beside George today, but she wouldn't comment. "You missed the community announcements," she told him.

"Really? Anything important?"

"Not much. There's to be a dance next weekend. The young people are quite excited. They'll have it in the schoolhouse on Saturday night. We have some first-rate fiddlers in this town, you know, and I am to play piano for them, too."

"Splendid." Robert tucked his free hand into his pocket. "Do you enjoy dancing?"

"I've done my bit of dancing, I guess, in my day."

"Well, you must come, too, then. With the summer work beginning, this might be our last for a while. The men will all be too tired of an evening."

Robert smiled. "Come now. There's never a young man too tired to come out and dance with the pretty ladies, is there? And you have some beauties in this town. The boys must show them the good times they deserve."

"Or what? They'll depart for lands unknown?"

"You never know. I may squirrel one away with me yet, when I leave."

Violet looked down at her shoes. "When will that be, do you think?"

"I'm just teasing."

"But when do you think you'll be leaving? For good?"

Robert lifted his chin to the idea. "I can't really say. I've only just begun to sell here. It was unusual circumstances when I arrived. Some places never really take off for me, and I'm only there a few weeks. Other places I'll spend as long as a year. So I guess we'll just have to wait and see."

"But you are coming to the dance."

"Of course I'm coming."

"And how do you plan to keep your distance from Evelyn Dawson the whole evening?"

"I hardly think Mrs. Dawson is in the mood to go to a dance, do you?"

"No, I suppose not," said Violet.

★ ★ ★

"You really want to go?" George blew on his tea and put his mouth to it even though it was still too hot. He slurped, and Evie frowned at him.

"Yes, I think I will. Not for the dancing, just to help put out the food. Or serve lemonade. I can bring some of my raisin squares."

George smiled at her. "Well, I must go, too, if your raisin squares will be there."

"Of course you'll go, too. It will be a nice time. I like to see all the young people, all the little love affairs breaking out."

"It's nice you can still enjoy their fun in your old age."

Evie snapped her napkin at him. They drank their tea while a silence rolled itself between them like a lazy cat. It was startled away by a knock at the door. Without waiting to be let in, Rose Whiting opened it for herself and stepped into the hall. Evie stood and went to be embraced by way of welcome.

"Hello! I see I'm just in time for tea, perfect."

"Yes, you are. Let me get your coat. We have a huge tin of cookies from Mrs. Blackwell. And a cake from Irma Jones. And scones from Mrs. Bachmeier."

"My goodness, such a feast," said Rose, rubbing her hands together as she came into the kitchen. George stood to hug her, too, and pulled out a chair. Its feet scraped the floor between them.

"We don't need to worry about going hungry, do we?" said George.

"Kindness needs an outlet, doesn't it? All wishing they could help you in some way."

"Oh, yes. I hope they don't mind letting out my pants for me as well, when the time comes."

Rose studied her daughter. "Evie, my dear, you don't look as if you are suffering from too many sweets."

Evie raised her eyes. "Well, Mother, I haven't really had a big appetite lately."

"But you must still keep up your strength."

"I have plenty of strength. Plenty of it. I never was a big one for sweets, you remember."

"Well, I'm going to stay and make you my fried chicken for supper. You never could say no to it."

"What about Father? Where has he got to?"

Her mother waved an arm. "He has so many cases right now I hardly see him. Flu's coming and going everywhere, making a circle through town and starting over again, seems like. Poor Jenny Simms has come down with it, and half the Jones and Cartwright children—it's just that time of year." She plunked herself down in a chair. "There's nothing much to be done for them except lots of rest and fluids, but your father wants to lay eyes on each and every one of them once a day, listening for pneumonia, you know how it is. He's a good doctor."

"Yes, he is."

"So I've come here to check on you."

"All right."

Evie poured her mother's tea and refilled her own and George's cups.

The silence returned, curling at their feet and bedding down.

"Well, I wouldn't say no to a fried-chicken dinner, that's what," said George.

As Rose cut up the chicken and Evie peeled potatoes, Rose watched her daughter. The chicken skin was slippery bumps under her fingers, and the knife was sharp. She peeked sidelong at Evie while trying not to butterfly her own hand. Evie seemed to be having a good day, going about her business and even humming to herself here and there. They stood side by side and listened to the crunch of stubborn bird bones separating.

"It's a strange feeling, you know," Evie said.

"What is?"

"These days . . . there are these days when it loses its hold on me. When he seems to lose his hold. It's as if he is the one who has to let me go and not the other way around. Like I don't get any say in it myself."

Her mother stared down at the chicken. "I guess that's how it feels to grieve, isn't it? The mind, well, it just doesn't want to wallow, not forever. Sadness is like an ocean. It must move in and out."

Evie nodded.

"And you don't have to let him go."

"You know what I mean. I have to let go the wanting to see him. I was lucky to have him, yes. But I wanted to see him grow up."

"Are you sleeping?"

Evie's look was quick both ways. "When I do, I . . . have dreams."

"It's normal for sadness to make us tired. It will pass."

They worked in silence for a while.

"I don't suppose you've run into that man, that . . . dream peddler."

Evie looked up. "No, not really. I've seen him at a distance, that's all. I think George knows him, but I've never spoken to him."

"Good. I can't imagine what Violet Burnley thinks she's doing, letting a man like that live in her house, cooking for him, doing his washing."

"What kind of a man?"

"A charlatan. The kind who comes to small towns thinking the size of our brains is in direct proportion to our population and tries to take advantage. Takes money from people who work hard for it and don't know any better."

"I don't know about that, but I haven't heard of anyone being disappointed. There might be something to it."

Her mother snorted. "There is no such thing as giving someone a dream. The only thing with the power to do that is your own mind."

Evie shrugged. "I guess there's no harm in it. If whatever he gives people affects their minds, they're still getting what they want, what they didn't have without him, so he's not really cheating them."

"Yes, it is cheating," her mother said sharply. "It most certainly is. I don't like his business. And I hope you never get so desperate as to try and buy a dream from the likes of him. He should let people's minds alone."

Evie hunched over her potatoes. She was slicing them now

and setting the damp, milky rounds into a pot of cold water to take out the starch.

"No, I'd never do that," she said.

★ ★ ★

Christina Blackwell was sitting in Cora Jenkins's bedroom, letting her friend test a series of limp ribbons next to her hair, one at a time.

"Honestly, Cora, do you really think it will make a difference?"

"We should not take any chances," insisted Cora, already wearing in her own hair the green she had chosen to match her dress. "This is all up to us, remember. We need to change the course of a dream. We are altering fate. Very hard to guess what small details may end up being of vital importance."

"Like a hair ribbon," said Christina sarcastically.

"Exactly like a hair ribbon. Let's see this one."

She held up a twist of periwinkle blue next to Christina's head. They looked in the glass together, through its pale spores of age. The ovals of their faces blurred out of its silver like surfacing mermaids.

"I approve," Christina said, because as long as Cora liked it, she was happy they could stop looking. She was no longer really seeing the colors of the ribbons. She was seeing in grays like a photograph of themselves. Worrying about Jackson was having the opposite effect on her than she thought it would. She had expected everything to be heightened. As her pulse bounced through her wrists and her temperature rose, she thought she would find herself in a confusion of sounds and lights, like a carousel. Instead the world was fading and the color of things bleeding outward, away from her. Her senses had all been muffled, like they were wintering under a gray fall of snow.

She felt a tug as Cora pulled the silk through the back of her hair and it whispered in. Her scalp tingled with the memory of girlfriends in the school yard plaiting each other's hair, all in a circle working at one another's back, fingers weaving while the pleasure crept along their necks and over the tops of their ears. She closed her eyes to feel it better. Never mind that Cora was grooming her like a purebred dog for a show.

Cora tied a bow and smoothed the hair toward it like a mother would.

"This blue is heaven with your new red dress," she said.

Christina opened her eyes to look. Of course she could not see the ribbon now, at the back of her head; she had to take Cora's word for it. Even the scarlet dress was faded by the murky glass of the mirror. Christina had been surprised when her mother agreed to such rich, vivid fabric at the store. "I gave it to her on discount," Cora confided, nudging her, "and she did give in. She couldn't resist the price for such good lawn, of course. Don't tell Father," and she winked. Christina thought Cora was a good friend, making sure she had the brightest dress to give her the best chance of attracting Jackson.

Cora's mouth fell open a little over her white teeth as she fussed around Christina, who had stood up, suddenly impatient. Cora smoothed the back of her dress and fastened a button they had missed.

"Is it too soon to go yet?"

Cora glanced at the clock. "Just a little bit. We don't want to get there and stand around while they warm up the fiddles."

"Tell me, Cora, who are you hoping to dance with?"

Now Cora checked her own figure in the mirror. She smiled at herself, and the points of her eye teeth came out.

"Robert Owens, I think."

"Robert Owens! He's old enough to be your father."

Cora smiled. "He's probably not quite that old."

"Even so. What would people think?"

"Oh, who gives a damn what people think!"

Christina was shocked that Cora would curse. But with no one else in the room to hear her, the word wafted harmlessly up like a curious moth.

"Why would you want to take up with a man like that?" she asked.

"A man like what?"

"Well, that nobody knows. Someone who travels from town to town selling things, living off of luck with no steady job. He doesn't even have an automobile. Or a horse of his own."

"I don't expect him to whisk me away to a castle. I just thought he might dance with me, is all." She patted her hair and watched her reflection do the same.

"But what's the point of it?"

"I would enjoy it. That's the point."

Christina looked at Cora in her pale green dress and thought how easily she would turn the men her way when she went through the room. Even if Christina's dress was brighter, she would never turn heads like Cora. She shrugged. "Well, have fun dancing with him, then."

Cora pointed at her. "And you will be dancing with Jackson Banks."

Christina tilted her head. "What makes you think that? He doesn't pay any more attention to me than he used to. And since I started ignoring him, he can just go ahead and forget I exist. I think this plan isn't working."

"Nonsense. I told you. Jackson hasn't made up his mind yet who he wants. He doesn't have the first clue what he's about. All we have to do is spin him around and point him in the right direction."

"We might as well be spinning him and pointing him at Pin the Tail on the Donkey. He could so easily blunder off to the side, and miss the mark."

"Of course he won't. I won't let him. You just have to trust me."

Christina sighed. She had never really gotten anything she wanted badly by trusting Cora Jenkins, but that was not for Cora's lack of effort. She remembered when they were little girls and Christina had her heart set on playing Mary, for once, in the Christmas pageant. Every year she was an angel or a shepherd, something that could be easily herded about unnoticed within the larger assemblage. Cora knew how much, despite her shyness, Christina secretly coveted that role. Wearing the old blue velvet robe, that chosen girl would come silently down the aisle with Joseph (sometimes riding the back of a papier-mâché donkey head stuck on the end of a broom, for effect) and sit gleaming in the candlelight as she gazed solemnly down at her newborn babe, magically produced when the time came from behind some bales of hay at the altar and sailed into her lap.

Cora was not afflicted with Christina's shyness and put up her hand when the question of Mary's role came up at Sunday school in early December. "I know who would make a beautiful Mary, Mrs. Heebner," she called out, and before she could say another word, Mrs. Heebner, glancing up from her clipboard, said briskly, "Cora Jenkins, that's just fine. Why don't you be Mary this year," and dismissed them all. Christina knew that her friend had not acted out of malice, and she let Cora drape a sympathetic arm across her slumped shoulders as they walked homeward together. But alone in her room, she cried her hot tears and wondered why, why she did not have the same courage, why she could not speak up and take things as other girls did.

The spring night was chilly, so they pulled their shadowy coats on over their dresses, like smothering fires with blankets. All around them others were heading to the schoolhouse as well, and the sun hung low and haunted them from within the trees. Horses made their way among the crowd, and even occasional motorcars honked their way through.

Robert Owens came up alongside the girls, as always with Violet Burnley on his arm.

"I think she's hoping he might save her from old-maidhood after all," Cora whispered to her friend. In spite of herself, Christina tittered. She wouldn't have hurt Miss Burnley's feelings for the world, but she was too nervous to help it. Robert turned coolly toward them and tipped his hat. "Ladies."

"Good evening, Mr. Owens. Miss Burnley," called Cora.

"Hello, girls. Beautiful night for a dance, isn't it?"

"It is. I hope you are coming to play the piano for us?"

"She might," said Robert. "If I leave her any free time between all the dances we intend to have."

The two of them laughed and left the girls dawdling behind them.

"It's looking like you'll have some competition for your favorite tonight, Cora," Christina teased.

Cora sniffed. "I always felt a bit sorry for old Violet Burnley before, but now I feel it even more. She finally has this friend— you can see how much she likes him—and why wouldn't she? But eventually he'll be gone, and then she'll be even more lonely."

"Well, her life is like that, I suppose. She'll get another boarder eventually."

"Sometimes I'm afraid of that, you know, for myself. Of ending up somewhere alone."

"That could never happen to you in a thousand years! You'll be married and probably have heaps of children."

"I plan to be married, of course. But what if I don't have any children? What if I end up like Evelyn Dawson? I could grow to be an old lady and have my husband die and be all by myself."

Christina looked at her. It was not like Cora to ponder and brood. "When your husband dies and you're an old lady by yourself, you can come and live with me." She slipped her arm around Cora's waist. "Now, cheer up! Forget Violet Burnley and all the old biddies. We're going to have a marvelous time."

"Marvelous . . ." Cora murmured to herself as they lifted their delicate shoes on the wooden steps and entered the busy hive of the dance.

Lantern light seemed to deepen the cracks in the walls, as if they were only photographs forgotten in trays of developer. Paper streamers buckled over the window frames, swinging with every breath of the opening door. Greetings called across the room were caught in them like flies. Cora and Christina were taken into the crowd and eddied around the room. Violet sat at the piano, waiting while the fiddlers drew their bows across the strings, tuning, tightening their voices to each other. There was Evie Dawson behind the punch table filling cups and trying to smile. Robert Owens leaned at ease against a wall, talking to some of the men; he hadn't noticed her there.

Christina tried to scan the room but was hemmed in by all the taller, jostling shoulders; she could see no sign of Jackson Banks or his group. Maybe they wouldn't bother to show until later on, she guessed, didn't want to seem too eager. And always Rolf Baer's eyes tracked her from wherever he stood. Once in a while, he stopped to look down, shifted his feet, looked up, and found her again. Christina stared back at him now, feeling bold, taking stock of him as she had never done before. Yes, his face was strange, she thought; she had not been mistaken in that. But his eyes within the face were clear and steadfast. The freckles were interesting. Something about their pepper of darkness on the white skin made her want to go over and trace them with her finger, feeling if there was any design there or drawing one of her own. It was not attraction she felt, but a curiosity was born in her. Why did he find her so fascinating? He was the only one in town who did.

Behind her a commotion broke out as Jackson Banks and his friends arrived, making a lot of noise getting themselves some food and crowding the punch bowl. Jackson, she noticed, was not above winking at Mrs. Dawson when she handed him a glass. He turned in Christina's direction, saw her, raised his punch to her by way of hello. She forced the corners of her mouth to go upward.

Cora was busy fielding many offers to fill up her dance card. She stood like a twisting forest vine in her green dress, with the dark trunk lines of the men closing in around her. Her first partner led her into the reel, and the edges of the room blurred to a ring of clapping hands. Men and women at the center jumped with her, with the sweat beginning to polish them. The windows were open to draw in cold air, but the heat of the bodies stamped any freshness down and killed it underfoot.

Evie watched the dancers while George wrapped his arms around her from behind. "Maybe you'll have a dance with me?" he asked her hair.

"I might," she said. From the cuff of his arms, she saw the crowd part briefly in a wavering line that gave her a view of Robert Owens across the room. He was smiling and clapping along with everyone else. His shirtsleeves were rolled up, and she saw the round bone of his wrists and the hair curling over them. Was it her imagination, or did he nod in recognition at some of the people? She looked around, and it seemed to her so many of them must have dreamed his dreams by now. And were they different as well, happier? She watched Violet at the piano and wondered what she might have bought for herself. Did she sail away into an oozing sunset on the prow of her brother's sunken ship? Evie watched the couples dancing, then the wallflowers, edging the room with their hope like a fine ring of salt, and tried to guess what each of them might most desire. She wondered if any of them wanted the same thing she did.

As the dance ended, Cora Jenkins appeared by the dream peddler's side. She said a few things that Robert answered, but in between his responses he looked around until his eyes found Evie standing behind the punch. His happy smile fell back, as if Evie had somehow hurt him. He touched Cora's arm lightly without looking at her and left her there while he nudged through the moving crowd. Couples were splitting apart and re-forming for the next song. Evie could hardly see them; she saw only Robert dividing them like so many stalks of wheat. George had gone across the room for some talk; with his arms no longer around her, she felt the cool blue dark of the open window.

When the dream peddler reached her, he fitted his smile back on and nodded. "Could I have two cups of that, please?"

"Yes, of course," she said, filling the glasses with her ladle, dripping a little down the sides. "Let me get that." She stopped his hand before he could take them and picked each

one up in turn and wiped it with a napkin. "Mr. Owens—"
she began.

"Pleasure to meet you," he said smoothly, and turned and
crossed back to the other side of the room before she could
say any more.

"Damn," she said to herself.

She watched Robert busy himself with Cora, the two of
them drinking their punch. She studied them so intently she
did not even notice George smile at her from across the
room or the way his smile faded when he could not get her
attention. When he took in who she was watching.

Once Robert and Cora were done with their glasses, he
set them on the nearest bench instead of returning them to
Evie's table, and that thoughtlessness annoyed her. He took
Cora's hand and entered the dance, but Evie hadn't seen his
mouth open to speak any invitation. Like it was understood
between them. He couldn't possibly be courting her, thought
Evie. He was much too old for her. The townspeople wouldn't
like it. And whatever else he did, she knew, Robert Owens
must please the town.

She watched the couples dancing, Cora's beauty flashing
like a lighthouse beacon as she spun. Robert held her loosely,
as though cupping some feathery insect that must not be
crushed. She was tossing her head back when she laughed
and showing the long curve of her throat.

When the dance ended, Robert bowed slightly and moved
away, while the space he had left beside Cora quickly filled
with another hopeful young man. She danced with them all;
she never stood still. George came back and took Evie's hand,
and he led her across the boards. With her body tucked into
his, she could no longer see very well, and she couldn't tell
where the dream peddler had gone.

★ ★ ★

Christina was drinking her punch without enjoying it. It tasted too sweet; when you were this hot and thirsty, you did not want something so sweet. She had watched Jackson Banks dance with three different girls, and to each he had whispered something that made her smile. Maybe the same thing to each girl, she thought. Maybe he would do that to her? She wished he would ask her to dance, if only so she could find out what it was he said to them. From deep within her thoughts, she didn't notice Rolf Baer sidling up beside her.

"Christina. Would you have a dance with me?"

He held his arm out to her, and she found herself taking it. There was that steadiness in his eyes. He did not know how to flirt; his gaze was too slow to move. He clutched her hand until he found a clear space for them, and then he shifted his grip slightly without letting go as he placed his other palm at her waist. She set her hand lightly on his shoulder the way she'd been taught.

"You can look away sometimes, you know," she told him.

He smiled, something she suddenly realized was rare, and many of his freckles folded in on themselves or disappeared. "I don't want to look anywhere else," he said.

"Well, it can make a girl kind of nervous."

Their feet circled a pattern around the floor. She felt the movement of his hips even through the space between them, their bodies touching only at their hands.

"How's this?" he asked her, and he stared off into the distance, frowning.

"Are you making fun of me?" she asked.

"No. I want you to like me."

He said this to the air over her shoulder. She had no

answer for him, so she looked away, too, to the side, where
Evie Dawson was holding tight to George, and Jackson was
busy charming the ear whorl of another giggling girl. For
some reason she felt glad to be there in Rolf's arms. He
wouldn't tease her like Jackson. Now that she had seen his
eyes up close, his staring didn't seem so bad. His pupils were
wide and black, and she could see herself reflected in them
in perfect miniature, like a stereograph. She looked down at
her own hand cupped in his large one, with freckles even
there sprinkled across his knuckles. While he steered her in
a slow ellipse, she found herself losing interest in what anyone else did around them. She stared at the middle of his chest
and imagined she heard there the thump of his heart like
footsteps.

★ ★ ★

Robert hid outside in the shadows. The moon raised her
scythe of light over the fields behind him while he peered in
through the yellow window, watching Evie. The ornery hair
was escaping her pins as always, and she seemed happy, clapping her hands over her head, making a hot diamond space
between her arms, and bringing them back down smartly to
her hips. Taking George's hand and whirling away into the
corner. Robert turned his back to the dancing and lit a cigarette, folding his hands protectively over the match as if in
prayer.

"Could I have one of those?"

A young man stepped out beside him, his back brightly
furred by the schoolhouse light, snuffed out again as the door
closed behind him. Robert couldn't remember the name, but
he knew the boy, the grinning one, the one the girls all crit-
icized, whose careless compliments they craved.

"How are old are you?" Robert asked him.

"Old enough." He winked.

Robert shrugged and handed him the pack. He was struck by how much that smile reminded him of Cora, charming to get what she wanted. It was almost flirtatious. He held out the box of matches, too, and watched as the boy dragged one into fire and held it to the brown tufted end of the cigarette he'd put between his lips. To cup one hand against the breeze, he dropped the box onto the ground and Robert stooped to pick it up. The boy's lips trembled, and the tobacco, which was rolled as tight as the tiny center of a black-eyed Susan, jiggled up and down trying to take the flame.

Robert ignored him, tucking the matches and cigarettes back into his pockets and staring out at the drunken rectangles of light cast onto the grass from the schoolroom windows. At last the boy was successful, plucked the paper tube out of his mouth, and released a satisfied vapor into the air.

"Hot in there, ain't it?"

Robert nodded. "Sure. Good to get some air."

"Perfect night."

Again Robert nodded, silently.

"You're the dream peddler."

"That I am."

"I'm Jackson."

They breathed in the smoke side by side, the hearts burning in their chests.

"What's that mean, exactly, dream peddler? What's that like?"

Robert blew out before answering. "It's just a gift I have. Anyone wants to dream a particular thing, something they don't usually dream, they come to me. I make a mixture, the customer drinks it before going to sleep. They have the dream."

"Sounds like a good racket."

"I assure you it's not. Money-back guarantee."

"Oh, really? Well, I might have to try it sometime."

"Whenever you like." Robert watched the mist of their talk dissolve over the edge of the steps. "What's your pleasure?"

The boy tried tapping his cigarette out into the bushes down below, but it was too soon, and there was no ash. Eventually they found the same rhythm, of hand to the face and rise of the chest, then the downward arc of the orange stars while their breath escaped with the light.

"I'd just want to get out of here, plain and simple. I'd go to the city in my dreams, do something great, become really rich. Something grand like that."

"Why don't you just go on and do that in real life?"

"Maybe I will. But a dream would be all right, too, for now."

"Sure."

The young man looked out at the tarnished darkness, gnawed through here and there by a distant lantern. Robert smoked and pictured Evie twirling in the light behind him. He could almost feel her shadow slant through the glass and graze his neck.

"Do you ever dream anything you don't understand? About yourself, I mean? Ever dream that you're someone you don't even recognize?"

Robert smiled at that. "Constantly."

Jackson smoked quietly for a while, passing the cigarette from one hand to the other as if he didn't know which one to favor.

"So you're not married?"

"Well, I bring no wife with me, so it's what people assume."

"Oh." He looked away. "So you are married, then."

Robert sighed. "I was, once."

"What happened?"

"It's not something I talk about. It didn't work. I was a bad husband to her. So I left."

Jackson looked at Robert intently. "Yeah. Me, I don't know if marriage would be for me. I don't think I ever will do it, get married." He held up the cigarette and stared into its burning eye. "I guess my parents would be awfully disappointed." He leaned his head back against the boards of the schoolhouse, and his wide-open eyes picked up the moving light inside and shone as if he were crying, although he wasn't.

"It's a funny thing, you know," Robert spoke eventually. "I've been to many towns like this one before and known many people who thought of leaving but never did. And maybe if they did leave, sure, their lives would be better, but then again maybe not. Life is a matter of routine, in a sense, no matter where you are. Big city, small town, it doesn't make much difference." He pulled thoughtfully on the cigarette. "There's no adventure in leaving, when you come down to it. I've built a life on leaving, and I can tell you now, even that becomes routine."

"So what are you saying? That there isn't any point to it all? There's nothing out there to find?" Jackson tossed his unfinished cigarette into the dirt, and its glow embered down to a single spark.

"Not exactly. Sure there are things and people out there to discover. But your life is the adventure. Your life. Whether you choose to stay or leave." Robert reached over and placed his hand on Jackson's chest. "It's in here, son. The adventure is in here."

He moved to take his hand back again, but Jackson quickly covered it with his own. Robert's head jerked up in surprise, and then both hands dropped at the sound of a scuffle approaching the doorway, and a few more boys jostled out onto the steps.

"Come for a drive, Jack?" one of them called out, recognizing him.

"Yeah," he said, without looking up. He stuffed his hands into his pockets and scuttled down the stairs with them into the school yard.

"I'm sorry," Robert said to his back, but he did not think the boy heard.

Chapter 14

That night the cool evening went cold and a strange spring snow came down, fat as cotton.

On Robert Owens's elixir, Laura Bachmeier went away on an African safari. She watched a caravan of elephants move with glacial slowness across the savanna, like wrinkled hunks of stone. Alice Gertson's son Mortimer had grown up to be an airplane flier and was gliding her skillfully through a sunset pink, while little Mary Watkins had spent her pennies on a longed-for trip to the circus, which she had never in real life taken. Tigers went through flaming hoops, and monkeys in red velvet jackets danced over the dust, and the face of the ringmaster was painted and greasy like a clown's. Rupert Shaw had married someone else, just for one night, a woman who always smiled vacantly and never nagged. And Elmer McBryde had gone to the Yukon for a pan full of gold, and he rolled the glints of it, choking the wet sand like stars, under an undulating sky of northern lights.

In the morning a warmer air passed over the snow, drawing up a low stubborn fog. All day it would resist the burning sun and never lift. In the sitting room, Benny's handprint could not be seen, but Evie went and put her hand over the place where she knew it to be, not touching the glass.

Why is it like this? she wondered. It would hurt less to

come out slow in a long, straight climb, but it didn't seem to work that way. She broke the surface for air and then went down again, coming out and falling back in, over and over and over and over.

"Cows have been done," George said to her from the kitchen, and she returned to him.

"Good," she said. "I'll have breakfast on in just a minute."

He had left her the day's eggs on the counter, so she cracked a few into a bowl while the water was heating for their coffee.

"That was a fun time last night," she said while she cradled her bowl and looked at him, whisking.

George nodded. "Awful lot going on, it seems."

Evie smiled. "I told you. There's always plenty to see at a dance. Did you see John Shaw's father taking him out at the end by the collar?"

"What was that all about?"

"He showed up drunk. He and some friends got their hands on something. So drunk he didn't have the good sense to go home and sleep it off. They might never have known it then."

She turned and poured her eggs into the hot buttered pan. They shriveled in and right away began to bubble.

"You're still a beautiful dancer. I'd forgotten."

She scraped at the eggs. "You're not too bad yourself."

When they were ready, she brought them to the table, and a few thick slices of bread and the dish of butter. She had served herself a small plate and took no bread.

"You should eat more."

"I know. I'm just not very hungry."

The curdle of eggs slipped down her throat, and she gagged. She reached for her coffee, chasing the food down with it. The hot coffee helped, scalded her insides clean.

George pulled his eggs around the rim of his plate with a fork. "And what did you think of Robert Owens carrying on with the Jenkins girl like that?"

Evie swallowed and grimaced. "I think it might have been more her carrying on with him, actually."

"Either way. That's trouble, there. He's too old for her and not the proper sort of man at all. He's practically a vagrant."

Evie smiled. "All they did was have a dance, George. I didn't see him get down on one knee and propose."

"You know what I mean." He lifted the forkful of eggs in the air, and some fell back to his plate.

"I do. And I think Cora Jenkins might be the silliest girl ever born to this town. But there you have it. If she will run after the likes of Mr. Owens, people will talk, and her reputation for flirting will be even worse for it. But he's not the type to stay around forever, is he? I think all that could possibly come of it is that Cora will be very disappointed when he does leave."

"She'll end up with a broken heart."

"Maybe. But it will probably be her own fault."

While George shoveled his food, tearing at bread and mopping his plate, Evie drained her coffee cup and put it down. "And what happened to him after that dance, do you think?" she asked. "He seems to have a strange habit of ducking out early from everything."

George looked up. "I'm surprised you would have noticed."

Evie rose, fussing with stacking their plates and clearing the table. "He took some punch for Cora and never brought the cups back to me. And when I saw the cups sitting empty where he'd set them down, I looked around for him. He was gone."

George folded his arms across the table where his plate had been.

"Are you picking on the poor fellow for not carrying the cups back? You don't mind about Cora, but this . . . this bothers you?"

"Never mind."

George looked at her carefully. "You're not thinking of . . . giving him any business, Evie?"

"No, I am not."

"Because if you are, I don't recommend it. Waste of money. I've heard all the tales, of course, but I don't think he could really be manufacturing dreams. Luck, I expect, is all it is."

"For goodness' sake, you sound like my mother. She warned me off him, too. Why does anyone think I'm even interested in it at all?"

"Because," he said. He stood and carried his empty cup to the sink. "Because for some reason you've got your eye on him."

★ ★ ★

"Don't forget, Evie and George are coming up for dinner tonight," Rose called when she saw Sam taking his hat off the rack by the door.

"I'll be back in plenty of time to see them. Zeke Olson broke his leg a while back, and I'm going over to take the cast off for him, that's all."

She nodded and went into the kitchen to mix up a meat loaf and peel some potatoes. She would coax out Evie's appetite with one of her old favorite dinners and an angel food cake for dessert. While she worked her hands into the mixture of ground pork and beef, massaging in spices, she gazed out at the orchard. Neither she nor Sam had taken the trouble to prune the trees these last few years, and they tangled and twisted together, every year giving less fruit. Different varieties of insect and disease were flourishing in the abundant shade and creeping over them.

She molded the meat loaf into her pan and pumped fresh water to wash her hands. Her wedding ring sat on the windowsill where she'd left it, spiraling the afternoon sunlight. As she slipped it back over her finger, the skin puckered around her knuckle. When she rubbed herself, it slid across the back of her hand, as if the skin were slowly separating from her, detaching as though it thought she shouldn't need it anymore. How easy it was to grow old, she thought, easy as a raft along a river.

The meat loaf in to bake, she went outside to sit on the porch and wait for her company. At the sight of the tulip masses, she felt a phantom ache in her back from all the hours she'd bent over the soil. Last fall when Benny was visiting, she'd shown him how to plant his own little patch of flowers and shown him, too, how to sprinkle them with cayenne pepper to keep the squirrels away. He'd wanted to taste a pinch to see how it worked, and how she'd laughed at him as he ran back into the house for water. She let him choose whatever colors he wanted, and he'd surprised her by planting only pink. "Not for me," he said. "I don't like pink, you know. They're for Mum."

As if in answer to her thoughts, there were Evie and George jostling along behind Chester down the road. She wanted Sam to buy them an automobile but Evie kept saying no. She didn't want to ride that fast.

"Half the fun for me is watching everything go by," she said. "I like things to go slowly so I can take it all in."

"You'd be so much more comfortable in a Ford," Rose told her.

"My rear end would be," she agreed. "But my soul would not."

Rose didn't argue.

Evie climbed out of the buggy down by the road and walked up through her mother's tulips. In the bright evening sun, their cups glowed gumdrop colors, and the colors seemed to hum. Evie didn't look at her, but Rose waved to George as he drove the horse over to the shed, and then she walked down to meet her daughter. She cordoned Evie with her arms, hands meeting easily now in the middle of her back. Evie wore no corset, and Rose could make out the ridges of her spine. She held her daughter tighter in case there might be something to read in them, some unseen future pushing up like a pattern of runes. Keeping one arm around her, Rose walked Evie up to the house, and the scent of the meat loaf met up with them.

"That smells good," Evie said, just as if she had every intention of eating it.

George crossed the porch toward them and took a chair.

"Let me go inside and get us some lemonade," said Rose. "Sam's out on a call, as always, but we can sit out here and wait for him."

They watched the sun reddening the west. The lemon tartness spread across their tongues. They all turned the other way when they heard the motor of the Whiting automobile in the distance, and it came around the bend as if they had willed it, were all dreaming the same dream of Dr. Whiting blowing cigar smoke into the windshield glass, the road wincing under his wheels. He drove past them, and his smile, formed around the big teeth clamped on the cigar, came off like a grimace.

When the meal was tucked away (Evie's pushed to the rim of her plate), Sam stood up and patted his son-in-law's shoulder.

"Going to take some of our canned nectarines over to Mrs. Coldbrook. You come with me, all right." It was phrased like a question but not spoken like one.

The men went outside while Evie and Rose cleared the plates. Rose washed, Evie dried, just as they'd always done. While they worked, Rose started talking. She preferred to have weighty conversations side by side, not face-to-face. She was like a man that way.

"I've been having a feeling about you and that dream peddler," she said.

"You have a feeling? What kind of feeling?"

"Just a bad sense that he is somehow going to cause trouble for you."

"Trouble for me?" Evie emphasized the "me." She turned her plate over and rubbed its back in circles, as she would have done to a colicky baby. "I don't see how he could. I've never even said hello to him. Except once, at the dance. He was there, and he did come over to me for some punch. For himself and Cora Jenkins."

"Cora Jenkins? He bringing punch to her?"

"I think he was only being friendly."

"He shouldn't be so friendly with such a young girl. It's all right for him to dance with the ladies who are married— or unmarried but still . . . sensible. And that Cora Jenkins is not."

"Cora can be very persuasive."

"Don't I know."

Rose was up to her elbows in soapy water, and the dishes lifted and moved around the bottom of the sink, scuttling away crablike from her reaching hands. Evie looked out the window while she waited for a clean dish to surface.

"I'm tired of hearing about him, to be honest," she said. "I'm tired of being warned away from him. I don't even know him. It's not like I've been seen walking around town with him. I haven't bought anything from him." Evie heard her voice growing petulant. "And what would it matter, really, if I did? Everyone else is trying the dreams."

"I'm not concerned with everyone else. And I'm not trying to give you orders at your age. I can only tell you it gives me a bad feeling. I don't know why. And my feelings about things are usually right."

"Not always, though."

"No, not always."

Rose hefted the dishpan, and Evie went to open the back door for her so she could pour the used water out into the garden.

"Let's go sit out front again. We can watch for the men to come back," Rose said crossly.

They sat next to each other on the porch swing, and it pitched one side forward and then the other as they settled into it. Eventually they straightened out, though Evie found for the first time that the tipping sway of it made her feel ill.

"Did you see the tulips Ben planted? They came up beautifully."

Evie nodded.

"Before you go, don't let me forget I have something of Ben's, if you want it."

"You do?"

"Just an old ball glove. One of the Schumann boys came over with it. Some story of how Ben had loaned it to him or you'd got him a new one and he didn't need it anymore. His mother wouldn't let him walk all the way out to your place with it, so he brought it here."

"Oh. He should have just kept it."

"Well. He didn't know if you might want it back."

"I understand. But I don't." Evie folded her arms across her chest.

"I think you will have another child sometime," Rose told her.

"I don't think I could bear that."

"Nonsense. It would be the best thing for you."

Evie did not want to argue, so she said nothing.

★ ★ ★

Sam and George sat together in a comfortable puffing silence as they smoked and jiggled down the road to Mrs. Coldbrook's.

"You taking care of my girl, George Dawson?"

"Always."

"This is worse for her than it is for you, you know," said Sam. "I don't mean to make light of your end of things. I know if anything happened to Evie, I'd be a changed man. So I can imagine how you feel, but women . . . well, that's just how they're made, I guess. They feel it worse, feel everything worse. Being a father is a wonderful thing, an important thing, too, but it's not the same as being a mother. I'm sure you know that."

George nodded noncommittally, waiting for the doctor to continue. He could never know if it was really worse for Evie than for him. He didn't think it mattered. They both braced their broken hearts inside their chests. Grief surged in their limbs and then soaked through them and inked everything they did. Every task on the farm for George was a punch in the gut. His dented heart hovered over the fence rails he mended and the fresh hay he pitched into the stalls he'd cleaned. It swung under the cows as he milked them, like his lantern. And Evie carried her heart over all she did inside the house, and every time she walked away from him to town, she walked that heart in with her and cradled it, like she'd hold two halves of a cracked eggshell so its contents didn't spill out.

"Hard for us, too, of course. Don't know what it is about this family—we only seem to have the one child. And it doesn't matter, except when you lose him . . . well, you might feel like there's no point to going on. There's no other little ones who need you."

He had one hand on the wheel and the other free to worry the cigar in and out of his mouth. He always smoked while he drove. Rose wouldn't allow it in the house. "But don't forget, you still need each other."

"I know that."

"Course you do. That's how it is for me and Rose. Evie's been grown a long time now, but we still take care of each other. This is hard on Rose. She misses her grandson, but she doesn't think about that. She's too busy wishing she could fix things for Evie. She's very worried about her."

"I can imagine."

George was looking at his own cigar like it was some creature he'd pinched up off the side of the road, rolling it over between his fingers, trying to fathom its nature.

"She's got it in her head Evie's going to get hold of that dream peddler and nothing good will come of it."

George wasn't sure what to make of this turn in the conversation. He had some concerns about Evie in that regard himself, but he didn't think it was any of Rose's business. He remembered what he'd told Evie about the dreams, but if he were honest with himself, he wasn't worried that Evie might waste some of their dollars. He was thinking about her being taken in a different way. He'd seen the dream peddler skulking nearby after the funeral, staring. Had a look passed between them? Maybe not then, but after the dance he was sure of it. He made light of it to Evie because he had to. If he took the idea seriously, anyone might. It might even be true.

"What does she think will happen, then?" he asked Sam.

"Oh, I don't know. Evie's vulnerable right now, you both are. You remember Rose lost a younger sister when she was a girl? Did you know about that?"

"Yes, I guess I did."

"I don't think Rose ever told Evie how hard that was for her. Not just Mabel dying, but what happened to her mother afterward. She couldn't get over it. Started taking something, think it must have been laudanum from the way Rose remembers. After that her mother just drifted. Cried at night, slept much of the day, and it left Rose feeling alone. Her mother never really got better."

"I didn't realize."

"Like I said, Evie doesn't know. But now you see what Rose must be thinking. Here's Evie with the exact same grief, same wound in her heart, and along comes some dream peddler with his promises and potions. Maybe it's not laudanum, but what if it acted the same way? What if we lost her?" He threw the end of his cigar out into the ditch. "And if she did get stuck in something like that, dreaming special dreams or what have you, it would be that much worse for her when Robert Owens decides to move on. It's not what we want for her."

George hadn't thought of this. What would he do if buying dreams took Evie away from them? If she couldn't stop, would she follow the dream peddler when he left? He shook the thought away.

"You know, Robert Owens was very good to me when we were out looking for Ben. He walked with me, and . . ." George decided to go ahead and confess. "He gave me a dream, too, free of charge."

Samuel whistled a long, sly whistle. "Don't let Rose hear that. She'll skin your hide."

"She already knows," said George sheepishly. "She caught me, when I was . . . when I was drinking the dream."

"That's something, isn't it? To think of drinking down a dream like that. I never could have conceived of such a thing."

"He made no promises. It didn't prove to be useful, but after Benny was found . . . I don't know, I started thinking about it. Because I did go into the water—in this dream I had. Not into the bay, but there was a river, and I was chasing after this beautiful glowing woman who was like a kind of ghost or . . . a water sprite or something. I'm sure it's nonsense. We did worry about whether he had gone down there, and I told Evie no, he would never do that, because I thought he knew better. . . ."

George felt his throat clamp around the last words, while his fingers slowly turned their unwanted cigar. "Maybe it all just got mixed up, somehow, in my head."

"Well, I've heard plenty about Owens from my patients, I can tell you that," said Sam, chasing off George's heavy silence. "All kinds of dreams, all kinds of crazy nonsense. Seems this man and his potions are all anyone can talk about lately, at least to me."

He turned the wheel. "'Dr. Whiting,' they'll say, 'you would not believe the dream I bought from that man. I was crossing the Arabian Desert in a long caravan with camels and elephants, and then a giant whale was beached there even though there was no ocean for miles around. And then a row of monkeys began to dance across the sand, and they were blowing horns, too, and waving flags. . . .'"

He humphed not quite a laugh at his own retelling. "I don't listen that closely, tell you the truth. What all kind of dreams they want . . . well, it doesn't concern me. I tell them that's wonderful and to go ahead and enjoy it, know why? Because people who have good dreams are more content with their life, and those kind of people don't call for my services as often. Don't know why exactly that should be, but it is. No harm in having a little fun in your sleep, I say. But Rose . . . well, Rose, she's dead set against Evie getting into all that. And I don't suppose Evie'd want to waste your money on it either."

"I don't know what it costs. He never charged me."

"I can imagine. There's a good price for that kind of thing. It can't be too much or people won't pay no matter how great they think it might be. Or if they do pay once, they'll judge it harshly and they won't come back again. Can't charge too much. But it has to be just enough to convince 'em it must be something special."

"Well, I don't know if you can put a fair price on magic, though, can you? Seems like he's got something in him. I don't know how else he does it."

Finally George put the cigar he did not really want to his lips and sucked in. He'd accepted it to be polite, but he never was very good at smoking a cigar properly. He wanted to breathe it all in, didn't understand how to take a shallow taste of it into his mouth without letting it all down to his lungs, where it made you queasy. George only knew how to breathe one way, big and deep. So he always felt a bit sick trying to enjoy one of Sam's cigars with him after supper.

Then Sam asked him, "So it surprised you a little that Ben would have gone out on the bay? When spring was near and he knew he couldn't trust the ice?"

George thought a moment. "Well, I don't know if 'surprised' is the right word. I was disappointed, and then I was angry. Because it needn't have happened, you know. We thought he knew. We've told him however many times. He wasn't a real small lad. Didn't wander out in the morning like a tot when we should have had the door barred. We thought we could trust him to have more sense. And he didn't, and now I can never forgive myself, and Evie can't either. Senseless. I can't see the sense of it."

Sam nodded, but he was already onto some other idea.

"Do you ever think it strange . . . that Robert Owens should have shown up in town the very morning Ben went missing?"

George looked at him, eyes wide.

"I guess I didn't know it was the same morning, not the very same. We heard of him because Violet told Evie he wanted to help us, with the search. We never knew exactly which day he was at Violet's house. I never thought of it."

"Well, it's a funny thing, but it turns out it was the same. Violet mentioned what day to me when she came to me about her rheumatism. She remembered the day, and she put it together. Evie said something to her about thinking Robert might have been sent here to us, or some such nonsense. Like he showed up the same time providentially, because he could help her."

"Did she say that? She say providence, did she?"

"Oh, I don't know if it was that word exactly. Just that she seemed to think there might be some reason."

George turned away then, hoping his profile would betray less of his surprise. He didn't know that Evie had stopped in on Violet, although she told him she'd been going into town seeing different people—the Joneses, people like that. He thought it was a good idea, something to cheer her, some distraction. But he couldn't imagine Evie saying anything about Robert Owens having been sent to them. God didn't exist for them anymore. That was George's understanding. He continued to go with Evie to church every week because it was what you did, not because he believed anymore that there was anyone out there to worship.

"Boy," was all he said when he realized he was expected to say something. "Sometimes women get silly notions, don't they?"

"That they do. I have not repeated what Violet said to Rose, and I'm sure you won't either. It will cause her unnecessary worry. I'm sure Owens's potions are harmless, but I'm not inclined to think his showing up here at such a time is a good thing. I'd just keep an eye on him, is all. I'm not sure he'll be good for our girl."

"No, doesn't seem that way, does it?" George watched the fields trundle by.

They pulled in to the drive of the peeling Coldbrook farmhouse. Sam hopped out of the car, reached over the running board, and pulled out two fat mason jars of slithery nectarine slices, curled up together against the glass. He walked up the steps and used the bottom of one jar to tap against the door.

Chapter 15

Robert was hiding in the apple orchard beside the grave-yard. He'd been coming out of Jenkins's store when he caught sight of Evie Dawson heading toward him down the street. He must ask Violet to go shopping for him, he thought. He could pay her extra. Then he could never be caught inside the store, waiting to be served. When he was quite sure Evie had seen him, he darted across the road, into the apple orchard with his satchel as if he were going off for a picnic. He resisted the temptation to look back, hoping Evie would continue into the store rather than follow him. When he thought he'd gone in far enough, he sat down and waited. In fact there was nothing much in the satchel to eat, just some shaving soap and to-bacco and another batch of sugar hearts to dole out to the girls. He wanted to go home to Violet's for his dinner.

Ahead of him the blossoming apple branches splayed out into the grassy rows, so low to the ground he was covered over with white. His scudding heart began to slow, and he felt the bark of the tree he leaned against through the back of his shirt. He imagined the roots of the tree spreading out through the ground below, drawing its water from the earth, and it calmed him. He took deep breaths that pressed his spine into the trunk.

In the distance the whole horizon was white-petaled and trembling. Then, through the curtain, somehow with no parting of it, she was there, coming toward him. She had found the right row, the one where he huddled, and she had no trouble spotting him. It was as if he could not hope to hide from her, and all his weeks of trying had been a waste. She walked through the trees with the chalky blossoms lighting at her feet where the breeze carelessly dropped them. Even though it was the time for blossoms to loosen, it still seemed unfair against her, as if every beauty of the world must fall down around her.

He stood up, resigned, and took a few steps forward through the grass. When she reached him, he drew breath; he wanted to speak first.

"Mrs. Dawson, I think I know why you've been following me, and I have to tell you frankly, I just won't do it. I am not going to sell anything to you. It wouldn't be right."

Her pink eyelids slipped down slightly over her eyes. Her hands gathered her skirt quietly at her sides.

"I'm sorry," he said, wishing she'd go away. "I can't give you any dreams of your son."

At that she looked up at him, reading his face.

"I think you misunderstand me, Mr. Owens," she said. "I do want something from you. . . . I've been trying to ask you for weeks, but it's not dreams I want. I was only hoping you could give me something that would make me stop dreaming of him."

Robert stared as if he could not comprehend.

"Sleep is hard on me," she said. "Every night he is alive, and every morning he dies again. It makes me wish I didn't have to sleep. And I thought you might have something I could use for that. I'd really rather not have any dreams at all. If I didn't, maybe then I could stand the waking up."

Robert put a hand to his face and palmed along his jaw, like someone who'd been slapped.

"In that case," he said slowly, "Mrs. Dawson, I think I can help you."

★ ★ ★

"Did you lie to me, Evie?"

She turned from where she stood at the sink scrubbing the supper dishes, hands held down in the milky little pond of soap and water. She twisted like a statue, head turning full across her shoulder without her body, because if she removed her hands, they'd drip all around her.

"What?" She tried to wait in stillness while she listened for what he would say. Listened for what came sliding under, if it were a breath of fury or fear. After so many years, she was practiced at hearing the undersides of George's words. They were trusting, like dogs who rolled over willingly for her and exposed their bellies.

"About the dream peddler, did you lie to me about him?"

Evie turned back to her work and tried to think fast enough to answer without delay.

"I'm not sure what you mean."

He couldn't know about the orchard, could he? She didn't even have what she'd asked for yet. Robert had agreed to meet her there again in a few days' time. She tried to figure out if anyone could have seen them. Even if someone had, she thought, how could word have traveled to George out on the farm faster than her own feet had carried her there? It couldn't.

"Did I say anything about the dream peddler?" she asked.

George sighed. It was not in his nature to peck at his wife, not to be jealous. He felt it like a fist pressing hard to his chest, trying to plunge in through the bone and reach something else.

"You told me you weren't interested in going to him for anything. You agreed it was all nonsense, about the dreams. But Violet Burnley was talking something about you telling her maybe he's come here to save you. And that's the opposite entirely." She heard him shuffle a step behind her. "So I was just wondering. You know I'm not the kind of man to put my foot down. Jesus, Evie, if it's that important to you, just go on and try it. You didn't have to lie to me."

Evie took a towel and dried her hands.

"Violet Burnley? She told you what I said?"

Evie couldn't imagine the two of them in private conversation. It seemed so unlikely she almost laughed.

"Not me, no. She told your father, and he thought I might want to know."

Evie's mind was skittering over her memory of how many times they'd been to her parents' the last few weeks, and it wasn't many.

"When did my father talk to you of this?"

"Does it matter?"

She fingered the edge of the towel in her hands. "No, I guess it doesn't. But if I said that to Violet, I must have been thinking about it later on, after we talked, and just wondering . . . if maybe I was wrong."

She wanted to yank the conversation back from this ledge but could not figure out how to do it.

George looked into her eyes, trying to read something in them that she would never let rise there. The gray pools had iced on him, sealed over the lights he was used to.

He spoke quietly. "Why don't you go ahead and get your dream, then? If anyone deserves one, it's you. Your mother

and father are worried about what might happen, and maybe
they got me worried, too. But then I started thinking . . .
what if you need to have your dream, to get past this? Go
ahead and have it. You don't have to tell me what you want
it to be. Just have it and then . . . be done with it. Then you
can forget."

Evie was still. "Forget what?"

"About the dreams. The dream peddler."

She nodded at him, willing to let the matter rest there.
There was a settling, as if she'd taken a pot of boiling water
off the stove.

★ ★ ★

Evie went into the forest because she felt safe there. She returned to the woods when there was nothing on her stove
that needed watching, no task that couldn't wait for her. The
pile of mending nestled in its basket, and the dust paled the
dark furniture, the neglected corners, while she walked out
into the past. The tall trees had become a different kind of
shelter. In the forest she could sit still, put herself down small
and folded at the base of the towering pines. The whispers
led her in there, and the world turned over, and the light disappeared from the forest floor. It rose into the treetops, while
Evie felt she was watching an unbearable brightness from a
safer, shadowed place.

Only once had she been frightened away from her ref-
uge, sitting in stillness while the forest movements surged
around her. The sky was darkening, and a storm was coming; as it crept closer, the leaves began to agitate like animals
bristling. Everything stiffened to the nervous static charge of
the air building to lightning.

Then she saw, at a little distance, a dead leaf left behind
by the autumn before. Crumpled, like a lost note browned

by the winter, it hovered. It was not just kicked up by the wind, though the wind was growing stronger. She had never seen a dead leaf behave like this. Picked up by the air but not put down, it fluttered at her as if trying to speak and expecting her somehow to understand its message. She stood up and felt the back of her housedress snagging on the bark of the tree. She went toward the leaf slowly, so as not to startle it away.

"Benny?" she asked it. "Ben, is that you?"

Her voice was lost in the greater rustle of the whole forest buffeted, waiting for a storm that would not break. She stared at the leaf while the pulse of her heart took over her senses, and even her hands and feet swelled more and more with every beat.

The sun pushed out of the clouds then and slanted down into the forest through a break in the canopy, and Evie saw, because of its light, the silver filament of a spiderweb strung between the trees. There was the leaf, caught in the web and trembling as if it feared her.

Evie realized it was not disappointment she felt but relief.

As she walked home, she remembered the little-boy smell of him, after his bath on a summer Saturday evening when his hair was still soap-wet and the dirt still staining the fresh-scrubbed caps of his knees. She pulled into herself that memory of holding him, when he was almost defenseless, and the pleasure of his nearness and skin and hair was so intense it was like desire. That memory moved over her like ants on a mound of sugar.

The late spring was painful with color, the purple of rhododendrons and the insistent yellow banks of forsythia lining the roads. As the round buds came out and the ground was spattered with petals, the world appeared to Evie as just a mass of dots and blobs. She had read once of a kind of paintings that were like this, and back then she had not understood. Now she recognized the passing time dotted down in them as seconds, the endless prick of the brush tip, the moments, all the colors that would never after bleed together. Now she thought this painting must have been invented in the spring, for she looked out and it was all there was—the buds and blossoms and bumbles of bees, everything painted and verdant and about to burst and full of holes.

And the grass changed now when the sun was lying low in the sky. If she looked down at the right time, she could pick out every single blade of it, and it was like something you weren't supposed to see or be able to count. The fields of violets, too, were some kind of trick. You couldn't see their endless blue when you looked right at them—you had to look just above to catch it, gaze off at the horizon. Only then did you discover how blue they truly were. As soon as you looked at them head-on, the spell was broken, into that scattering of flowers on the grass. She wondered if she had made this mistake with everything in her life. Was she looking too closely at things, at everyone around her? Was she doing this and misunderstanding who they all really were? She had missed Benny, maybe. She had stared at him so hard, loved him so hard, when she should have been looking just to the left of him; she should have been free with him and at ease. If she had been more forgiving, less exacting, less needful, more willing to look away, he would not have been taken from her.

Chapter 16

"You came to his funeral," Evie said. "I saw you."

"You were leaving. You were climbing up into your buggy."

"George had my hand. And then I saw you . . . under the tree."

"I'm sorry I didn't go in. I just didn't know . . . because I never knew him."

"It doesn't matter. I don't remember any of the faces. . . . They all looked the same. I only noticed you because . . ."

"Oh, yes. I understand."

Robert pushed his hands into his pockets. They felt safer there.

"So if I take this?" She held up the glass vial he'd brought her.

"You drink it right before sleep. It should take away your dreams. If it doesn't—"

"Yes, I know. Money back." She looked away, at the shivering orchard beyond him. "I hope it doesn't come to that."

Robert watched her. "I wonder if I should warn you . . . I've never done this before."

"I understand."

"I only make dreams. I've never . . . I'm not sure what's

going to happen. What your sleep will be like. Or your waking. It might change things."

"Don't worry. It couldn't make them worse."

He leaned a little, looked into her gray eyes, as if he might see something in her she did not yet know was there. "I wonder."

She opened her hand and looked again at the vial, then closed it tighter. "You didn't ask me how he died."

"Of course not. I could never ask you that."

She looked up. "We don't know," she told him. "He was found . . . under the ice. He'd gone through the ice on the bay out there." She gestured at the distance with her empty hand. The bay, invisible from where they stood, was surely lapping and winking in the sun, the ice long vanished. "But we don't know why he went out. Why he went out on the ice to begin with."

"I'm sorry."

"It doesn't make sense, does it?"

"No," said Robert. "He was how old? Eleven? I wouldn't think that could ever make sense."

Evie rolled the potion between her palms. "He was only nine," she said.

★ ★ ★

Toby was holding court on the back steps behind the store. The dream peddler had changed everything for him, and now the boys who had so often laughed at him were listening while he spoke. Toby had always been popular in his way, wanted for shooting or fishing expeditions, but he'd never garnered any respect for his words or ideas. He wasn't quick-witted enough to say much when the boys gathered and joked. He laughed loud when he heard others laugh, even if he didn't understand. And when he talked, he kept his voice low. That way he felt like he was a part of things but didn't have to worry the fellows might hear and laugh harder at what he said.

Now they were all paying attention. There was a taut, stretched respect for what he'd discovered. Of course it was not right to give details, but a few were enough: where, how long, how many times. What color the dress, before she removed it.

They leaned against the porch rails or sat on the steps, and Toby regaled them with talk of how lucky he was to have money set aside, how relaxed and easy he'd become around the girls. Robert Owens was a man you could trust, he told them. A quiet man. Discreet.

"Sounds about right," said Ansen Smith. "But I'm saving up just now. Wouldn't spend my money that way."

"Saving to marry Jenna?" asked Barto McBryde. The group hollered as if it were funny, and Ansen was clapped on the back.

"I might think about it," John Shaw said. "Not guilty like Ansen here, if you know what I mean."

"I wonder some of the married men don't give it a try. That'd be the ticket. No getting tired of just one. Great solution if the wife's feeling poorly."

They all laughed again.

"What about you, Rolf? You gonna try it?"

"He figures he'll wear Christina down one of these days. Get her to kiss you, that right?"

Rolf went scarlet to his ears.

All too soon they were bored, and tired of Toby's big talk. Most of them stood and jumped down off the steps, pushed off the wood and away. They all had chores to do, and they were all hungry.

Jackson lingered behind the rest. He leaned at the porch

rail, resting his forearms on it and looking out at the green-ing land behind the store. With his eyes on the horizon, he asked, "Those dreams work for you every time? For sure?"

"Haven't failed yet," said Toby.

"That's something." He pushed back and forth as if test-ing the wood. "You got any to spare?"

"Well." Toby jammed his hands into his pockets. "As a matter of fact, I do have one I've been saving. Got it the other day."

"Oh, yeah? You could do that? I mean . . . what if it isn't fresh?"

Toby licked his lips. "Don't think it makes any differ-ence. I done it before. I have to buy them on the sly, when-ever I can, and that isn't so often. So I don't always use them on the same day."

"Huh." Jackson laced his fingers together. He tapped his thumbs.

Toby grinned in his slow-dawning way. "You want it, don't you?"

Jackson glanced at him. "I wouldn't mind."

"I guess I could sell it. I mean, I don't think I could just give it away."

"No, I don't expect it for free. I just . . . I don't want to be seen knocking on that door, you know? Miss Violet prob-ably answers. It's embarrassing."

"Oh, she won't know what you're there for. I mean, of course she'll know, but she'd never guess what *kind* of dream."

"I've just been thinking . . . you've done this before, and you've got used to it. I'd feel strange about it. I don't want any girls in town to see me there. Or for it to get back to my parents that I was, you know . . . consorting with him." Toby didn't know what "consorting" meant, but he could guess. It was too long a word to mean anything good. He watched Jackson stand up straight. "But I have money. Always have money. What if I made you a deal? Since you go there regular anyway, would you buy some for me, too, when you're there? Next time I can even pay you in advance."

"Well, sure. That'd be all right with me." He quoted Jackson a price just slightly higher than what he'd been paying. That was his rightful fee, he imagined, and thought himself pretty clever after all.

Jackson counted out the money, and Toby pulled a tiny vial from his pocket and held it up.

"Looka that," said Jackson. "That's a lot smaller than I thought it would be."

"Yup. Really just one swallow, that's all they are. Take a swig at night, go right to sleep. You won't be sorry."

"I just bet I won't." Jackson took the vial, held it gingerly up to the light, squinted at it. He shook it a little to see the liquid move, and it was more viscous than water but still seemed to spit bits of rainbow. "Thanks." He put it into his own pocket. "I guess I'll let you know if I'd like any more."

Toby grinned. "I think you will. Every dream I've had has just been . . . swell. All different girls. Different kinds. Most beautiful girls I've never seen." He smiled wider at his own joke.

"We'll see." Jackson took the porch steps all in one leap and loped around to the front of the store and the street. He almost hoped to see some acquaintance and stop to shoot the breeze, the warm dream rolling in his pocket, but he saw few people. Only the old men who spent all their last, stiff days folded on benches in the storefront shade. Instead he whistled, lightly at first and then louder. *Whistle and I'll come to you, my lad,* he thought.

The dreams would be the thing, he knew. He could feel a change coming, the liquid growing warmer, promising that the change would soon be worked inside himself. He would buy as many as it took, and then he would dream of women, only women, each more beautiful than the last. Their beauty and passion would overwhelm him, and there would be no more confusion.

★ ★ ★

Evie met Robert almost every week to get her medicine. He tried not to charge her at first, but she insisted. He also tried to give her a lot of it. Unlike the dreams he sold, what she required could be made in larger batches to last her longer, he reasoned. She didn't want to take a big bottle, she told him. The small glass vials could be easily tucked into a drawer of linens, even stashed in a pocket, and she wanted to hide what she was doing from her husband. And the weekly payments worked best for her as well. The small bits missing from her grocery money would go unnoticed at home.

"Tell me about yourself."

Robert expected her to shrug off the question, stand up brushing her skirts in that way she had, and say something about getting her husband's supper, as she always did.

"I didn't think I'd ever get married," she said.

What a waste that would have been, Robert thought. He studied the side of her face, the dark line of lashes shading her eyes, the way her lips curved into each other. Every so often a flush came into her cheek, but it never stayed. He found himself waiting for it. "You didn't?"

"Not really. I was always so independent. I never had many friends, even. My mother made people uncomfortable."

"Oh, yes. I don't see much of her. I gather she doesn't care to come often into town."

"No. She'd rather keep her own company. The women here . . . well, they don't like that. I think they don't understand how a woman could be happy without all the quilting bees, the church socials, the endless gossip."

"Vi told me a little about her. She left me with the impression some people think she's a bit . . . that she might be . . . simple."

Evie smiled. "Or she is altogether too deep for them. They think she's in touch with dark forces, the occult, something like this."

"Ah. Just like me."

"Yes, exactly. Like you." She bent and snapped up a long blade of grass. "Always on the outside."

She said it lightly, but the words pulled on him, drew off his smile.

"They don't like that she won't go to church, of course," Evie said.

"And why won't she go? Does she not believe in God?"

"She says the minister droning and the tuneless singing interfere in her communion with him."

Robert laughed. "So . . . which is it? Does your mother know witchcraft? Does she have the second sight?"

"I'm sure you don't expect me to tell my mother's secrets. Unless you tell me yours."

"Well, no. I can't do that. A magician must never reveal how he does his tricks."

Evie put one hand behind her, leaning back on the trunk of a tree. "Sometimes it's as if she knows things. And it's strange. She was the one who told me . . . when I'd be expecting. With Ben."

"A mother's intuition?"

"We've always been close. Maybe she does have a special sense when it comes to me."

"So why did you think you would never be married?"

"Just because . . . that's how it was. I was closer with her than anyone because of how she was—not mixing in, people thinking she . . . I didn't have anyone else at times. There were some little girls who weren't supposed to come to our house or even play with me."

Robert pictured little Evie Whiting, long dark braids bouncing along her back while she ran through the woods by herself. Little Evie tossing a rubber ball or making mud pies in the road, alone. He remembered his own boyhood and the many friends he'd had, how easily they joined together at school and how year by year he had shed them until now he was more alone than she could ever have been.

"That's sad," he said.

"Mm. I've never been sad, about that. My mother was my best friend. And she still is. And now I have George and his family."

"So George didn't care about your mother? Like everyone else?"

"I don't know. When George started coming into town to see me, it was all decided pretty fast. He knew her a little by then, and he knew what people said about her, but I guess he ignored it."

"He wanted you enough it didn't matter."

She seemed to stiffen. He wondered if she didn't like that word, "want," coming from him.

"I was the one who approached him, you know, the first time we met. We knew each other from school, but this was later on."

"Now I see." Robert smiled. "You bewitched him."

"Like mother, like daughter. Yes, that's probably what they say."

★ ★ ★

Sam Whiting had been up most of the night with a croupy baby, and he was tired driving homeward from the Thomson farm. His eyelids wanted to close, but the feeling of sand underneath them kept him blinking and lifting them up again. He turned in at the graveyard gate and stopped his motorcar, looked out across the jumble of stones as if he might spot Ben's little resting place. He had wanted to pay for a large monument, something that would tower over the graveyard, carved with corner cherubs and one big angel, maybe, huge scalloped wings of stone banking out over the grass, but Evie refused. He wanted something grand, a tribute that could be easily seen from the road. Evie was adamant and seemed to think that towering gravestones were unsuitable for children, like too much rich food. Instead she chose a small slanted stone, low to the ground, that curled back on itself at the sides like a partially read scroll. She embellished it with no carvings or Bible verses. Just his name, "Beloved Son," and the dates of Benjamin's short life.

Sam felt himself stumbling over the uneven ground. It seemed so far away, this unassuming grave hidden among all the taller ones. Everything between the stones was brilliantly green, like some distorted land from a dream. When he reached the scroll, he stood for a moment, looking down at his grandson's last gift. The lettering was incised clean white into the granite, and the stone itself freckled the light. Starry spots within it glittered like a clear night sky. He crouched down and ran his fingers lightly over the letters without really reading them. His eyes were blurring straight edges and starting to close.

He had spent his night at the Thomson house, where their

third, a little boy named James, had croup and scared them all witless. The night air was not cold and damp enough to ease his breathing, they said, though they'd been running out with him at intervals and propping him up with his face turned to the high moon. After examining him Dr. Whiting knew it was the true croup and explained to them the cold air would not have helped anyway. He showed them how to lay out a pan of hot coals and sprinkle it with sulfur. He tied flannel over his own face and held poor James above the dark smoke while he writhed and choked. Finally the boy began to cough up a messy grayish membrane and was laid down breathing much easier. Dr. Whiting stayed and smoked the little boy twice more in the night to make sure all the infection was gone, then left them all dazed over their pale bowls of porridge in the morning. James was resting soundly, and the other children waved bright metal spoons good-bye at the doctor from the breakfast table.

There was always some kind of illness running through these large families, he thought. He was sitting now on the grass, although a faint dampness of dew was trying to find his skin through his clothing. They'd all had a case of the measles, too, shortly before Mary was due, and Sam had been concerned about her passing it on to the baby. The baby still seemed right as rain, but the little two-year-old, Lila, was worrying him now. He had noticed a change in her on his last two calls to the house but couldn't put his finger on what was wrong. Lila had been growing strong and healthy and like most children her age was starting to string her words together into short sentences. She enjoyed games of patty-cake and pressing her cheek hard against whatever she hugged.

He noted again how low to the ground Ben's modest stone was, how it sloped perfectly down to meet the grass. He remembered something about the ancients having stone pillows, didn't he? He had read that somewhere, he was sure, the Greeks or Romans using them. The grave seemed to be guiding him onto itself, as surely as if it had arms. He decided to try it out, and he took off his coat and spread it over the dew, then lay down with the tops of his shoulders slanting back onto Ben's memorial. He watched the sun floating up in the sky, a bubble so bright it forced his already heavy eyelids down over his eyes. As he closed them, he saw a phantom sun scarred red across his interior darkness.

Lila's words had been going out like things with a tide. She was as laughing as ever, happy, always singing tunelessly some endless song known only to her. But her words washed back in less frequently, their edges softened down like sea glass. Something told him he should know what was wrong, but he struggled to hold that idea against the physical perfection of her childhood: her hearty appetite, straight back and limbs, untroubled sleep. Even as he closed his eyes, he thought he could stay awake to puzzle it through, but he fell asleep with his body stretched out over the length of Ben's earth. The grass under him flattened, and the sun wormed across him, warming the dark wrinkles of his clothing.

Evie came into his dream, not the gaunt daughter of today but the chubby toddler of many years ago, sitting on a blanket in the front yard in her dirty play dress, patting her surroundings with the tender palms of her hands. There are dimples in each of her fingers smiling up at him. He bends down to observe more closely what she is doing and finds she is picking up fallen tulip petals from the beds in the lawn and examining each one carefully. She puts every petal through the same series: smells it, tastes it, rolls it between her fingers. Then she pokes it into her ear, and he's surprised to see it disappearing completely from view. He kneels to check her ears, but they are empty, unharmed by the petals.

In his confusion over where they could have gone, she seems a tiny magician, fooling him with the simplest of tricks.

Then he notices her putting a small pebble up to her mouth, and he snatches it away, afraid she will choke on it. She smiles at him and shakes her head silently, entertained by his inability to understand. She puts her now-empty fingers into her mouth and pulls out a pebble, glistening wet from her saliva, and places it carefully beside her on the blanket. Mystified, he watches as she pulls a whole row of pebbles from her mouth and lines them up across the pale fabric He studies them, certain this is a message she has made, in a code he cannot decipher. Running his fingertips along the surface of the stones, he is still troubled, trying to understand, and Evie, out of patience, begins to climb across the hump of his bent back and giggles down into his ear.

He woke, with the feeling he'd sunburned his face and no idea how long he'd been sleeping. The dream was still with him; he could feel the tug of Evie at his shoulders and half expected to see the little rank of pebbles waiting for him there in the grass. With an unexpected ease, he realized he knew what was wrong with Lily Thomson. She'd lost her hearing, probably from an ear infection caused by her bout with the measles. And now all the words she had so carefully collected were leaving her. In her head they were still perfectly cut, as if from ice, but in the round hollow of her mouth they began to melt and lose their shapes, and when she tried to breathe them out, they were already gone. From now on she would make only barks, wails, and a hazy, heartfelt kind of panting.

The sadness of his discovery made little impression on him as he raised his head, trying to twist the stiffness out of his neck, and rolled over onto one elbow and looked underneath him. He was overcome by a sense of gratitude, a certainty that his dream had been a visitation even though he had never before in his life experienced any magic. He palmed the surface of the gravestone with the hand he was not leaning on.

"Thank you, Benny," he told it. "Thank you for helping me."

★ ★ ★

The only trouble with Evie's new way of sleeping was how she woke, with the itchy feeling of having slept not at all. There might be a darkness, a vague sense of George ruffling the air behind her or the moon tickling in at the window, but always a sense that no time had passed and whatever sleep she got had been only a few minutes. She decided it was a matter of will to get used to it, to keep her mouth clamped shut while yawns stretched hard at the back of her throat, to keep her eyes open wide so there would be no hint of sleepiness when George spoke to her.

Evie didn't like to go back to Violet Burnley's after that first time. She realized now that if Violet saw her there, buying who knows what from Robert Owens, it would get back to her parents, and George. She was glad for the summer, because there were so many places to hide. You could disappear into the sheaves of corn, leaving no wake behind you. Every field and grove was a shifting cover for private meetings, and eventually she came to think of Robert as everlastingly dappled with shade, his face a wobbling patchwork of light and darkness. He came to her in the same orchard where they had met, beside the graveyard, and everything they said to each other was tinged with the verdure of leaf shade. He always held out a half-pound bag of sweets, sugar hearts from the store, as if she were a creature that had to be lured. One time he brought her an apple, and she turned the waxy skin in her hand as if considering all its surface before biting, hunting for the deepest red she could find on it.

"It's strange you came to town the time of year you did," she said. "We don't get too many salesmen coming through here in the winter."

He folded his arms. "Guess I wouldn't normally have come that time of year either. It's no fun walking through the blasted cold, that's for sure."

"So why did you? Come here then?"

He watched her rolling the apple in her hand.

"Sometimes things just don't go right. There was a young woman, in that last town. She drank one of my potions before she went to sleep, and then she never woke."

Evie didn't look up at him, but the apple stopped.

"I promise, there was nothing in that potion that could have hurt her. It must have been a coincidence, but people in that town, they blamed me."

"Why did they blame you?"

He looked away. "No one could tell what had happened to her. Maybe she had a bad heart? They didn't accuse me directly, of course, but you understand there always comes a time when I have to leave. Everything starts off fine, people think up the dreams they want, and when they buy the potions and they get them . . . well, they like that. And they keep coming back for more, so they can go on having dreams.

"But the problem, see, is they've all told me what they want. They've all told me what they want most to dream of, these secrets they have, that they haven't told anyone else. They're uncomfortable after a time, knowing everything that I know, and they maybe think they can't trust me to keep quiet about what I know. So even if they'd rather keep coming back to me to have dreams, they resent me being around. The price gets too heavy."

Now they looked at each other.

"When I come to town a stranger, people don't think much about telling me secrets, I guess. They don't know me, and I don't know them. But after a long enough time, see, I do come to know them. I am in danger of becoming part of their town. And when I feel that, when I feel people starting to hold it all against me, that's when I know it's time to leave."

"Sounds like a lonely life."

He shrugged. "I s'pose it can be lonely, yes. But in a way I also feel like I'm good for them. Like a doctor, maybe, like your father. I take money for a while, and it's good business for me and all, but then when I leave, I don't know . . . they are able to let those parts of themselves go with me. They've shucked off a burden, somehow. Sometimes it's a good thing, to let go of some part of yourself."

Evie was shaking her head. "But the part of themselves that leaves with you, then, is the dreaming part. What do we have if we let go of the dreaming part of ourselves?"

"And what about you?" he asked her. "I've helped you to silence your own dreaming mind. Probably I shouldn't do that. But I find it hard to say no to you."

"Because of Ben."

"Well, yes." He looked as if he might say something more, but all he did was go into his pocket for cigarettes.

"It's different with me," she said. She swallowed the bulb of yawn blooming under her palate. "Right now I don't have any other choice."

"As you wish it." He held out her medicine, and she walked away from him into the wind. When she had gone out of his sight, he looked down and noticed she'd dropped his apple into the grass, and it was smooth and unbitten.

★ ★ ★

It was George's birthday, and Evie had decided to bake him a cake.

He was out haying in the fields and would not come in for supper until the evening milking was done. She had collected the eggs from the hens that morning, but she stepped out again for a last look as she sometimes did in the afternoon. As soon as the days stretched out a little, the quiet winter hens began laying again, as if the process needed light. Evie enjoyed the hens, the broken silkiness of their feathers under her hand, the comical rolling of their yellow-ringed, beady eyes.

In the half-light of the henhouse, she felt at home, as if the dust motes in her sleepy mind suddenly showed themselves to her here. She yawned in the twilight and shook her head. She was still having trouble, moved through the day in a stubborn stupor she could not shake off. Putting her hand into the warmth under each hen, she stopped for the first time to wonder at how easy it was to take their eggs from them, as long as none of them were broody. Since she had already collected earlier, most of the soft, hot hollows were empty. Charlotte, she noted, had another broken shell, and her straw was sticky with egg slime. Evie had cleaned up yesterday's mess as soon as she discovered it, but she'd probably been too late. Now that Charlotte had a taste for the eggs, she'd be no good. Evie would have to break her neck and dress her for the table.

With two new eggs she found, Evie climbed back up to the house and began the cake. Her apron turned white and floury as she measured and mixed. By the time supper was ready, the cake sat, petaled with frosting, in the center of the dining table. Evie had spelled HAPPY BIRTHDAY across it, using a knife to carve careful letters. In its serene roundness, it even seemed hopeful, like a cake for a little boy. Evie left it and went upstairs to change into her good yellow summer dress. She took out her hair, brushed the curls, and pinned them back again. She realized she had grown used to the shape of herself. She could anticipate her reflection now, so the image she ferried in her mind could meet up with what she really was.

When George came in from the field and saw Evie and his cake, he smiled, and it creased the grime across his cheeks.

"It's a celebration," he said dubiously.

"Happy birthday, George."

"Well, look at all this. Look at you."

Evie had set a roast chicken to rest on the sideboard, and the smell went down into him. She'd made rolls and butter beans and roasted carrots. He rubbed his hands down the front thighs of his overalls and pulled them back up, curling and releasing his fingers.

"I'm not fit for all this," he said. "I'd better go clean myself up."

In a clean shirt and forearms, George ate hungrily while Evie nodded over her plate. He looked up at her now and again but saw only the same thing each time: Evie drawing a fork agonizingly slowly through her food and once in a while lifting a bite and holding it in her mouth. He could see her taking a drink of water to make the food go down, as if she could not swallow without it.

They could have gone to her parents', he thought. Or even his parents' next door. They would have been pleased to put on a little supper if she'd asked them. And then the two of them would not be here alone together. With others around maybe he wouldn't be feeling this anger churning upward from his gut, this sudden need to make her eat. Evie stared dreamily out the window, unaware of the flush working up the back of her husband's neck. As soon as his plate was clean, Evie jumped up as if a bell had sounded. She cut George a big wedge of the cake and a smaller piece for herself.

"It's delicious," he told her.

"I'm so glad. I remembered at the last minute you'd rather chocolate, and I just didn't have any."

"No, no, this is good like this." He ate some more. "You going to try some?"

Obediently Evie raised her fork again. George had an impulse to reach across the table and grasp her hand, shove the fork into her mouth and down to the plate again, again, and again until the cake had gone into her. Hold her mouth shut over the gagging. He imagined himself pressing his hands behind her head, pressing her whole face down into the cake. She yawned, and he saw himself bending her yawn into the soft frosting before she could close her mouth.

George shifted his weight in the chair, and his hands brushed across the tabletop, crumbs snowing down to the floor. He cleared his plate and Evie's as well, with the cake unfinished. She sat at her empty place, leaning her head on her hand, paying no attention to him. George went over and forced himself to kiss her on the cheek.

"Thank you for that wonderful supper. I'm very tired. I'm going on up to bed."

Evie looked up at him. "Oh. All right."

As he lay in bed watching the tide of daylight go out, he listened to the movements of Evie washing their supper dishes below. The work seemed to go on for a long time. Most nights Evie and George went to bed together, and when she slid in beside him, he waited for her to turn onto her side and then he drew her body in next to his. He liked to fall asleep holding her, but tonight the sounds of her work carried him off before she came up. As if he were rocked by a ship and all her movements sounded like the clinking of wind in the chains.

Chapter 17

Toby was having a wonderful dream. He had them frequently now, thanks to the extra money from summer work he took on the busy farms. Under the sun he strained his muscles and the blue veins surfaced into his sweat, and under the moon he slept. Most of the time he didn't recognize the girls in these dreams, and it was a different girl every night. He hoped Robert Owens would stay in town a very long time.

In this dream, though, he knows at once the woman waiting for him at the edge of the field. The wheat is high, and as she backs away from him, he fears he could lose her in its sighing folds if he doesn't follow fast enough. But she is not running, only leading him into the center. Her gray eyes check over her shoulder every so often, making sure he's still behind her. The growing wheat gasps and parts around them, then closes in on itself to erase their path.

Her hair when she unpins it is thick as an attic darkness and lined the same way with the daylight. He will put his face into it, then lie down, catch the tips of it along his skin like rain. Her body is the one from before, the round, muscled thighs closing around his hips when he enters her, the large breasts shifting their brown nipples slightly away from him as she arches her back. His eyelids half close over his vision, his chest moves down to cover the glance of her breasts, and she is slippery around him. He'd never realized that he wanted her when he was waking; it only comes to him now, in the dream field. The sun crosses over his back and bends down between his shoulder blades. It lifts the sweat beads one by one, harvesting them from his skin.

Even in his dream, he is surprised to feel her bucking hips against him. As she starts to call out in her pleasure, he hears himself shushing her like the swaying shafts of wheat, because he can't help thinking that even this far from the town someone might hear them. . . . No time passes in the dream. He rolls away and feels the crackling stalks tickle, while the sunlight never moves from its midday stiffening in the sky. Eventually it becomes clear to him that they are frozen now, and only if they separate will time resume. So he rises and looks for his clothes, tossed into the wheat and clinging there, and the chaff peels away with them as he pulls them out. She makes no move to dress herself, only leans on an elbow and watches, one leg pulled over the other and hiding the place where he has just been. The faint staggered stretch marks of her abdomen glimmer like lightning.

"Come back," she tells him from the ground. "Come back to me every day, and I will soon have another baby to love."

He laughs, delighted to be able to help her. Then he woke, to the gauzy swell of the curtains at his window, and the smells of hay and jasmine beds and horse rose into him. He found himself returning to her many other times, at night when the blankets snaked tight around him and then slackened again. He never tired of her.

★ ★ ★

The days of summer dragged long and hot, and the orchard clicked and buzzed with insects. Evie had paid Robert his fee and was now pushing her vial of medicine into her pocket, watching that the tip of it did not stick out.

"Is it so important, to keep it a secret?"

Evie looked at Robert as if the question were absurd.

"But why?"

"It's just easier this way," she said.

"For you."

"For everyone. I'm tired of being watched and worried over. Mother has a crazy idea that if I buy dreams from you, I'll . . . I'll disappear into dreamland or something. She really seems to hate you. I don't know why."

"And your husband? George? I shouldn't give advice about marriage, I guess. But it seems to me that keeping such a secret from him . . . Are you so sure he won't understand?"

Evie watched a butterfly come close to landing on Robert's shoulder, then veer away into the deeper cavern of leaves. "He told me I should come to you. He told me I should buy a dream. But I don't want him to know."

"I don't understand."

"He thinks it's over and done with. He thinks . . . he thought it was just a matter of one dream, that I could buy it and dream it and move on. He has no idea what I'm doing. And I don't want to try to explain. How it feels . . . to wake up every morning and realize again, to be smothered with that. I can't stand any more dreams that Ben is alive. But George, he shouldn't have to know."

"Why?" he asked gently. "Wouldn't he want to know? Do you not worry if you keep all this hidden . . . it could drive him away from you?"

"I don't know. Without Benny . . . I can't feel. I don't know what hurts. Everything hurts. And all I can do about George is carry on what we've always done, but the feeling is blotted out. I'm sure I must still love him, because I always have. But I don't feel anything. There's no difference, in distance or closeness anymore. We are both alone." She sighed. "All I can do is protect him."

Robert would have liked to reach out and touch her, but instead he played with his pack of cigarettes. He tamped it down in one palm, studying it closely. "I don't normally snitch on my customers."

"I'm sure you don't."

"I'm going to make an exception in this case."

Evie looked at him, her eyes dark.

"Your husband already took a dream from me. Many weeks ago, before—"

"He did?"

"He must have heard through the store. Toby or Cora. And the day I went out with him and the search party, he asked me."

"He talks like my mother," she said sharply. "He talks about you like only a fool would give you good money."

"Yes, well. I don't suppose he dreamed what he was hoping. Although I tried to warn him. . . . I didn't really think it would work."

"Warned him what?"

"He thought maybe a dream could help him find your son."

"I see." She smiled slightly, as if embarrassed. "We never used to keep secrets from each other."

"I'm sure you didn't."

She put her face in her hands. "And it didn't work."

"I guess he didn't tell you because he didn't want to raise your hopes."

She lifted her head and looked at him. "People always say that, don't they? People think hope can be raised or lowered like a flag, and it's not like that at all. It's in your chest no matter what. I couldn't have pushed it off if I tried. I'd been stabbed at the heart, but the hope . . . No, it was just like a rock."

Chapter 18

It was after church one Sunday, and the townspeople were busy taking leave of one another, unhitching their horses and driving away from Violet's reproachful postlude. As the crowd's edge began to thin, Cora Jenkins surprised the dream peddler by squeezing herself in beside him and asking if he'd walk her back to the store.

Her parents had already begun to make their own way down the street while Cora said good-bye to her friends. There was no one with the authority to pull her aside or hiss at her under their breath. The mouths of the young girls fell open, wet with listening.

Robert touched the brim of his hat.

"Of course, Miss Cora. If you've no one to see you home, I'd be glad to."

He held his arm out for her, as he usually did about this time for Violet, and Cora took it, as demurely as if she had not just asked for it herself. Over his shoulder she winked back at Christina, whose hanging lower lip clamped back up over her surprise.

The walk would not be long, and Robert was glad for it. She pressed his arm lightly with her fingertips. The green leaves wiggled at them, and the midday sun was broiling the tops of their hats.

"This is a pleasure, Cora," he told her. "But I'm a little surprised you would not rather walk with some of your friends. Or perhaps a young man your own age."

She tossed her head. "Of course I wouldn't. They're all silly. The boys and girls alike."

"Oh, I see."

"And besides, I'd like to ask you a question, and I want to be in private."

"All right, then. Now you have me."

She smiled. Her pace slowed, as if she feared they'd reach the store too soon. "I was just wondering. I've heard all about your dreams, of course. And I wanted to know. . . . Everyone is always asking for dreams for themselves, but what if you wanted a dream for someone else?"

"I'm not sure what you mean."

"What if, for instance, I had a friend and she was in love with a boy but he didn't like her. But he *could* like her, he's just too busy being a stupid boy to pay any attention to her. I've been wondering what if, say, he was given a dream about her, a dream where he loved her and maybe they were happily married or something—that might put the idea in his head, wouldn't it? I mean, it might make him notice her when he was awake, if you could make him dream about her when he was asleep."

Robert was thoughtful.

Finally he said, "Well, a dream can certainly have that effect. A dream like that, about someone you didn't realize you liked, is usually just your mind's way of letting you know how you really feel. But the way my dreams work . . . well, it's partly about the relationship between me and the dreamer. I've never tried to give someone a dream he didn't ask for, see. He's supposed to be expecting it."

He considered her disappointment.

"I'm not saying it couldn't work. But I've never tried. If you wanted one . . . I'd make it, but I wouldn't be able to offer my money-back guarantee. You'd be on your own with that one. Probably shouldn't be trying to give dreams to someone who doesn't know what you're up to anyhow."

Cora tilted her head. "It's not like we'd be poisoning him, you know."

By now they had reached the front of the store and stopped. She let go of his arm and stepped onto the first stair, so she might look down on him just a little.

"I'll think about it," she told him. He began to turn away, so she said quickly, "Before, you know, when I told you I wouldn't rather walk with someone else."

She was waiting for him to say something. "Yes."

"You've missed my meaning, I think." There was a set to her mouth. She put him in mind of a schoolteacher whose forbearance might be wearing thin, who would at any moment now rap his knuckles with her ruler to drive out the stupidity.

"I didn't realize there was any meaning to this."

"I danced with you," she told him. "At the dance." As if the word needed repeating in order to be absolutely clear.

"I remember. You are light on your feet."

"And now you've finished walking me home."

"So it seems."

"I think you should court me," she said, turning her shoulders slightly away from him so she was almost in profile. He realized it was not embarrassment. She was showing herself to him.

"I'm much too old for that, my dear. Your father would not like it at all. And I must admit I'm not really looking for a wife."

"Well, maybe you just don't know what you want," she tried. "I could go with you, you know. I wouldn't mind, I'd love to travel all over. I could help you sell your dreams, you know I could."

"My business is fine."

"But it could be better."

"It doesn't need to be better. I make a living. There isn't anything I want for that I don't have."

Cora sighed impatiently and sat down suddenly on her step, tucked her chin into her hands, resting her elbows on her knees. Her childish pose of frustration made him smile.

"Don't you just ever get *lonely,* though?"

Robert pulled his cigarettes from his shirt pocket and searched for his matches.

"Sure, I feel lonely plenty of times. But it doesn't mean I want to marry someone I don't love."

Cora brightened, lifted her changed face up to him. "You could learn to love me, I'm sure you could. Everyone says I'm very lovable."

"Everyone says you're lovable because you're beautiful and they want to make a beautiful girl like you smile. But the two things are not the same."

He lit a cigarette and waited for her to rise and go inside the store. She looked up at the smoke he blew over her head.

"Well, thank you for walking me home, at least," she said as she stood up.

"It's my pleasure," he answered, but he didn't sound like he meant it. By the time Cora opened the door, he was walking away from her, and she turned around in the shadowy doorway and watched him shrinking down the road.

All she heard was that he had called her beautiful.

★ ★ ★

Strolling back slowly the way he had come, Robert smoked. As he passed by the manse, Pastor Arnold popped out, rushing down the steps as if he'd taken the puffs for a signal of distress and crossing the short lawn just in time to block the dream peddler's path.

"Mr. Owens, excuse me, but I feel I must speak to you about something."

He'd used up so much breath in his dash that the words sputtered unevenly. Yet he pulled his chest up and out in a gesture of dignity, thrusting all his authority of church and holiness in Robert Owens's bemused face.

"It is not the usual thing, in our town, for gentlemen who have no ties here to walk the young women home from church. Or any event. Certainly not gentlemen who are a good deal older than the young women are and when their families have not consented."

He tugged his collar. Robert smiled at him.

"I think 'gentleman' may be an undeserved compliment in my case. Don't you?"

The pastor blinked at him.

"I apologize for walking Miss Cora home, but I assure you it was an innocent act. She asked for my company, you see, and I make it a point never to refuse a lady's request."

"Be that as it may, and I might argue that she is not a lady because she is still only a girl, I admit I'm glad to have this opportunity to speak with you, not only about the relationship with the young girl, of course, though—of course that is important—and I'm glad to see at least that you seem to understand it was not something that should have been done and is not something that should ever be repeated—"

"Oh, I don't say I think I should not have done it. But I realize other people will view it that way. It's the appearance of things, I see. I understand that completely." He drew on his cigarette, then angled his mouth slightly to avoid blowing smoke in the minister's face. "I'm sorry for making the wrong impression, but really, you know, it's otherwise out of my hands." And he spread them wide apart as if he had dropped the matter at the pastor's feet.

"Humph. Be that as it may," Mr. Arnold continued, uncertain now exactly when he'd been interrupted or how the impudent dream peddler had somehow retracted a most necessary apology. "Be that as it may, it is not all we need to discuss. I feel it is my duty to inform you, since most of our responsible citizens seem unwilling to, or, heaven forbid, have actually purchased what you are selling, that you are in fact not welcome here. Not welcome by me, among my flock."

Robert rocked back and forth on his heels. "I'm sorry to hear this," was all he said.

"Times can be hard, I know that. And I have tolerated drifters before who came through this town, selling tonics and elixirs of all kinds, that might have been genuine medicine and might have been syrup, for all I know."

Robert smiled into his chest.

"And if I felt I needed to speak to them, you can be sure I did. It's not as if you are the only one, you know. But, sir"—in spite of himself he lifted his forefinger here, and it waggled in Robert's face, as if it could not remain still when perched on the end of such indignant rage—"you are a cat of a new color altogether. Dreams, my boy, dreams, these are a private matter between a man and his soul, a man and God. If you truly are selling them, then it can only be Satan's work. I can imagine no other way. And if you are not, you are a typical charlatan. Maybe the rest of them can't see it, I understand that. They are good Christians and believe the same of others. They are trusting. They trust you. But I don't."

"There's nothing sinister in my magic. It is a partnership between myself and the dreamer, nothing more."

"Whatever it may be, I think it's about time you took it elsewhere. I don't know if you are familiar with the words of Zechariah."

Robert looked at him blankly.

"Chapter ten, verse two. 'For the idols have spoken vanity, and the diviners have seen a lie, and have told false dreams; they comfort in vain: therefore they went their way as a flock, they were troubled, because there was no shepherd.'"

When Robert made no response, the young minister did not stoop to explain it to him.

"I have my eye on you," Arnold told him. "And you must keep away from the young women especially. Any misstep there, my man, and I will not be the only one in town to take notice, I can assure you."

Robert tipped his hat, much as he had to Cora.

"I thank you for the warning. Good day to you."

And he held his face steady while Mr. Arnold scuttled back to the manse, and then he let go and chuckled to himself and patted his belly, thinking about dinner.

Cora ran her oiled rag over the bedroom furnishings. She moved slowly, gazing at the ghostly smear of her own face in the top of her dresser and rubbing the knobs at the head of her bed until they shone like gazing balls. There wasn't much furniture to fuss with, but she wanted the chore to last and to be alone with herself, with her new thoughts. It was a sign she was becoming more womanly, she believed, this need to be alone in the quiet instead of surrounding herself with laughter and the smitten stares of boys. She studied the well of her heart while she worked, but it was like churning her feet around the edge of a tide pool, and the more she dug in, the cloudier the waters became.

Her mother was resting, and Father was making Toby help him with the inventory down in the store. Cora would have been quicker at it, but Toby was the boy and Toby must learn the business, no matter how slowly he might. It was like moving the heaviest furniture every spring to clean underneath, the business of dragging Toby's mulish mind into the light.

She went to the neglected windowsill and worked there, where she might look out. People passed down below on the street, always nodding, touching hats to each other, never a stranger among them. She flicked the rag at the window, folded it to a clean spot. She had rubbed all the dust away and was now just massaging the newly oiled wood, wondering if anyone would chance to look up and see the red hair haloing her pale face in the window. She was prepared to lift the rag and wave.

Robert Owens came into view, arm crooked through Violet Burnley's as if he'd brought her to town for shopping. They disappeared from sight, and Cora waited to hear the store bell jangle, but it didn't, and presently the pair emerged again from the other side of the porch roof. She'd been mistaken; they were only enjoying the day after all. She dropped her rag and gripped the inside of her elbow with her hand, pressing down where she imagined his fingers touched Miss Burnley. She pushed hard, wondering what it would feel like if he grabbed her in a moment of passion. When boys danced with her, they always held her too lightly, as if they thought girls bruised easy, like fruit. And Robert when he had seen her home had kept a slight distance between them, instead of taking her arm. Even so she had felt the heat build in the space between their hips as they walked. The one side of her had flushed with it, as if she'd stood too long by a fire without turning.

When she could no longer see his back moving away from her down the road, she let go of her arm and stretched her hand. The blood ebbed back into the places her fingers had been. She bent to the rag, then moved across the narrow hall into Toby's room. It was just the two bedrooms up here above the store, while her parents slept in a room off the kitchen downstairs, where it was warmer. In Toby's room she worked faster, ignoring the passersby outside his window, pausing just to tug at the haphazard way he'd made his bed.

As she straightened up, she realized his big form had silently filled the doorway behind her without her knowing.

"What are you doing up here?" she snapped. "You startled me."

He stepped into the room and held out his arm. "I dropped a jar of beets. Dad said I should come up here and change my shirt." He thrust the sleeve closer to Cora, and she looked at it, the purple stain running up from the cuff as if he'd cut himself and was bleeding right through the bandage.

"That's never coming out," she scolded.

He shrugged and began to unbutton the shirt. "Thought I'd grow out of being so clumsy by now. Guess not."

Cora watched him for a minute. She had heard a few whispers about her brother and the kinds of dreams he'd been buying from Robert Owens. And supposedly Toby was not the only one. A small idea uncurled itself in her mind. Day by day her feelings for Robert grew, and she could feel herself growing as well, passing from girlhood into womanhood. But he didn't see it. She studied Toby, wondering about his dreams, wondering if he thought they had made him into a man.

She stepped toward him, gave him a slap on the flank as a farmer would with a lazy cow.

"Out of my way, then."

"Sorry." He shuffled aside, still working on the shirt.

"Goose."

She rushed out to the stairs, the oily rag clenched over her heart.

Chapter 19

Ali McBryde was a farmer's boy like Benjamin Dawson had been. His unripened life was a round of school and chores, and on summer days he learned to bale the hay and pitch the gold-dust piles of clean straw into the mucked-out stalls. He saw what cultivating was and watched the grubs come struggling up out of the earth when it was turned over and turmoiling their way back in. In his scant free time, he played baseball in the school yard with friends or practiced his carving on forest twigs with the treasured pocketknife he'd been given last Christmas.

With a blade that opened out smoothly on its hinge from a shiny case like a bullet, it was the envy of all his knifeless friends. The tool itself was precious to him, but not as much as what it meant—that he could be trusted, that he was man enough not to cut off his own finger by accident. Whenever he walked with the silver weight of it in his pocket, this was really responsibility he carried, keen as ice against him. It would have burned his skin if not for the flannel pocket lining between them.

Ali McBryde was blond and slight, with a freckled face and hands, a tiny slope of a nose, and large eyes that gave him a look of innocence, but innocent Ali was not. Ali needed money, and to get it he had robbed the till at Jenkins's general store.

For many weeks he had watched the church collection plates each Sunday, floating back and forth along the pews, filling with the shallow flash of coins like untested boats taking on water. Every week the ushers brought the bloated plates up to the front of the church, and they were never left unattended until everyone had gone out. After Mr. Arnold had said good afternoon to the last parishioner, he always turned immediately and went back up the aisle to his money and carried the plates to some mysterious location in a part of the church Ali had never seen. He had always assumed this was how Mr. Arnold was paid, at the mercy of congregational whim and prosperity from one week to the next.

Finally Ali had decided there was no opportunity here. Even if he could stay behind one Sunday, if he could somehow separate himself from his parents and dash up toward the money as the last few people left, before Mr. Arnold quite turned away from the door, there was always Miss Burnley at the organ playing the postlude. He never could be sure she wouldn't suddenly pop up her head and catch him stealing.

Besides all these considerations, part of him thought it might be worse to steal from the church than somewhere else. While he knew that theft was always a sin, stealing from God himself, from God's worker on earth, seemed like going a mite too far. His crime, he imagined, would otherwise be forgiven. It was for a good purpose. It was only for justice, after all, and no greater cause could there be in the heart of an eight-year-old boy.

At Jenkins's he figured the way would be smoother. When Cora minded the till, she was easily distracted and trusting. She was always going back into the stockroom to check on this or that, even when there was no one else to watch the register. Ali had seen it before, sitting alone in its big-buttoned arch of importance. The bell that was supposed to ring up the sales was broken now, but Mr. Jenkins never bothered to fix it, since no one except his own family ever worked the store. Cora also turned her back on it when she was busy talking with some young man she liked.

One dusty, hot afternoon when the distance was hazy, like chalkboard erasers clapped together in the classroom, his kickball game was breaking for supper when he saw his best chance walking into the store in the form of Jackson Banks. Ali slipped in after him, before the door had quite closed, and watched slyly and listened.

Cora was finishing up selling some ribbon to two young ladies, and when they left, there were only Cora and Ali in the store, and Jackson Banks. Ali stood silent by the penny candy in the clear glass tilted jars. Cora was used to the children hanging around in this attitude, undecided, one finger crooked in the side of the mouth.

"Well, Cora Jenkins, as I live and breathe," Jackson drawled, leaning one elbow on the counter and smiling at Cora.

"I don't know who else you'd expect, when you come into our store."

Her voice was tart, but she was looking down at the counter trying not to smile. When Jackson said no more, she sighed as if already exasperated with him.

"What can I get for you today, Jack?"

"I don't know, I haven't decided. I just came in to pass the time."

"Well, let me know when you make up your mind."

She grabbed a feather duster from under the counter and stalked over to the shelves, reaching up and dusting all the rows of jars and cans, methodically making her way to the front window and away from Jackson and Ali. Ali didn't think she had even noticed him come in.

"What if I wanted . . . a kiss from a pretty girl?" Jackson called to her. "What would the price for that be?"

She turned, brandishing the feathers like a weapon. A fairy-tale knife or sword, changed at the last moment by some sorcery of Jackson's.

"I don't find that very funny."

"Aw, come on now." He shifted his elbow along the counter as if leaning had become uncomfortable, while the pose of nonchalance could not be abandoned. He grinned, but he made no move toward her.

"You know Christina Blackwell is my very best friend, don't you?"

"I guess. I never paid that much attention."

"Well, she is. And she's a wonderful girl, and it's about time you saw sense. Start paying attention. You should have asked her for a kiss long ago."

"Christina Blackwell?"

Ali almost laughed. Jackson sounded as surprised by the suggestion as if Christina Blackwell were an eighty-year-old widow with no teeth left in her mouth.

"Certainly Christina. Why not?"

"I don't know. I never thought of her that way. I just never really noticed her."

"Well, you should. A callow boy like you doesn't even deserve her."

Jackson only grinned harder. "I'm sure I don't. So you won't put me out of my misery, then?" Now he left the counter and walked toward her.

"Don't be ridiculous. You are not in any misery over me."

"Oh, but I am. I've been thinking about you all the time. You're the sweetest girl in town."

Ali was so fascinated watching them he almost forgot his purpose.

"Christina fancies you. . . . I never will. And I won't betray my friend."

"You never will like me? Not even a little?"

"No."

Ali moved soundlessly around the counter. He was so short he almost disappeared behind it. Jackson had his back to him, and as he stood in front of Cora, he was now blocking her view of the till as well.

"No harm in one little kiss, then. Just for fun."

"Yes, there is harm. You're being silly. Go chase someone else."

Carefully Ali pulled open the drawer of money and began helping himself. Not to very much, not enough to be missed until it was being counted and compared with the ledger at the end of the day.

"I don't want to chase anyone else, I told you."

"Jackson Banks, if you take one step closer, I will call out, and Mother and Dad will come in here. They're right in the back, you know, having their tea."

"I don't think you will."

Jackson was almost beside her now, and something like a static charge was building between them. Ali felt it, like the ground waiting for dry summer lightning to strike. He had come back around by now to the candy jars, lifted one silver lid, and treated himself to a jawbreaker. While he sucked on it, he watched Jackson bring his lips to the air in front of Cora's mouth, without ever touching her skin. Ali tried to see the sense in that. Maybe he just wanted to find out if she would stand still? This was like a game of Truth or Dare, Ali thought. Jackson was daring Cora to do something, but no one in the room was sure what.

Ali was at the door now and slipped back out. The peal of the bell snapped the air like a rubber band, and Ali imagined the puff of it blowing Cora and Jackson away from each other. He would never know. He didn't turn back to look, because there, sitting alone on a bench just outside the store, was the very person he was looking for.

"I'd like to buy something from you, sir," he said, sitting himself down on the empty plank beside Robert Owens, breathing in the faint poison of tobacco smoke and holding his chest tight and still, so he would not cough like a baby. The dream peddler turned and peered down into his earnest, peppered face.

"Well, now. I shouldn't have thought a young scalawag like you could afford any of my wares. How are you going to manage it?"

For a moment Ali feared that Robert Owens had somehow caught him out, by watching through the window or simply by some magician's intuition. But as he made no direct accusation, Ali plunged on, figuring he was in it now and nothing as yet had been said. And maybe a traveling man like the dream peddler didn't care too much where his customers' money really came from.

"I have a grandmother, far away, who sends me money every birthday," he fibbed.

"I see. And what would you like to spend your granny's gift on, then?"

Ali leaned over, resting his elbows on his knees. Robert tried not to smile, while under the world-weariness of this posture the little brown shoes dangled, unable to touch ground.

"I want a nightmare," he said finally. "A real gruesome, scary one, where I'm running away all night from something terrible."

Robert tapped his cigarette thoughtfully. "Something terrible."

"A sea monster, an angry ghost, or a band of pirates. It doesn't really matter, as long as it's really, truly scary."

"You like to be scared, then, do you?"

"Sure." He sat back up again. "I was reading *Treasure Island* last week, and that was just a ripping good book. Maybe not quite scary enough, though."

"*Treasure Island*, eh? That is a great book. You must be a smart reader, to get through something like that at your age."

"I am a good reader. Taught myself a few years ago. My older sister, she helps me with the words I don't know yet."

"Aren't you lucky to have such a kind big sister?"

"Yes, sir, I am."

"And what's your name, young man?"

Ali studied him. "It's Alistair. Ali McBryde. Don't you remember me?"

"Oh, I see. Yes, now I remember. You made the snowman?"

"That's right. It didn't melt for a whole week."

"Well, Ali McBryde, you might as well come along with me. I stay at Miss Burnley's, and it's close by. I can have a fantastic nightmare ready in time for you to go home for your supper."

Ali smiled brightly. "Really, Mr. Owens? I didn't even think it would be so easy."

He hopped up off the bench and took Robert's free hand, pulling him down the grooved board stairs and looking pleased, like he'd just leashed an escaped circus bear. The bell rang again behind them, and Ali turned to see Jackson Banks skipping down the steps. With his hands as always in his pockets, it didn't appear as though he'd bought anything, even for all that time he'd spent in the store. Jackson was going one

way down the road while the dream peddler and his new client were going the other. But Jackson did turn and look at
them over his shoulder, the two arms linked in the space between the tall body and the short, an odd swinging joint
where Ali's small hand disappeared into Robert's large one.

★ ★ ★

Later, as Ali made his way home, he munched a blueberry
scone Miss Violet had sent along with him and thought
about the nightmare he'd purchased. It was blue-black in its
bottle, like translucent ink. He told Robert Owens he didn't
need to know the details of the dream—it would be scarier,
he explained, if he could just be surprised. And now he felt
a satisfaction like a slosh of water in his belly.

When he entered the house, it was full of the salt air of
his mother frying ham and cooking corn bread in the pan.

"Ali, come and wash and tear the lettuce for our salad,"
she called, without looking over her shoulder. She always
knew when he'd come home, no matter how stealthily he
thought he'd entered.

"Aw, Mom."

A cackle fluttered down from the stairs above him. "Looks
like it's women's work for you again, Allison."

Just the sound of Barto's voice fell down hard across his
narrow shoulders like a yoke. Ali did not have an older sister.
Or a sister of any kind. All he had was an older brother, Barto,
who was stupid and cruel.

Ali moved through the hall to the kitchen without looking up. If he did not look up, the disembodied voice wouldn't
exist and he could walk out from under pretending he hadn't
even heard it.

Obediently he washed the lettuce head. It took a long
time, because the fine grains of dirt were all trapped down in

the tight snarl of leaves. While he worked his fingers through the rubbery mess, he plotted. His glass of milk and Barto's were already poured and at their places. When he was sure the lettuce was clean and he had sliced the tomatoes and scooped it all into the big salad bowl, he waited for his mother to turn away from the table. As soon as she did, he walked over, uncorked the vial from his pocket, and poured the contents into his brother's glass.

At first, while the dark drops pulled apart and spiraled through the milk, he feared that it would be stained blue and he would have to spill it to hide what he had done. The dream would be wasted, and instead of revenge he'd have only punishment for his carelessness and his brother would laugh even harder, gusting out of his gut. Sometimes that laugh fizzed around Ali's head long into the after-silence, like an angry horsefly.

As he watched, though, the ink-blue threads whirled down into the milk and disappeared, spun out like twisters. His mother was still banging around the stove top behind and did not notice him. Gingerly he picked the glass up with his fingertips and worried it. The milk was a little off its color, but not enough for anyone else to notice. He had heard that the potions had no flavor except for a subtle sweetness, and he counted on that, too, being lost in the folds of cream.

His bedtime was earlier than Barto's, but he did not go to sleep. He wanted to lie awake all night and listen to Barto struggling with his monsters in the other bed. The only instruction Ali had not been able to follow was making sure Barto drank it close to bedtime. He was a few hours early instead, and he would just have to wait to find out if it mattered. Eventually Barto came in with his lamp, and Ali lay with his back to his brother, facing the wall, breathing as evenly as he could and watching the ghoul thrown out of

Barto's lantern shadow its way up the wallpaper. It stretched across the ceiling as his brother bent down to pull off his socks, bounded with every small movement, then yawned upward again. He heard Barto creaking into his bed and tossing until the blankets had settled around him comfortably. Ali lay still, waiting, waiting, and waiting until he forgot to wait and the sleep came in and took him.

When Ali awoke the next morning, Barto was already gone, the bed made and the quilt smoothed over whatever troubles he might have tossed in during the night. Ali dressed quickly, dragged his own bedclothes up carelessly, and bumped downstairs.

In the kitchen Barto was having a big yawn over his bowl of oatmeal.

"You've had a sleep," his mother told Ali, sliding his own bowl into his place and briefly resting her hand on the top of his head.

Ali looked across at his brother. Barto's mouth was stretched open pink and dark, and every time he closed it again, he shook his head like a wet dog drying.

"What about you?" Ali asked him. "You look like you hardly slept at all."

Barto stretched out, big fists searching the air like a baby's. "Mind your own business," he said.

"What's that?" their mother asked. "You sleep bad last night, Barto?"

"I went right off," Barto told her. "Weird sleep, though. Bad dreams. Like something was chasing me down all night long. I woke up feeling as tired as if I'd really been hours running." He bent forward again and began to scoop the steaming oatmeal into his mouth. Ali sprinkled brown sugar over his bowl and shrugged as if he couldn't understand, but he put his head down and smiled to himself. He poured in cream from the pitcher and watched the sugar crumble.

After breakfast they went outside to their chores and the long summer day of work. Still in the grass by the porch were the broken wood-chip pieces of the carving Ali had made the week before. With his pocketknife he'd been whittling sticks he picked up from the woods, saving the straightest ones from the kindling pile. He had cut his hands a few times, but he was learning not to. When he found a long, bowed, shallow piece of wood, he'd sat with his knife and begun to hollow it out, narrowing the tips and shaving off the bark, fashioning a perfect toy boat to float down the river. The boat had come out long and fine and light, and then he'd spent hours digging carvings into its hull, swirls and stars and moons, whatever he could manage. Barto had waited until all those hours had passed and then grabbed it out from Ali's hands in an instant.

"What's this?" He'd grinned, turning it over in his fat palms and examining all the lined surfaces, the work of it. All the time.

"It's a canoe," Ali had told him.

"Not anymore," laughed Barto, and he'd dropped the wood on the grass and stomped it with his foot, hard, and it had crunched and broken like bone.

At this late afternoon hour, the Reverend Arnold liked to sit in the manse parlor, behind a small desk tucked into the corner, making notes for the week's sermon and contemplating his message. Mrs. Arnold would be busy with supper preparations in the kitchen, and it was one of the few hours in the day when he did not have some female—his wife, or the leader of the Ladies' Aid, or Violet Burnley pestering him about hymn selections—thrumming at his ear like a persistent mosquito.

He settled into the straight wooden chair, not too comfortably, and flipped through his Bible. He tapped his fingers along the blotter. Finally he readied his pen, changing the nib and testing its flow against a spare page. When he was poised to begin, a rapping against the front door from its impressive brass knocker interrupted him. Mrs. Arnold emerged from the kitchen, wiping her hands on her apron, and moved past the open doorway of the parlor to answer it. He heard high, womanly voices, the dreaded words "Of course not, please come in," and he steeled himself, laying his fountain pen down precisely parallel to the edge of his paper.

His wife, still nervously wiping her now-dry hands, ushered Mrs. Schumann into the room and closed the door behind them.

"Abigail, what a pleasant distraction." He stood, edged his way around the desk corner, and motioned her to the sofa under the front window.

"I hope I'm not interrupting you at work," she said.

"Not at all, not at all. You, and all my parishioners, you are my work," he said. Then, thinking this didn't sound quite right, he added, "I welcome the diversion. Researching and writing can be so dreary." He smiled, easing himself into his favorite armchair across from her. "What's on your mind?"

Mrs. Schumann folded her hands over her knees. Her hard-set face looked almost upset. "I hardly know where to begin. It's all so . . . I don't know if I can explain. . . ."

"Take your time, take your time." Mr. Arnold lowered his voice to its most soothing tone.

"It's all begun with the dream-selling character. This Robert Owens."

Mr. Arnold's back straightened. "Yes?"

"Do you know him?"

"Not precisely. I certainly haven't patronized him."

"Oh, no, of course not."

"I had occasion to speak to him once. Only once." As he didn't know how to describe that encounter, when he had the distinct but crazy impression Robert Owens was laughing at him, he decided against saying anything more.

"A few months ago, maybe around the time of that dance, you remember? I became aware of a . . . a change. In my Johann."

"Oh? What sort of change?"

"Well, for one thing, he moons around."

"Moons a—"

"It's just so hard for me to explain, without sounding . . . It's not that I don't want him to be happy, you understand? But this is not normal happiness. This isn't the same as after the price of corn goes up or the boys shot their first bird, and he was so proud. This is like . . . well, it's like he's a different person. I don't even recognize him. And he's so forgetful. He was supposed to be mending the back-pasture fence the other afternoon, but he never even came in for dinner. . . . I had to send the boys out looking for him, and when they found him, he wasn't mending anything at all!"

"What . . . what was he doing?"

"The boys said they found him wading in the creek. Just paddling around, trousers rolled up around his knees, and he'd built a campfire on the bank for no reason, in the blazing heat. And he said they should all sit around it and play cowboys. . . ."

"Cowboys. Well, my. I'm sure the boys would've liked—"

"The boys are too young to handle this! They have their own chores—they can't be keeping track of him, too. They can't run the darn farm." She put a hand to her mouth. "I'm so sorry. But I'm just at my wits' end. The work this time of year is all we can keep up with, and you know Papa hasn't been the same since his stroke. . . . I have him to dress and feed on top of everything—it just isn't fair! Johann can't take time out in the middle of the day to play Indian tepee!"

"Is this the only . . . I mean, have there been any other—"

"Oh, there've been countless of these incidents. That's just the most recent. Leaving the milk pails out to spoil in the sun. And he plain forgot to order the thresher for the wheat. . . . Thank goodness he goes in with Coldbrook and the others, and they reminded him in time." She paused and put a hand to the back of her neck. "I can feel him slipping away from us, day by day. He's just not the same man I married. He was always so . . . responsible."

"Abby, I'm still not sure what all this has to do with—"

"I'm getting to that. I've been asking Johann for weeks and weeks what's the matter. Where is his head? He won't say, he won't say. Then, a few days ago, he finally told me the truth. But only part of the truth." She paused here, making certain the minister's eyes had not wandered from the new worry lines in her face. "He admitted to me he has been taking the dreams."

Mr. Arnold leaned forward in his chair. "I see. What kind of dreams are those?"

"That's just it. He won't tell me." Here Mrs. Schumann's rigid posture collapsed, as if her whole body were a sculpture of ice that had finally caved in in the late-summer heat. "How can that be? In all our years together, he's never kept a secret from me before."

That you know of, thought Mr. Arnold, then quickly dismissed it as unfair.

"Well, I'm not sure how to proceed," he said. "Perhaps if I paid Owens a visit. I'm in charge of your husband's soul, after all." He smiled a tight smile, curtailed by the responsibility. "There's a chance Mr. Owens might be persuaded—speaking in confidence, of course—to tell me what this is all about." He sat back, wondering if he was about to make promises he couldn't keep.

"Do you really think so?"

"At any rate, he can't stay here forever. The man is practically a vagrant. And when he leaves, his dreams will go with him." He tapped his fingers together hopefully.

"That could take many months!"

"In the meantime why don't you send Johann over to see me. I'll talk with him about all this, the . . . mooning, his responsibilities to you and the children, and of course the waste of good money." He noticed with some discomfort that Abigail was still wringing her hands.

"That's not all," she said. "I think he's been around my children."

"Pardon me?"

"Do you know what I found under their pillows when I stripped them to wash the sheets? *Stones*." She could not have laced the word with more horror than if she'd said "guns," or "poison." "Dark little stones, smooth as satin, gold veins in them. Looking up at me like two eyes."

"And they. . . . you believe they have something to do with Mr. Owens?"

"I know they do. I scolded the boys and asked where they'd got such strange things, and they just as bold-faced as could be told me the dream peddler gave them to them. He stopped at our place, first thing on his way into town, asking for somewhere to put up. And I sent him on to Violet's." She wrapped her arms now across her chest. "He told them something about the rocks, some dreaming nonsense. They've been sleeping on them ever since."

"Have they . . . have they been acting differently as well? Acting strange?"

"No." She sounded almost disappointed. "They're just as rambunctious as ever. But I tell you, it makes me very uncomfortable. He never asked my permission to give them anything. And the boys just don't know what they should think of their father. He's so . . . so pleased all the time, whistling, grabbing at me to dance around the kitchen. The boys have been terrible, trying to get his attention. Pulled a pile of hay down out of the mow and made a big mess, jumping into it. And the worst was when I caught them trying to light cigarettes in the barn. Cigarettes! In the barn! They could've burned it all down. They expect him to whip them, Reverend. They're looking for signs of the father they knew. They need to be punished, but he pays them no mind at all. Laughs at them. I'm at my wits' end," she repeated.

"Do you . . . do you have the stones?"

She blinked. "No. I threw them into the river." They looked at each other. "I couldn't keep them in the house."

"I see. No, of course. I was only curious."

"And all this . . . this is not all."

"Surely . . ."

"I overheard the boys talking in their room. This was after I took those rocks away." She closed her eyes. "I'm not sure how to say this."

"That's all right. Take your time." He rubbed his temple.

"It seems . . . at least, from what I understood of what they were saying . . . it seems the dream peddler has quite a following among the young men. Toby Jenkins, and all them. That they have been giving him . . . an awful lot of business."

"I'm not sure—"

"It sounds as though he has been selling dreams of an *inappropriate nature*," she said darkly.

"Oh, dear," said Mr. Arnold. "Oh, dear."

"I could not think what to do, but I felt I must bring this to your attention. It's all in fun, everyone says. What could be the harm? Well, I'll tell you what. I think this is scandalous. And to think my young boys, who are very young, should even hear about something like this . . . But you see, they have friends with older brothers, and I have no reason to doubt . . . And then, once I heard this, I had to ask myself . . . what if this has something to do with my own husband? And his dreams, and why he won't tell me about them? How can I not wonder? If Owens is selling all kinds of . . . magic, would he have any compunction about selling that to a married man? Johann could be . . . for all I know, in his dreams, where no one could ever catch him! Where he believes it does not matter."

"I see. But it does matter."

She nodded tearfully. "Yes, it does. It matters to me. I feel like a fool."

"Now, now," said Mr. Arnold. He leaned forward and patted her hand, hoping the tears would not spill. "Let's not lose our heads. I know this is distressing. But let us not forget, despite what you overheard . . . you don't know for certain what your husband has been dreaming about. You don't yet know." She shook her head. "Now, then. I don't want you to worry. Send Johann over to see me, and we'll get to the bottom of it. I'll sort him out."

Chapter 20

The dream peddler was walking through the graveyard stillness when he began to have the feeling he was not alone. It was a fleeting thing, like the flash of a bird's shadow as it darts from one tree to another, gone in the moment of recognition.

He had never come across anyone else here except on the days when he and Evie had planned to meet. Robert walked here because he enjoyed the orderly rows of stones and the little haphazard flowers growing up wherever the wind had dropped their seeds. The long green fronds of weeping willows hung down, protecting the silence within their dreamy, hairy branches.

He walked to the end of a row, then spun fast and tried to catch whoever was there. Only a startled bird flew at him out of the bush, while the quiet, dappling green that floated the headstones went on undisturbed. It was not until he had wandered all the way to the southwest corner that he saw her, hunkered down like she was reprimanding a child. She seemed unaware of him, and he realized she was not following him at all but here for her own purpose, and everything turned on him then, and he was spying on her across the patchwork of graves.

She lifted her head, and stood. Her hair was just like her daughter's, forever loosening itself from its knot, frizzled with gray but otherwise just the same. As if he were meeting with Evie again, he walked to her, and it dawned on him he'd never seen the new grave in the back. She had kept him away from her son, had always led Robert down into the orchard where their footsteps would not disturb him.

"We were able to bury him, when the warm weather came," Rose said.

"I see."

He looked down at the stone, surprised by its modesty. In this attitude he could see the sparse new grass coming in over the fresh black earth like feelers, and he could see Rose's feet. They were naked except for dirt, toughened and callused. She had walked all the way here, he realized, with no shoes. She walked everywhere in the summer months with no shoes, and her feet had grown a hard crust like a shell. One small toenail was torn half away. The feet made her seem crazy, he understood suddenly; it was the feet more than anything else, more than thoughtless words or absentmindedness. Because they were so uncared for, because she cared not for them, their cleanliness or pain, as if they were somehow disconnected from herself. If she could walk what it took to make this of her own feet, she could not be normal; that was what people must think.

"I know my daughter goes to see you."

Startled by the flint sound of her voice, he looked up at her.

"It's not what you think," he said quickly.

"You don't know what I think."

"Tell me, then. Do you think I sell dreams to her, take advantage of her for my own pocket?"

"Don't you?"

"No. It's not like that with us."

She dented her hips with her hands. "Are you . . . involved with her?"

He leaned back slightly from the question. "No."

She surveyed him a moment, then looked past him to the deep green orchard.

"It might not be the worst thing. She needs to feel something again. She needs to wake up."

"But she . . . her husband . . ."

"George is a good man," she said. "But he's a simple man, and a quiet one. He's not going to pull Evie out of this. He's only going to watch her disappear."

"Maybe the trouble is . . . it's not for George, or even you . . . or me. Is it?"

"I've seen the two of you meet here. More than once. And she never notices me. She never notices because she doesn't come back here. Doesn't look over here, her son's resting place."

"You think she avoids her pain? Ignoring the grave?"

"I imagine it probably helps."

Robert hesitated. "She has a handprint, you know. There's a handprint of Ben's, left on a window in the house, which she never wipes away. I think she feels him there when she looks at it. Maybe she doesn't need to visit his grave."

Rose looked at him directly then, and her eyes were much like Evie's, except they were brown. "You know my daughter quite well."

"In some ways, yes."

"Do you take money from her?"

He smiled slowly. "Only because she insists on it."

"If you can do her any good . . . at all . . . I told her to stay away from you, you know."

"That was probably sound advice."

They stood looking at the dates of Ben's life. The wind went through the trees around them, and the branches woke, wondering.

"This has been very hard on her."

"I can only imagine."

"Can you?"

He shrugged. "I could try."

"When someone has been this badly broken . . ." Rose shook her head. "There's no fixing it, you know. One just learns to live with the brokenness. How to walk and talk in spite of the cracks. How to feel without tearing the seams."

"I suppose so."

"Do you know why I'm telling you this?"

Robert looked up at Rose then. "I guess you want me to be careful of her."

"I want you to understand you can't heal her."

He wasn't sure what to say to that.

"Maybe you—" he said. He started over. "People don't exactly come out and say this . . . but somehow I've heard things. . . . They think you're some kind of a witch."

Rose smiled and lifted her shoulders. "I'm just a person who does not care what people think." She gestured down to the filthy feet as if she'd been reading his earlier thoughts. "Maybe that's as strange as being a witch, I don't know. I've always talked to myself, ever since I was a girl. I can't seem to help it. And I light fires because they are warm and beautiful, and I go without shoes because the grass feels good on my feet."

"You've never come to me for anything."

"I'm content with my dreams as they are."

"I think you have more power than you admit."

"Mr. Owens, I have absolutely no power over anything but myself." She leaned in toward him as if to share some secret. "I think I understand how your products work. And I am not in need of them."

★ ★ ★

George and his father, Harold, helped each other harvest the sweet corn. Harold led his horse, Maisie, up and down the rows while George pulled the corn, shucked it quickly, and tossed it into the wagon. Mostly they worked in silence, as they were both quiet men. George concentrated on the work, thinking mainly things not lawful to be uttered about the heat and listening to the corn leaves hiss and the blackbirds caw, the thud of cobs when they hit the bang board at the top of the wagon.

If Ben had been there, he would have been chattering away like the birds, ripping at corn silk with his small fingers, and talking endlessly about baseball and fishing. George imagined a whisper in the green beneath the corn, but he did not know whose voice or memory of a voice he was straining to hear.

They had not spoken since early in the day, when Harold asked after Evie. George had opened his mouth to say, "Just fine," like he always did. He thought about Evie and her new ways, eating so little, sleeping late some days, yet still moving through her tasks in a daze as if she slept not at all or had nightmares. There wasn't anything his father could say, so he went ahead and offered his usual answer and got the usual nod in return.

The sun climbed higher and smaller into the sky and spread its heat over the blue all the way into the rubbed white edges of the horizon. Halfway through the morning, June came and found them, with her basket of biscuits and stone jug of cold lemonade. They sat in the shade of the wagon and took turns drinking.

"That hits the spot," said Harold.

George agreed. The jug was smooth and sweating under his hands. It would keep the lemonade cold for hours.

"Got to get the quilting frame out later on, for your mother's bee," Harold remarked.

"Need any help?"

"Sure. Come back with me before you leave, you can help me set it up. Have to move some of the furniture around."

"In the front room there?"

"Yup." Harold drank. George noticed the way he handled the jug, turning it in his big hands as if he needed to grasp a certain spot before he could heft it. He seemed to tremble a bit with the weight, and his lips didn't meet the opening just right, so a wet trickle of lemonade escaped his mouth and went down his chin, onto his shirt. George wondered how many years of hard work his father's body had left. Each season had etched its own aches and failures deep within, around the bones, like rings through the trunk of a tree.

George expected Evie would be along to help with the bee, though he'd never seen her quilt at home, only the piecework. It was one of those secret things only women could do, like twisting shapeless masses of yarn into sweaters and mittens and turning a dense bag of flour into airy loaves of bread. Everything Evie made was for George in some way infused with magic—George's own work by comparison was blunt and plain. He knew how to plant and tend what he'd planted, but it was the ground, the sun and rain in turns, that worked all his miracles.

He thought about Evie steadily, but he did not know how to help her. Should he talk about Ben or stay silent? Should he hold her close or let her keep her distance? At night, while they lay in bed, he listened to her breathing. Despite its evenness and her lack of movement, he knew she was awake. He would wait and wait in silence for the change of sleep to engulf her, her breath to go deeper, her body to twitch, but he was so bone tired from the day that he always went off first. He was never able to catch her at it. Then, in the day, she seemed to confirm his suspicion that she did not sleep, not really. She yawned when she didn't think he was looking, great gaping yawns that seemed as if they would crack the corners of her mouth. She sat with knitting or mending in her lap and stared into space, as if dreaming with her eyes open.

George felt helpless. Evie was taking no laudanum, but she was almost as lost to him now as if she were, glassy-eyed and vacant like Jenkins's candy jar emptied out. He almost wished he were the kind of man who would slap her or shake her, though of course he never could. Surely something would come out of her then, her eyes roll forward and really see him—a yes or a no. He almost thought he could bear either answer, if only she came back into herself long enough to tell him. If she could, instead of this washed-out ghost of herself, just bring him the truth.

★ ★ ★

The monthly meeting of the Ladies' Aid Society was being held at June Dawson's place, and Evie went over early to help her get ready. Corn was coming up high in the fields where she walked, its stubbly green gathering tighter in the distance where it rolled away from her. The color of it cleaned her. George and Ben would have harvested together, Ben leading the horse between the rows while George pulled and husked the ears of corn, throwing them against the bang board into the wagon. Ben had thought that was great fun, begging turns to toss the corn like baseballs into the board.

Evie was carrying a tea cake she'd made, and George waved to her from his far-off post in the field, watched her for a stiff moment until she waved back. She shifted her basket from one hand to the other, and gradually her footsteps pushed George behind her. Ahead was the solid square of the Dawson house and George's old window over the front parlor. After they were married, he had told her about the nectarine, sitting on the ledge like a lookout, losing moisture.

She was annoyed with him when he told her that. She had given him the fruit to eat, had pictured the juice when he broke its skin tickling into him because of her. Instead he had kept it like a lock of hair. He had taken something she had not given, in a spirit fundamentally different from the one she'd intended. She had long forgotten it was she who'd told him, however jokingly, not to eat it, and eventually she accepted his choice. He had tried to sculpt a permanence where there was none, and she realized, in fact, this was her own definition of love.

Now the windowsill was empty, and the white folds of the curtains drifted up from it in undisturbed lines. What had come into the world because Evie met George had so easily gone out of it again. The treetops flashed out of the window as the sun fixed the sky's reflection there, and Evie's chest pulled itself in. Her heart within her was like a stone cast into the sea, traveling down through the depths until it reached darkness, where pressure took the place of light and cracked things.

She arched herself, trying to shift the stone. Sometimes when she lay down at night, this internal structure tilted and her sorrow moved again, like a water bubble in a glass sliding away from an open mouth. She wondered, if it ever escaped from her and touched the air, would something change, the temperature or the wind, and burst it?

The big quilting frame was stretched out across June's parlor with dining chairs banked around it in a square.

Women sat at the quilt in all their aspects of concentration, quick needles bowing back and forth under the silver thimbles. The plan was to have it done in time for the county fair. It would be raffled off and the money to go to the mission. Evie was wedged in between Mrs. Jones and Mrs. Cartwright, and she felt a gathering of shyness like a drawstring, women trying to close ranks against the sadness.

Evie bent sleepily over her work while the conversation settled into her, stocking her mind the way the women did their cellars, potatoes and apples and onions and jars and jars and jars and jars. She yawned continually, as if she were riding an automobile up into the mountains, but her ears remained cottony.

"Did you see the shiner on Myrtle's little boy last Sunday?"

"What was that all about?"

"They say one of the Boudreaux boys got him. That new young wife of his is overrun. . . . She's lost all control over the children."

Clucking tongues.

"Boys will be boys."

"Try taking fewer stitches, Cora. It will be easier until you learn to make them smaller."

"I think Harmon is buying dreams and not telling me about it."

"No. What makes you think?"

"Something secretive about him when he's getting ready for bed. And he's always been such a grump. Suddenly he's cheerful?"

Laughter.

"I should send Matthew to try it!"

"I could never go to him in a million years. It'd be too embarrassing."

"I wouldn't even know what to ask for."

"I think it's a cheat. But if it makes some people happy . . ."

The conversation was dropped and clattered to the floor like a tray when Cora stood up among them with a hand on her mouth, trying to excuse herself from behind it and leave the room. With the closeness of the chairs all wedged in around the work, she struggled and stumbled. They heard her footsteps scrabbling against the hall and dying down toward the back of the house. As the pull of her sounds fell slack, heads turned back toward the waiting patchwork.

June shrieked her chair back and announced in a bright, loud voice that she would go check on Cora and instructed them to carry on. She moved stealthily for a large woman, snuck up on her own kitchen, and found poor Cora retching into the sink.

"Oh, dear! Oh, my dear!" She rustled over and placed the sympathetic plumpness of her hand on Cora's back while it heaved.

"I don't know what's the matter," Cora gasped when her stomach was empty. "It just came over me. I'm awfully sorry."

"Never you mind, dear," said June, working the pump so Cora could splash her blotched face and rinse her mouth. "You did well not to be sick all over that quilt. Could you imagine?"

Cora managed a smile.

"You must have got a touch of that flu that's going around. I think the whole Jones family took it, one after the other. We all thought it had finally run its course, but you never know with these things."

She guided the girl upstairs and made her lie down. Cora was holding on to herself like a child, making her narrow shoulders seem even smaller. When June thumped back into the room of quilters, they had closed easily over Cora's absence like water. The chatter continued, crawling nimbly over the spread-out history of the town—there was Sam McBryde's old shirt, the one with the red checks his wife had hated. And Lucy Pearson's good blue Sunday dress with the flowers she was so proud of, ruined when her jealous sister Rosie threw the inkwell at her in a fight. The bright flickers of all the fabrics that had skimmed those bodies, stuck to them sometimes through sweat, swirled around the excitement of ankles dancing, were all stitched now into a banner of their past. The busy needles poked it without mercy.

When the quilt was finished and the ladies were taking their leave, Cora was brought down, blinking her eyes hard as if she could squeeze the sleep away from them.

"I'm fine," she kept insisting.

She and Christina got up behind their horse, and Christina took the reins.

"I feel much better now that I've rested. I'm not sure what came over me," she was still murmuring as they drove away.

Evie stayed behind to help June clean up. She carried cups and plates from the parlor to the kitchen, and the two women worked the finished quilt out of its frame. In toward each other and back out they walked, marrying its corners between them. When the quilt was folded small enough, June held it to her chest.

"How are you getting on?"

Evie covered a yawn with her hand. She leaned over a displaced chair, picking it up.

"Well enough." She straightened, the chair back framed in her arms. "We missed you while you were away. How's Jim and the family?"

June was busy tucking the quilt onto a high shelf in her corner wardrobe. "Well, Isobel's expecting again, and the little ones do run her ragged. I was glad to help for a bit, while I was there." She closed the wardrobe door and moved to help Evie with the chairs. "I do hope that Cora makes it home without being sick again. I'm afraid bumping along behind that horse will just unsettle her worse."

"Christina will look after her." Evie went back to the kitchen and started on rinsing cups at the sink. "And Cora's always been so hearty. No matter what everyone else is sick with, you'll always see her minding the store. Even with all those people coming and going, sneezing and coughing on her, nothing ever seems to take." She wiped at the blood-dark ring of tea stain on her cup's interior.

"Strong as a horse, that one," said June. She flapped out a towel to dry the cups Evie had finished. "The Jenkinses are all like that. Cora might look slight and bony, but she's tough as leather inside her. Wiry, I guess. She has a kind of heart that burns real strong. She's bright with it. Oh, well, guess it was finally her turn."

"I guess so."

"I hear she went walking, home from church not long ago, with that Mr. Robert Owens."

"Did you?"

Evie rubbed hard at her cup. She grabbed the salt shaker and sprinkled it, rubbing again.

"Lands, child, it's been that way for years, just leave it. You'll scrub the color off yourself before ye've any effect on it."

Evie ignored her.

"I wonder if that's a match, there?" said June.

Evie looked up. "Cora and Mr. Owens?"

"That's who I'm speaking of."

"I just can't imagine. Tom and Mary aren't going to let her go off with him. He'd have to stay here."

"So he could stay. Maybe he could decide to settle.

Keeping the town in dreams, seems like he could do all right for them."

"I'm not sure he makes so very much money from it. I wonder if he could support a wife, a family."

June shrugged.

"He has no house to live in. I just can't picture it," Evie went on. She didn't know why she was insisting, when it didn't matter one way or the other.

She finished rinsing the dishes and picked up a towel.

"A house could be built for them," said June. "The Jenkinses could do it."

"They could. But Mr. Owens is a traveler. That's the nature of his business."

"It just seems to me . . . well, none of my affair. I can imagine that Cora with an older man. Someone to guide her. Someone to settle her down."

Evie smiled. "You may have a point there."

"You off to home, then?"

"Yes, I think I will. Supper won't make itself." She folded her towel and placed it gently next to the sink.

"I'm sorry, what I said earlier, about all Jim's family. Isobel being pregnant. I wasn't thinking."

"It's not your fault. That's just how things are."

June was stacking the saucers and cups together again carefully. "And how are things, with you and George?"

"They're fine," Evie said quickly. "Just fine. He's very busy with the crops, of course, and he's tired when he comes in. We just stay quiet. We're doing all right, though." Evie watched the way one teacup rolled on its side to fit into the other, like a tiny ship capsized.

"Well, don't stay too quiet. George is like that, you know. Well, of course you know. He doesn't always say what's on his mind, but inside he's thinking away, thinking and thinking.

Talking is good for him, but you have to make him talk. Otherwise he forgets." She closed the cupboard door on her dishes and let her hands rest on the countertop. "If you remember Ben together, if you talk him over sometimes, that will be better, I think. For both of you."

Evie looked at her. "I don't know if I can. . . ."

"I've been missing Benny's visits this summer. He used to run over all the time, hoping for cookies or cake. I always gave him something. I told him he'd spoil his supper, and then . . . I gave them to him anyway." She rubbed her eyes.

"You did," Evie said. "You did spoil his supper."

Chapter 21

Now whenever Robert went into the graveyard, he turned furtive, but he never did see Rose Whiting there again. Evie always met him in the afternoon, when George had come for dinner and gone and would be out in the fields until suppertime, and no one would miss her. Robert never mentioned the conversation he had with Rose, and neither did Evie, so he still wondered if she knew about it.

Today he stood at the back and waited, on the side away from Ben's grave. He watched her coming and thought now that she knew what to expect from him, she walked differently, winding her way through the stones and taking her time. Then it was a simple exchange, a vial for some coins, and sometimes they sat together and talked about things. When she was close enough for him to make out her face, she smiled, because she knew what would happen and how he would be. He couldn't decide if that made him happy to see her or not.

She sat down on a stone beside him as if she expected him to stay with her for a while. He saw she was often yawning and how it brimmed a pinkish wetness in her eyes.

"The potion is supposed to help you sleep better," he said. "But now you seem tired all the time."

She turned to him with one cheek resting in her hand.

"It takes time to fall asleep, and then I sleep the night through," she said. "But there is something different. The sleep is so dark, like a blindness, but I'm half aware of things all night long. I remember in the morning the house-creaking sounds and all the times that George turned over. So when I open my eyes, I'm not sure if I'm waking up. I don't know if I've really slept at all."

Robert pulled in his chin. "I'm afraid that might be the price you pay for giving up the dreaming. I don't know if it's ever the right way. Sleeping without them."

"Why do you think we can sometimes remember our dreams and sometimes we forget? I've had dreams in my life I can remember so clearly, even years later. Do you know why?"

He lifted a fallen leaf out of her hair. "Maybe there are some we just don't need to remember and some we should. Some dreams that try to tell us something about ourselves, so we remember, even if we don't understand why."

Evie thought for a while, turning the glass cylinder over in her hand, rolling it down one palm and then the other.

"Do you ever make dreams for yourself?"

"No, I never do that. I just let whatever dreams would like to come to me come in. I don't usually remember them. Sometimes I suspect I might have dreamed of the past. Except it wouldn't really be the past, just one that should have been. And then, when I'm awake, I don't choose to remember that."

"Why do you do what you do?"

She had put her vial into a pocket and sat now with her hands around her knees, her skirt pulling up and her waxy white calves showing themselves.

He shrugged. "It's a way to make a living."

"There are lots of ways to make a living."

"You think there's some better one? Something else I should have chosen?"

"Well, it just seems a lonely way to go through life. You never can stay anywhere very long. You're always alone, and no one ever really has a chance to know you. Wouldn't you like to stay in one place longer? To have friends who have known you a long time? Maybe have a family of your own?"

He squinted up into the distance, as if he must take his answers from the breeze or find them on the faint horizon.

"I had a family once. I had another job once."

"What was that?"

"I used to be a man of God." The look on her face made him laugh out loud. "I know, people find that hard to believe. But maybe you can believe me if I tell you I wasn't a very good one."

He pulled a long blade of grass from the ground and sat rolling it thoughtfully between his palms.

"The preaching part I was good at. I've always had a talent for selling things, you see. Convincing people. Charming them. The kingdom of heaven is a great idea, I think. It's a happy idea, it's easy to sell."

"Didn't you believe in it at all?"

"I don't know. I guess I did, at one time. I guess I became a minister because it seemed like a good thing and I never really bothered to think the matter through." He sighed. "I was a drunkard, Evie. Most of the time. I drank too much before I ever was ordained—I just hid it well. People thought I was gifted, joyous. But mostly I was just . . . intoxicated. The girl I was courting never saw, not until it was too late for her."

"What happened to her?"

"Well, she found out what it was like to live with me, once we were married. We started off happy enough, I think. But there are times when I am drinking . . . when I am not a good man. I could be mean, say mean things, and I was frightening. Many times I wouldn't remember afterward, but often enough I would. I would apologize and cry. My wife would forgive me. She would curl into herself and wait for the next time I would be drunk." He threw the grass blade back to its own. "I think she lived mostly in fear of me. We had a baby girl, and she was afraid of me also. She was two, last time I saw her. She had these big brown eyes. Her eyes used to fasten on me when I was across the room, like she thought if she looked away, I would change on her without warning, and maybe I did do that."

"Where are they now, your family?"

He shook his head. "I don't know. Still with her mother's people, maybe. That's where they went. There was this one night, I came home dead drunk, and I took a candle upstairs to go to bed and must have knocked it over onto the floor. Didn't even notice. I woke up when I felt the heat and saw the window curtains blazing and the wall beginning to light. Rachel wasn't beside me. I ran and looked into Emma's room, and she was gone as well. I ran down the stairs and outside to find them standing a little distance from the house. Rachel was holding Emma in her arms, and Emma was staring at the roof in flames, sucking her thumb like she always did. Rachel, though, Rachel was not looking at the house. Rachel was looking at me.

"When I got close enough to them, the fire had sobered me up quite a bit, see, and everything was clear to me then. 'Why did you wake up?' That's what she said to me. 'Why did you have to wake up?'

"The house burned. I stumbled into the field that night and slept there. Rachel must have gone to the neighbors' to stay. There wouldn't have been much anyone could do about the fire but stand and watch that the church didn't go up, too. Eventually Rachel took Emma to her mother's house, and I did not see them again. There wasn't anything I could do but let them go. . . . I didn't deserve to keep them. I couldn't ask forgiveness for a thing like that. I didn't want any."

He looked into Evie's face to see how she was taking everything, if it changed her feeling about him. He couldn't tell what she might be thinking.

"There is one thing I am grateful for. Emma was only two when I almost killed her—so she will never remember me."

For a while Evie played with the fabric of the dress bunched in her lap. "I didn't realize you were so sad," she said finally, looking up. "You hide your sadness very well."

"I don't think it's hidden," he said. "But sadness isn't really the right word for it, maybe. I'm resigned, is all. I was who I was, and I did what I did. I left it behind me because it was all I could do at the time. I like my life now. I like moving from town to town and meeting new people. And this might sound proud, but I really do think there are some people that I help. Certainly I help more people now than I ever did trying to minister to them."

"You don't know that."

"Maybe not. But it's what I believe. It's all in our minds, everything. The past. Now. Maybe heaven. That's what I believe in. A mind is a magic thing."

"And what about your soul?"

He was looking down at his own chest, as if divining what might lie within himself.

"I haven't got any soul. Perhaps I did, once. When I was

a child, I suppose. I can't imagine any child without a soul. I gave it up, though. I was never true to my soul. I didn't care for it, and it died."

As he was sitting right beside Evie, when he turned his head toward her, his eyes were so close to her own that she couldn't look past them.

"That man, you see, that man who drank and scared his own wife and child, he is still in me. He's still in here." He pointed to his chest. "So to answer your first question, no, I don't really want anyone to know me. I don't want to have friends who have always known me well. I can only be a decent man if nobody knows what I was."

Evie leaned forward and put her two hands on his shoulders and moved her face even nearer to his. She was so close he imagined for one dizzy moment that she might kiss him.

"Of course you still have a soul," she told him. "Maybe you don't feel it anymore inside yourself, but the rest of us can see that it is still there."

In the east the sky had darkened, and the air growled at them, low and distant. Over her shoulder Robert studied the livid storm rising up behind the trees. From the west the sun illuminated the forest, and the trees crackled like a growing fire against smoke.

"You'd better be getting home," he said. "You've much farther to walk than I."

Evie stood up and brushed at her skirt.

"Before you go," he said, "I wanted to give you something . . . well, loan you something."

Evie stood, unaware of the inferno of trees behind her. Robert was sliding a book from his bag and holding it out to her. She took it and turned it over in her hands. It was a small volume. *The Wind Among the Reeds* by W. B. Yeats.

"You told me you like to read, didn't you?"

"I don't know," Evie said. "I don't remember. But yes, I do like to read. Lately my concentration . . ."

Robert shrugged. "Well, you'll have it anyway. It's poetry. Most of 'em really short, one page at a time. Read it if you like."

"Thank you," Evie said. "Thank you, I will."

When she turned and saw the eerie light of the blazing trees, her breath caught, like clothing on a nail. She felt Robert watching her leave the graveyard for the road, but she didn't turn around.

Evie hurried home, trying to beat the storm. When she heard the sky crack from a slap of thunder overhead, she knew she was too late, and the warm rain began to fall and wiggle through her hair. She had nowhere to protect the book, so she rolled it into the front of her skirts and held it to her chest, rain streaking down the front of her petticoat until it was heavy and clinging with water.

Running up the path to the house, she met George on the front porch, also soaking wet, and they laughed at the sight of each other.

"What on earth are you doing with your skirt?"

"Nothing," Evie said quickly. "Just holding it up out of the mud."

She went inside, and when George was not looking, she tucked the book safely in among the others on the shelf.

★ ★ ★

Toby thought about all the things he'd rather be doing, from best to worst: putting together a game of baseball behind the school . . . crowding with the fellows onto the back porch, chewing tobacco, playing cards. . . . Even getting dressed for a dance would be better, his fresh-starched collar too tight, his face red from heat and the giggling girls. . . . Even marking down inventory in the dusty storeroom would be better than this. But the Reverend Arnold had asked him to come, and there was simply no way to refuse.

The minister himself answered the door after Toby knocked, and ushered him into the front room. Toby had never been inside the manse, and he thought it seemed quite fine. The furniture was worn, but the walls were all hung with paintings, and Toby admired them. They gave like windows onto warm, glowing scenes of mountain waterfalls and sheep in the pasture. And he had never in his life seen so many books all in one place—rows and rows of them, leather spines stamped in gold. Toby could not imagine reading this many books in one lifetime, even if reading were all he ever did until the end of his days. He was slow at it, and every time he'd put a sentence together, he had a hard time holding on to its meaning, remembering those words while he worked his way through the next one.

It made perfect sense to Toby that Mr. Arnold's room would immediately surround him with the things to make him feel nervous and small. He sat on the sofa, unknowingly in the same spot Mrs. Schumann had taken, but denting it deeper. He rubbed his hands on his knees.

"No need to be nervous," Mr. Arnold said. "I just thought it might be time you and I had a chat. A kind of a man-to-man chat."

Toby could feel himself sliding forward down the slick horsehair. He braced his big feet firmly against the floor. "All right," he said. Mr. Arnold had cornered him as he left the church last Sunday but had given him no idea what he wanted. Toby could not remember ever having a conversation alone with the minister. He could remember only standing awkwardly silent with his parents in the yard after service or sitting silently when Mr. and Mrs. Arnold came for supper. He didn't think he'd ever been alone with the Reverend Arnold, ever, even for a few minutes.

"My boy, I'd like to talk with you about Mr. Owens."

Toby looked away from the books. "The dream peddler?"

"The very same. This town is a small place, as you know. I sometimes think it must seem very small to a young man your age."

Toby considered. He'd never thought of the town, with its long dirt roads and its outlay of vast swaying fields, as small. To him it felt like an endless stretch of land and work, bordered only by the pale, low sky and the bay. He didn't know how to answer Mr. Arnold, but it didn't matter.

"It's natural," the minister went on, "to look for some kind of adventure, a little something more. Even a kind of escape, if you will."

If he would? Toby had no idea what the reverend was driving at, but he did not like to ask. He sat patiently instead.

"I've heard some talk . . . that is, I'd like for you to answer me honestly here. Have you been going to the dream peddler? Buying dreams?"

Toby's hands rubbed his knees again. "Well, I—"

"And your friends? Have they been buying dreams also?"

"Yes, I think so, sir."

"What I mean is, these dreams . . . there are . . . girls in them? Ladies?"

Toby dropped his eyes. "Oh. Yes."

"Aha. Toby, it seems to me this kind of patronage needs to stop."

"Sir?"

"I don't think it's right for Mr. Owens to come into this town and corrupt young people such as yourself. Do you understand? There are certain things you are not ready for, things you should know nothing about. Because although you may feel like a man, and you may have certain feelings . . . you are not. You have not fully become a man, and I believe this kind of indulgence—such dreams, as it were—can only serve to delay the coming of your full maturity."

"Yes?"

"There are things a man should not know until he is married. Do you understand?"

"Oh. Yes, I think so." Toby shifted uncomfortably.

"Now, I'm not trying to accuse you of anything. But my concern is with . . . the moral nature of such a dream. The sheer wrongness. I'm concerned with your immortal soul, the part of you that will abandon these . . . desires of the body in what is a comparatively short amount of time, if we take the long view. If one is thinking of eternity."

"Yes, sir."

"I know this must be . . . embarrassing. But you must be perfectly honest with me. Is it true that you and your friends have been buying dreams in order to . . . satisfy . . . certain corporeal urges?"

"Sir?"

Mr. Arnold looked exasperated. But his words were so strange, so slippery, that Toby couldn't grasp them to get at their meaning.

"What I'm asking is, have you been using the dreams to take care of certain urges of your body?"

Toby was now past embarrassment. He was beginning to feel worried. He felt bad, and guilty. He could not lie.

"Yes sir." He stared into his lap. "I'm afraid that's the truth."

Mr. Arnold sat back. "Well done, Tobias. I appreciate your honesty. You should know you can always come to me with these things, questions or problems. Even when you feel you can't tell anyone else . . . especially then. I hope you'll remember I'm always here, and I would never judge you. I leave that to God."

"Yes, sir."

"It's important that you know," Mr. Arnold went on, "even though these urges may be . . . natural, it's still up to us to . . . control them. To give them the right shape. God gave us these desires so that we might know the blessed union of marriage and the beautiful miracle of children. But these feelings . . . they are only intended for that. Do you understand?"

"Yes, sir."

"Now that we have established the truth of the matter, it's my duty to caution you, to guide you. This kind of indulgence, with you and your friends . . . it's wrong. There's really no way around that. For example, when you're dreaming your dreams, have you ever found that you know . . . do you ever recognize the . . . the objects of your affection?"

"Sir?"

"The girls, Toby, the young ladies. Are any of them residents of this town? Friends, neighbors?"

"Oh. Well, not usually."

This was close enough to the truth, but Toby was growing increasingly uneasy. He thought of his dreams of Mrs. Dawson and how much he cherished them. He wondered if Mr. Arnold could possibly read his mind. If maybe God, and not only the town gossip, had been whispering in the minister's cauliflower ear.

"Consider this: if you have a dream, or a fantasy, about a young woman of your acquaintance, then you have done her wrong. You have disrespected her, used her. It's very important you see this. A man who can't control himself, his body and mind, is a danger to us all."

Toby was nodding hard. "I understand, sir."

"I'm sure you remember the Tenth Commandment."

As he seemed to be waiting for Toby to say it, Toby looked down and started his lips moving, silently counting them off on his fingers. Mr. Arnold soon lost patience with him.

"Thou shalt not covet. And this applies to your neighbor's wife, but also to everyone you know."

Toby hadn't thought of this. How could he have forgotten? Mrs. Dawson was his neighbor's wife, and he had been dreaming about her right along as if it didn't matter who she belonged to. He felt a deep roiling in his stomach. His conscience must have been asleep in there, but now it had woken. Toby felt himself blinking, and he tried to listen as carefully as he could to the rest of Mr. Arnold's words.

★ ★ ★

"I've always wanted to ask you . . . how did you ever discover what you could do? Whatever gave you the idea of selling dreams?"

Evie had taken off her boots and stockings and was working her bare toes through the cool grass.

Robert smiled at her. "You are the first person ever to ask me that."

"I find that hard to believe!"

"It's the truth. No one ever asks, just like no one probably ever asked a fortune-teller when exactly they knew they were seeing the future. Does it have something to do with believing in me, I wonder? If you don't look too closely at a card trick, then it will seem like magic."

"Is that all you think it is? Like doing a card trick?"

"I don't know."

He passed her the cigarette. It wasn't ladylike to smoke, but she'd been sharing Robert's cigarettes sometimes, and she didn't know why. She came to like the burning they started in her chest. It was as if they fired her heart that had gone cold and brought it back to life.

"There was a little boy in my parish who'd been maimed. He fell out of a hayloft and broke his back. Father made him a clever little chair with wheels so's he could scoot around. But he never walked or ran again. Guess he was lucky to be alive, but boy, when you saw him sitting in that chair watching all the other children at tag or ball, it broke your heart."

"I can imagine." She thought of Ben. If he could have been rescued, only damaged somehow, broken but alive. She was run through with a hot envy for the mother of the little wheelchair boy.

"It was hard on him for other reasons, too. He was his father's only boy, and he was supposed to grow up and take over running their farm and all. And now he knew he'd never be able to do that. Guess he figured I was the one to come to, being the minister and all. After our children's Bible study one day, he stayed behind wanting to talk to me. In private, he said. And he told me he had a dream the night before that he was running. And how wonderful it was, to be in that dream. 'I was sad when I woke up and it wasn't true,' he told me. 'I cried.'

"What he wanted to know was, was that wrong? They told him it was God's will he be in a wheeled chair, so now of course he felt guilty. For wishing it were otherwise."

"And what did you say?"

He plucked out some grass where they sat and scattered it absentmindedly over the insteps of Evie's bare feet. "I told him never to think it was God's will. That's no way to explain things. Accidents happen. And I told him God loves him, walking or no walking. And not to be guilty for wishing a perfectly natural thing. He said to me then something that kind of changed my way of thinking." He took the cigarette back from her, with his fingers where hers had been.

"What was that?"

He drew on what was left of their cigarette and blew out. Watching him, she had the sense, briefly, that he was not really from her world but a kind of dragon-turned-man who breathed only heat and smoke.

"He seemed to understand. And he told me he wondered if maybe a dream like that was a kind of prayer."

Evie's look on him was growing heavier. Her eyes felt to her so strong she was surprised she was not actually pulling him closer to herself, but he seemed not to feel anything.

"And I told him yes, I thought it probably was. That was when I had the idea. I asked him if he thought it might be worth crying in the morning if he could run at night. He considered that and told me he thought it would. I didn't think anything of it, you see, wasn't trying to convince him I was magic. But I had this idea I could figure a way to do it. If he believed in me enough, I could give him his dream.

"So I pretended this thing for him. I pushed his chair over to the manse, where my wife kept all kinds of herbs and such in the kitchen. She thought I was drunk, of course. But actually I wasn't, not really. Or not any more than usual. I don't know what I was thinking of, just that if I gave the boy something real, something to take inside him, it would work. I don't know if it was magic or a miracle or dumb luck, but it did." He held the stubby end of the cigarette over the grass. "I gave him his dreams all along. Not every day, but a lot of them, and they seemed to bring him a great deal of joy that he didn't have before. He still envied the other children, but now he'd got something that they didn't have, see. And sometimes he went places in dreams they could never go.

And after all those years of trying to lead people to God, I felt as if I had finally done it."

"What did you do then?"

"Nothing. I never thought of selling 'em or even giving them to anyone else. It was just a special thing between him and me. But after the fire . . . after I left, I knew I had to make a living, and I didn't want to minister anymore. So I had this idea. And I went and tried, and sure enough it worked with just about everyone willing to buy from me. So I have my little living now. The End."

Evie smiled. "You've been successful here, then?"

"Sure. For starters I have you, you constant bother."

She hit his shoulder lightly. "Give me what's left of that," she said of the cigarette.

"You can have your own, you know."

She shook her head. "I don't smoke. I just like a little bit of it."

"Sure, sure."

She'd never been teased this way by any man other than George, and she spent some time considering how it felt. Good, and also wrong.

"Will you stay here a long time, then? Because you're doing so well?"

"It remains to be seen. I could, but it always depends on the people and how long they'll have me. Your minister is not terribly fond of me. I guess it depends on how much that will influence people, or if they grow tired of me, or bored."

Evie dropped the end of the cigarette in the grass and spoke again before she lost her nerve. "I've been thinking about your little daughter."

"Have you?" His eyes narrowed.

"Don't you think you might go back and see her sometime?"

"I don't think my wife would like that." He reached one foot forward and stubbed out the cigarette, eyes on the ground.

"But . . . you've changed. She would see that, surely, if you tried. You could get them back."

"How do you know?"

"What?"

"How would you know I've changed?"

Evie colored. "I only have your word for it. But I've never seen you drinking. You said . . . you stopped."

Robert sighed, and Evie could still smell the smoke on his breath.

"I know it's not my business," she said.

"No. But I did tell you."

"You wanted me to know."

"Yes."

Evie stood up as if she meant to leave, but she was still barefoot.

"I'll never see my son again. I don't have any choice about that. But you . . . you could go back and try. Instead you're choosing to suffer. You don't have the right. Not when you could go back tomorrow and see her again."

Robert looked up at her. "I don't pretend to suffer like you. I have the luxury of knowing she's still alive. You've no idea the pleasure I get, imagining the happiness of her young life."

"But you won't be part of it."

"She's better off without me."

A music of children playing dawned at the edge of their voices, and Evie stopped, listening. The child sounds bounced closer, laughter and arguing and a steady counting a little way off in the trees.

"One . . . two . . . three . . ."

The numbers sang loud as hiders peeled away and ran

shouting through the orchard. One by one they fell silent, not wanting to betray their positions, until only the count sounded off through the secret-whispering leaves.

"Eight . . . nine . . . ten . . ."

"I have to go," Evie said. She bent to her stockings and began to tug them on.

He smiled at her fear of being seen with him by the children. He watched her lacing her boots, then picking her way through the edge of the orchard to the graveyard, where the children were not allowed to play. He watched her until she disappeared, and he stood breathing as quietly as any hider, in the center of the children's game.

Chapter 22

There was a prayer meeting at the church one summer evening, when the lightning bugs swam in and out of the early twilight along the edge of the forest. Christina met Cora outside the store so they could walk the last together. Cora glanced at her friend sidelong, without turning her head. She touched her hand to the ribbon around her neck.

"Looking forward to seeing Jackson?"

Christina was staring down at her feet.

"I don't know."

"He rarely goes to prayer meeting, does he?"

"No, I suppose he doesn't."

"Rolf Baer will be there, though."

"Yes, I expect he will."

Cora waited for Christina to say more but found that her silence persisted.

"Jackson came into the store the other day, when no one else happened to be there."

"Mmm?"

"He was awfully forward with me. It took me a long time to get him to go away."

"Really? Well, that's not surprising, is it? He sees you're the prettiest girl in town. They all do."

Cora reached to flick a bee away from her friend.

"I hope you're not angry with me. I did nothing to encourage him, truly. He's just . . . a ridiculous boy."

Christina felt to check the security of the pins in her hair, then let her hand rest a moment on the back of her neck.

"You know what, Cora? I think I might have to give up on Jackson Banks. You were right from the start. He's never really going to like me. If he didn't ever notice me to begin with, we aren't going to trick him into it."

Cora pressed her lips together, and when she released them, the blood flooded them even brighter.

"I think you've made a good decision, Chrissy," she said. "I never really thought Jackson Banks was good enough for you. Even though I know . . . you wanted him to be."

"I know. I see now how foolish I was." She fidgeted with her church gloves. "But lately I've begun to wonder if maybe there could be someone else."

"Someone else?"

"You remember what you said? About how maybe it wouldn't be so bad . . . to be adored?"

Cora stared. "You don't mean to say it's Rolf? Rolf Baer?" She said the name as if he were known across the county for having murdered several wives and hung them up in the wardrobe at home.

Christina blushed. "I thought it was impossible to change my mind. But then we went to that dance, and . . . maybe I could."

Cora sighed. "I'm glad for you, Chrissy. The thing about Jackson . . . This is so much better, isn't it?"

"Yes, I think it will be. And you know something funny?"

"What's that?"

"My dream might come true after all. The one I bought from Mr. Owens."

Cora stopped and leaned against the hitching post outside the church. "That's right," she said. "Isn't that something?"

She leaned over and grabbed her stomach, as if she could feel it sucking all the color from her face.

Christina touched her shoulder. "Cora, are you quite well?"

She straightened up. "Yes, I'm fine. Just felt sick for a moment. Robert Owens strikes again, imagine that."

"You look very pale. Do you want me to walk you back home? I can just run inside and tell Mommy and Papa we're going back."

"No, no, that's all right. I think it's passing, just give me a minute. I really don't want to leave."

"Look at that. . . . Miss Burnley dragged Mr. Owens along with her. Wonder how she managed it?"

Cora smiled, perked up. "Maybe she convinced him to be concerned for his immortal soul."

Christina put her hand on Cora's back. "Is he the reason you won't just go home?"

Cora didn't answer.

"As your friend, Cora . . . didn't you try to warn me when you thought I was wishing for something I'd never have? Something I'd be better off without?" She watched Violet Burnley and her boarder mount the church steps. "You know Mr. Owens is too old for you, so why do you persist in hoping for him? Even if he did fall in love with you . . . then he would take you away. From your family and from me. I'd hate that. And I don't believe you'd be happy in the end either."

"Well, time will tell. Maybe I can't make him love me. But he said something to me once . . . something that made me think perhaps I could."

Christina considered her for a moment. "Well, if you

manage it I just hope it's what . . . how . . . you think it will be. I still think you're crazy."

Cora tried for a sly smile, but the dart of her eyes was too quick and seemed nervous instead. "I'm feeling much better," she said. "Let's go in."

The prayer meeting opened with the call to worship and the hymn "Abide with Me." The pews protested as the town settled into them. As soon as the music ended, the space it left was filled with a creaking and rustling of bodies while Mr. Arnold approached the pulpit, as if the church and the pews themselves feared the silence.

"Friends," he began, "we have just sung together, with all our hearts, one of my favorite hymns. 'I need Thy presence every passing hour. / What but Thy grace can foil the tempter's power?'" he quoted. "'Who, like Thyself, my guide and stay can be? / Through cloud and sunshine, Lord, abide with me.'"

The congregation shifted. He paused and looked out over them, searching for some sign his thoughtful repetition of the lines they'd just sung had offered them some new and startling clarity.

"I fear that one has come into our midst—a tempter, if you will—who may be leading some of you astray."

Robert's head, which had been leaning down toward his own chest while he listened, snapped upward, and for the first time he actually seemed interested in what was being said in church.

"It has long been held a sacred Christian belief that we must be wary of our dreams, for who knows whence they originate? How often do demons come into our sleeping hours to tempt us into sin? How many times has Satan inspired your dreams, or yours, or mine?" He paused to allow the words time to scurry all the way to the back of the room. "None of us can know. Let us be grateful for those mornings when we do not remember them upon waking and pray that this might be the case *every* morning. Do not take your dreaming lightly, and do not engage with those who would lead you to believe you should enjoy them! Any such person is no doubt a demon in disguise, sent by the devil himself to lead you into sin!"

Mr. Arnold's voice seemed to wear deeper grooves as it sanded the floorboards, the knees of the pews, and the softened souls of his parishioners. The dream peddler's face was still, like a mask of mud that might crack if he smiled. He glanced around and encountered a similar effort in the bodies of his friends, who kept their heads staring forward instead of turning to look at him.

"How do you know with whom you are dealing? Consorting, no less? Remember that St. Thomas Aquinas teaches us of the danger of interpreting our dreams, lest they be inspired only by demons. He cites Deuteronomy, chapter eighteen, verse ten: 'Let there not be found among you him who observes dreams.' Thus sayeth the Lord! This is what he commands you. Ignore your dreams lest you be tempted by forces you know not. And here you are, not only living through them but buying them, paying for them! We must pray for your souls and the soul of this sinner who has come among us. Remember Jeremiah, chapter twenty-nine, verses eight and nine: 'For thus saith the Lord of hosts, the God of Israel; Let not your prophets and your diviners, that be in the midst of you, deceive you, nor hearken to your dreams which ye cause to be dreamed. For they prophesy falsely unto you in my name: I have not sent them, saith the Lord.' Mark you: 'I—have—not—sent them'!"

Reluctantly heads began to turn, wanting to see what Robert Owens would do. He had rounded his shoulders forward as he listened. He appeared to be deep in private thought, as if he did not realize or care that the tirade was directed at him.

"Brothers and sisters," Mr. Arnold went on, "let me tell you a story about a man I once knew. His life was rich and full of good works. He had a loving family, an honest job. He was not a man of worldly goods, but neither did he want for anything. His house was solid, the butter at his table was sweet, and he was a friend in his community.

"Then one night he had a dream. In his dream he was no longer an ordinary man of friends and family and honest work. He was the king of a large realm, a desert kingdom that put him in mind of biblical places. His palace stood in an oasis surrounded by palm trees. Although he had a queen, in the evenings the most beautiful maidens of lands near and far were brought to his court to dance for his entertainment. He had a prince and a princess child, both, but he knew them not, for they had servants to care for them. And in the evenings when the maidens were dancing, an orchestra played, made of instruments he'd never seen or heard before, and its music was more exquisite than anything he'd ever known in his waking life.

"He came to me because he was so troubled by this dream. 'It seems so real,' he told me. 'I can't help thinking this was my true way in another life, or a path I was supposed to follow in this one and can't. All my happy circumstances seem like nothing now compared to those riches when I wake. The dream comes to me every night, and I cannot ignore it. I wait all day just to get back into that world I know at night.'"

He paused and surveyed the rows of listening parishio-

ners, their stillness undone here and there by a finger rubbing
the side of an itching nose, a pair of ankles crossed, a handkerchief lifting.

"I think it was the music that haunted him most. He could
almost capture its melody during the day, but never quite. I
insisted to my friend that it was just a dream, to pay it no
mind, but the dream destroyed his happiness anyway. He
could not have what was in it, and he could never be content
with his own life again after that. But his life was good. And
so is yours."

Robert's eyebrows went up under the front of his hair.
His body began to shift as if it would follow, and they all
wondered if he would be driven out of the church.

"Isaiah, chapter twenty-nine, verse eight: 'It shall be even
as when an hungry man dreameth, and, behold, he eateth; but
he awaketh, and his soul is empty: or as when a thirsty man
dreameth, and, behold, he drinketh; but he awaketh, and, behold, he is faint, and his soul hath appetite.' I know you know
these things to be true. The temporary satisfaction of a dream
can never be brought over into your real life or the life of your
souls. Only through worship and good works can we truly
satisfy ourselves. . . ."

The old wood of Robert's pew cracked as he lifted his
weight from it. He gazed around at the people as they turned
to realize he was standing in their midst. There was a long
hollow of silence while they waited for him to exit. Instead
he spoke.

"It is my understanding that God sealed his covenant
with Abraham's descendants by sending Jacob's ladder down
to him in a dream. That Joseph married the Holy Mother
because the angel Gabriel visited him in a dream."

The faces turned away from him and back to the front of

the church, waiting for more of Mr. Arnold's fine words to rain on them. They remained dry. Robert went on.

"Joseph was able to save our Lord Jesus Christ, wasn't he, because he was warned of Herod in a dream? I leave it to you all to work out these questions for yourselves. Perhaps God has spoken to some of you in your dreams, perhaps not. I don't claim to be a prophet. I don't sell miracles. But I think if we're going to call on the Holy Book for our condemnation, we'd better be sure of it, hadn't we?"

He made his way out into the aisle and stood face-to-face with Mr. Arnold, and the long planks of wood floor sank between them, worn away by the history of footsteps. Mr. Arnold, not to be daunted, was glaring down at him from the pulpit as if contemplating one of God's insects.

"Job, chapter thirty-three, verses fourteen to eighteen," Robert went on. "'For God speaketh once, yea twice, yet man perceiveth it not. In a dream, in a vision of the night, when deep sleep falleth upon man, in slumberings upon the bed; Then he openeth the ears of men, and sealeth their instruction, That he may withdraw man from his purpose, and hide pride from man. He keepeth back his soul from the pit, and his life from perishing by the sword.'"

The dream peddler turned away from his accuser and walked to the front of the church and out the door. After watching him leave, the parishioners turned back to Mr. Arnold. Without his dismissal they were unsure if this event had ended the prayer meeting. It was clear that Robert Owens had won the day, but Robert Owens was only a drifter, while Mr. Arnold was their spiritual leader. He married them, baptized the children of their unions, and buried them, too. They blinked up at him.

Clearing his throat, Mr. Arnold bent his head in a manner that seemed intended to erase the memory of any unpleasant disruption and carried on, saying, "Friends, let us pray." He led them in the Lord's Prayer because it was solid and gathered the voices of all the congregation beneath his own. Like water under a boat, they bobbed him up, while the familiar ancient words brought him back his composure.

★ ★ ★

Robert leaned against the church while the drone of prayer lapped gently on the other side of the wall. With it he was sending his own whiffs of smoke up toward the heavens. He was waiting for Violet, to walk her home as he always did.

Inside the church Cora Jenkins was listening to the reading of the announcements when she suddenly thought she would stifle if she couldn't get outside. The summer church was warm, but to Cora's skin it seemed as if the air had somehow turned to a different substance. Its molecules had swollen large as baseballs, crowding around her head and chest in a plea for entry she was now powerless to grant.

"May I wait for you outside?" she asked her mother, trying not to look sick. Mrs. Jenkins gave her a concerned look. "It's so hot in here," Cora said, waving her hand a little in front of her chest to show she was not getting enough air.

"It won't be long," her mother whispered. "Do you want your father to take you home?"

Cora shook her head. She slipped out of the pew and down the side aisle, stepped out into the humid twilight that rolled down over her dress. The light buffeting of the breeze was like a soft bedsheet taken off the line and drawn across her skin. She walked down to the street and around the side of the building, where she saw the starry end of Robert's cigarette floating near the wall. The back of his silhouette was hoary with light from the window. He saw her approach through the blue darkness and stubbed the cigarette on the wall behind him and dropped its ember into the dirt. When he turned toward her, only one side of his face showed the light, like a moon.

"You're still here," she said to him.

"I am. Waiting for Violet."

Robert looked at Cora without smiling. He was not in the mood for her flirting, though he was not very hopeful she would just go away.

"You were quite brilliant in there, you know," she told him.

"Nothing brilliant about it. I know the Bible very well. You can back up just about anything if you know the Bible well enough."

"Anyway, I was impressed. I think everyone else was, too. I don't think anyone had any idea Mr. Arnold was going to attack you like that tonight. How lucky you happened to be there."

He folded his arms. "I wasn't taken completely by surprise. Mr. Arnold made it clear to me some time ago that he looks forward to my departure. I guess he decided to see if he could hasten it."

"Hasten?"

"Speed things up. He's taking action."

Cora looked at him. "I can understand that." She moved closer to him and turned to share his attitude so she could follow his gaze, out into the field behind the church, where the fireflies hailed one another with their mysterious signals.

"Do you think you'll be leaving pretty soon, then?"

"I don't know. Why?"

"Because . . ." She gestured behind her, meaning the people behind the wall.

"Oh, I wouldn't let a little incident like that chase me off.

Not if people still want me around. When it's really time to leave, I'll know it. Always do."

"But it won't be much longer, will it? With the summer ending . . ."

"I don't know," he said again.

Cora was silent, looking down to where their feet lined up in a track, as if stitching the ground.

"Why do you know the Bible so well?"

"I used to be a minister myself. A long time ago. Another lifetime."

Cora moved away from the clapboards and turned back to him. Her face was ghostly in the fading light, and her eyes glimmered.

"Well, you see? You couldn't be bad, then. I knew you couldn't be a bad man, not really, and you can be with me. There isn't a thing wrong with it. Older men marry much younger women all the time. All the time." She gulped the air. "You can marry me and teach me everything you know, and I will love you so much, more than anyone else ever could, and when you're old and sick, I'll still be sort of young, and I can take care of you."

The more he seemed to shake his head, the more insistent she was, talking faster as if convincing him were less about the argument itself than about its momentum.

"You just have to make up your mind to it, as I have. You just have to be willing to take me with you. Don't say no because you think it isn't right. Just do what you want to do. When summer ends, you can take me with you—it won't be too late."

Robert smiled sadly. "You're so sure I'm a good man, Cora. But you haven't asked me if I was a good, kind minister, why did I leave?"

"It doesn't matter. You were, because there is love in your heart. All you have to do is turn it toward me, Mr. Owens. Robert. Just turn it toward me."

Her voice was rising now, and he was aware of a shuffling beyond the wall, and the steady light from the windows began to buckle and flicker with movement. Cora put her arms out and clasped her hands behind his neck, then pressed her lips to his. She did not know how to kiss him, and she kept them perfectly still, like a child, but pushed them into him so forcefully that his own lips were crushed back against his teeth.

He took her by the shoulders to gently remove her from him. His mouth felt numb from her, as if she'd injected him with a poison.

"Why can't you understand?" she cried. "Why can't you love me?"

The sobs jerked out of her chest while she turned and ran, toward the crowd now milling into the road. She ran past Violet Burnley and Mrs. Jenkins as they came around the corner of the church and found him standing there, arms hanging helplessly down at his sides.

★ ★ ★

It might have been only his imagination. One or two regular customers failed to come to him that week at their usual time. But summer was busy, the long growing days, and anyone might miss an appointment. Business was still steady; he would put it out of his mind.

After all, Evie needed him to stay. As long as she wanted his medicine, he wouldn't fail her. Had a few people looked deliberately away from him just now, when he smiled at them in the street? He was usually braced for this, and he chided himself for feeling one way or another about it. It wasn't up to him.

The prayer meeting had prepared him. No matter how clever his answers to the Reverend Arnold, his witty words wouldn't win in the battle with fear. Yet he couldn't shake the sense that it wasn't yet time. He went home and counted his vials. He waited for dreamers.

Chapter 23

"Miss Blackwell. It's nice to see you again."

"Hello!" Christina heard herself chirp, and then she went silent, like Violet's bird.

Robert Owens was alone today on the bench outside the store. Usually Christina could nod silently and politely at the usual collection of curved old men and walk by, but now she was caught in the web of his greeting like a fly.

"I'm here to meet Cora," she said. "We're taking a walk down to Mrs. Schumann's, who hasn't been well, to bring her some things."

"That's kind of you. I remember Mrs. Schumann was the first person I met when I came into town."

"Really?" *It's a wonder you stayed,* she thought. She did not dare say it out loud.

"Yep. She sent me on to Miss Burnley's. And Miss Burnley pointed me here, to the store."

"And you must have met Cora." She looked down at him.

He took a breath. "I always meant to ask, if we happened to meet, if the dream you bought from me worked out for you."

"Oh, I don't know," she said. She glanced at the door to the store, hoping someone might step out and interrupt them.

He smiled. "You don't know?"

She pulled a handkerchief out of her skirt pocket and played with it.

He patted the seat beside him. "Come have a sit for a while. Don't be shy."

Christina did not know how to refuse without being rude, so she walked closer and sat on the other end of the bench, wringing the dry handkerchief in her hands.

"I wasn't sure what to think," said Christina. "I did dream of my wedding, and a young man. . . . He just wasn't the one I was hoping for."

"I see." Robert was thoughtful. "But he was someone you know?"

"Oh, yes, it was . . . someone from town."

"How interesting." He pulled an almost empty sack of sugar-heart candy from inside his vest and offered it to her apologetically. She put out her hand, and he shook some treats into it.

"What do you think your dream meant?" he asked her.

She traced her finger through the candies in her palm, rolling them and reading the sweet red messages printed on them.

"I haven't been able to decide. This is a person who seems to like me." She colored. "I thought maybe, if no one else ever does, he might be my only future."

"Never, dear. I think I told you before, but I'll say it again. There isn't any one future. Who is to say you will even be married? Maybe you will do something else."

Christina looked at him as if he'd lost his mind. "I hope that's not possible!"

At that moment Jackson Banks rounded the corner of the building. He came to the bottom of the steps, took in the two of them sitting on the bench together, and paused only a heartbeat before bounding up the stairs and past them. He pulled the door open, winked at Christina, and went in.

When they were alone again, Robert spoke. "It would be better to remain unmarried than to spend your life married to the wrong person."

"Maybe."

"Most certainly." Robert was watching Christina's face carefully. "You needn't follow a dream you bought to find happiness," he told her gently. "Just follow your heart."

"I'm afraid it's not pointing a clear direction for me." She bit down on a candy version.

"Ah. Well. That can be a nuisance."

He rolled the top of the paper bag closed and set it on the bench beside him.

"Is that why you never married?" she asked him, before she could lose her nerve. "You thought you might make the wrong choice?"

A man opened the door from within, then stepped in front of it to hold it open for two women to pass him before following them down into the street. Robert waited until they had left before speaking.

"I would say I chose a different sort of life. That kind of love isn't a part of the life I've made."

Christina was thoughtful, looking into her lap. "What if someone wanted to marry you now?"

"I don't think that would change anything."

"What will you do if you ever fall in love?" She was surprised to hear herself asking him all these bold questions, she who was usually so shy. But there was something about Robert Owens that put her at ease with him.

He leaned back. They both turned their heads as Jackson exited the store with a paper bag under one arm. He whistled his way down the street.

"People don't just fall in love by accident, like you'd fall down a set of stairs. They have to be willing."

Christina wondered if that were true. Across the street she noticed Mrs. Jones drift in with the two women who'd just left the store, and they stopped together, talking. Except they all seemed to turn and face Jenkins's sign, taking in Mr. Owens and herself sitting there. Their words were lost to her in the dust, but their expressions had gone hard and seemed disapproving.

"I should go in now," she said, standing up. "Cora's expecting me."

"I wonder if you might want to give it another try sometime? Your dream? I could make you another one. You never know, it might come out different."

Christina hesitated. "I don't think so, thank you. I'm not sure I want to know what would happen if I dreamed it again."

Robert nodded, reaching an arm across the empty back of the bench. "Suit yourself," he said.

Evie knew she should start the supper, but her body dragged. The deep sleep she'd been avoiding hounded her always, trailing after her on soft paws and waiting for her to lie down. She went to her book, the one Robert had given her, and took it off the shelf. She wasn't sure how he had guessed, but poetry was the only thing she could read now. When she tried to pick up a longer book, she couldn't sustain the story in her mind. The characters and events bled through one another, and she would read and reread a page without taking in what was going on.

Over the summer she'd been reading one poem at a time from *The Wind Among the Reeds*, whenever she had an idle moment, although she hadn't decided if she liked it. It seemed to her there was an awful lot of sighing and a lot of nonsense about women's hair. There was frequent wandering into the afterlife and other places Evie did not want to go. When she read in "A Cradle Song" about "the narrow graves calling my child and me," she shut the book and decided she wouldn't go on with it. But then she found herself still picking it up from time to time, and now she saw she had come almost to the end.

"Aedh Wishes for the Cloths of Heaven," she read. Aedh was the one always moaning about love. It seemed to Evie he knew very little about real love. He was so busy flying among the stars and sunsets that he never came down to the work of it, to eating the hard, dry, overcooked supper you didn't want, digging out the needed smile no matter how deep it burrowed within you, the living with snoring and nagging and the just plain exhausting effort of it all. Her cobwebby mind was trying to clear as she fingered the paper. She noticed a crease at the top right corner of the page, as if someone had once folded it down.

> Had I the heavens' embroidered cloths,
> Enwrought with golden and silver light,
> The blue and the dim and the dark cloths
> Of night and light and the half light,
> I would spread the cloths under your feet:
> But I, being poor, have only my dreams;
> I have spread my dreams under your feet;
> Tread softly because you tread on my dreams.

Evie looked up, and her gray eyes went dark. Her daytime fog was torn away like a garment. She could not know if Robert had given her this book for a reason, but her tightening heart seemed certain that he had.

While she sat, with the outside greenery fluttering away at
her through the window, she heard a knock. Visitors had fallen
off over the summer, since that initial flurry of comforting and
shoulder patting and baking things had subsided. The handkerchiefs had been tucked back into the pockets and the tilted
heads straightened up; the stiff shoes had shuffled the friends
away. Evie was alone again, and knocks were rare out here on
the farm. When she heard it a second time, she realized she
must put the book down and go to the door.

There stood Cora Jenkins, her pale face mottled with heat.
She had swept the hair away from her ears halfheartedly,
although she usually combed and plaited it with such care.
Her eyelids were puffed, as if some strange infection had
bloated her taut young skin.

"Cora, dear, are you quite well? Come in and sit down."

Cora came in but said nothing. Evie brought her into the
sitting room and excused herself to put on the tea.

"You look very nice, today, Mrs. Dawson," Cora told her
when she came back.

They sat and listened to the water beginning its low hiss
in the other room. Evie did not look nice in her old housedress and apron and dark-ringed eyes, but then Cora didn't
seem fully aware of having spoken. Evie thanked her anyway.

There was a short silence between them, and they could
hear the imprisoned water in the kettle growing angrier.

"Would you like a cookie? I left them in the kitchen."

"No, I . . . My stomach hasn't been well lately. I can't
keep things down."

Evie tsked her tongue. "Not that nasty flu again? You
should be resting at home." When Cora didn't answer, Evie
prodded her. "It's not that I'm not happy to see you . . . but
why have you come all the way out here when you're feeling
so poorly?"

Cora looked up, over to the kitchen doorway and back again to Evie's face. "Have you not guessed? Does no one know yet?"

Evie leaned forward. "What do you mean?"

Cora's shoulders were rounded over her lap, and when she closed her eyes, she forced out the tears Evie hadn't noticed in them before.

"I haven't bled," she whispered to the floor. "I'm going to have a baby."

Evie was still. She had never faced such a problem before. It happened, of course, she knew it happened, to other girls in faraway towns and big cities. Bad girls? Girls who did not know any better? In either case they were sent away on trains before their bodies began to balloon, shuttled off in secrecy, alone but for the company of the other fallen girls. She pictured them all in dormitory beds like those of a hospital or a boarding school, slow, panting girls awaiting their confinement row on row in snowy nightgowns. Every so often one would be led away to give birth, and the others would remain, rolling over to lie on their other sides and waxing like pale-limbed moons. And here was Cora, just like them, with no outward sign yet of her condition, save for the fact that she was crying.

Evie said only, "Cora, you have to tell this to your parents."

She shook her blotched pink face. "They'll send me away. I'll be disgraced and ruined, and no one will want me. And"— she swiped a hand across her face—"I'll never see my little one. They'll take him away before I ever set eyes on him."

"I don't think they would do that. A wedding would make more sense. Have you not even told the father?"

Cora shook her head. "I don't want him to know. He's not . . . I can never marry him. And I was only with him because . . . because . . ." She put her head in her hands. "I just wanted him to see me as a woman. A lover. That's all I ever wanted."

Evie stiffened. "What do you intend to do?" Her question sounded hard to her, but she could find no way to soften it.

"I don't know yet," Cora said. "But I've been thinking about it. That's the reason I came to you."

She tried to rush on before Evie's mind could get ahead of her. If she presented her idea quick enough, she was hoping, she could force it in. In that moment of hesitation, before the wall of refusal went up, she'd sneak it past, and maybe it wouldn't be dismissed out of hand.

"I could stay here with you," she said.

"With us? What would we tell your parents?"

"Shh. Shhh." Cora put up a finger as if she were talking to a child, still trying to float her idea up overhead, prevent Evie from making the wall piece by piece with her questions, her doubts of stone.

"Yes, stay here with you. Just think of it. I could help you. We could tell my parents something, like . . . I'm just here to keep you company, because you've been sad. And I *could* keep you company, and help around the house. You could even tell her I'm helping you with a new business, like sewing or selling your pies at the store, and then—"

"For how many months? It would never work, Cora. You have responsibilities at home, too. They'd never say yes."

"Wait, wait, I haven't finished. We could tell them you've been ill, even, that you need someone to care for you so George can farm—"

"My own mother could do that. Or June. They know this."

Cora's pupils widened, and the extra darkness in them gleamed as she worked out her plan.

"We could tell everyone you're expecting. That your father told you you must stay in bed for the duration. And I'll
come and wait on you, and keep the house clean, and do your
cooking and chores. Even your mother might want extra
help for that. And then, in the end, when the baby is born,
you could . . . you could keep him."

She had kept her voice calm. She must not be upset. If
she seemed sad about any of it, the plan would not come
to pass.

Evie sat quietly for a minute. She hadn't thought of it until
Cora said the words. Now she understood why the girl had
come here for help, had chosen Evie. She was hoping to offer
her something she could not refuse, something she wanted so
badly it would outweigh all the lies.

"Cora," she said softly, "I can't take your baby."

Cora's face contracted to a strange maze of wrinkles,
which the young could amass only with a horrible effort.

"Yes you can. You can. Don't you see? You could raise
him, and then I would still be able to see him once in a while.
I could watch him grow. It wouldn't be the same, but . . .
he'd have a good mother, you see? He wouldn't have to be
ashamed. No one would have to know. And I know you
would love him, I can imagine how well you would love
him—your Benny was the happiest boy in the whole world."

Finally Cora's tears came down, and Evie felt her own
eyes well like a mirror.

"We are not going to do this," she said firmly. "We cannot perpetrate such a lie."

"What does it matter if we lie? When has anything good
ever happened in the world just because someone told the
truth?"

Evie put a hand to her forehead. Her skin was hot with

indecision. "I think if you leave your baby here, even if we could get away with it, we would both be sorry."

"If you don't help me, I don't know what I'll do. I have nowhere to go."

Evie got down on her knees in front of the girl and took her hands in her own.

"You need to go home. I told you, the best thing is to tell your mother and father. They'll know what to do."

"You don't understand. I can't tell them. They'll want to make a wedding, and I just can't."

Evie squeezed the cold hands with her own hot ones. "Why, Cora? Who is the father?"

But Cora mashed her lips together and said no more.

★ ★ ★

Cora had gone. In her mind Evie pressed the future over her past like a piece of tracing paper. All she knew of raising a baby was Ben, and when she imagined taking Cora's child, she kept seeing her own. She struggled to make the baby a girl, with red-gold hair, but her concentration would weaken and the dark outlines of Benny come through the paper.

There was the baby in a high chair, drawn up to the table at suppertime. Evie put squares of bread and cheese on the baby's tray while George pulled faces at her. She'd laugh, losing little chewed buds of her meal onto the floor. Then Evie was sitting up at night when the baby was sick, checking the hot forehead too often, until she'd taken so much of its heat into her own hand that she could no longer feel the difference. The baby cried in her ear, and then Evie skipped some years and was sending the little girl off to school with a pail and a new-made dress, copper braids down her buttoned back.

In Evie's future, Cora never married. Instead she stood endlessly behind the counter at Jenkins's store, waiting for her own little girl to come in with a nickel for the candy jars.

Her mind jumped again to the age of nine. By then the little girl would be learning to sew and could be trusted to cook on her own. What a help she would be. She might come home from school crying because the boys had teased her and pulled her hair. Evie would unwind her braids and gently brush out the sunset waves, clucking comforts at her. By now Evie could see this nine-year-old clearly, rescuing a lost kitten, bathing it by the fire with a wet washcloth. Cross-stitching a sampler. Sneaking into the pantry before supper. Jumping down the steps off the porch while Evie chastised her. She could see it all distinctly, but she could never see anything past the age of nine.

★ ★ ★

"Chris-teeeen-a."

She heard the singsong of her name and turned to see Jackson grinning at her. He had walked up so silently behind her in the grass that she'd had no inkling of him.

"Hello." She turned back to the bush she was harvesting, fingers fumbling along the raspberries.

"May I have one of those?"

She held her basket slightly away from him. "Help yourself. They don't belong to anybody."

Wild raspberry bushes had been growing against part of the graveyard fence for as long as Christina could remember, and the children often visited them after church and picked them clean while their parents stood talking.

Jackson reached into Christina's pail and crushed a handful into his palm. She slapped his arm away, but he only opened his mouth and crammed the berries in, and after he swallowed, he licked the juice from his palm and wiped his hand on his pants. Christina wondered if he was taking some boyish pleasure in trying to disgust her.

"That's not what I meant," she said.

"Oh, well, and what about you? Aren't you going to leave any for the children?"

"I just felt like making a cobbler. You know there'll be plenty more ripe tomorrow, and the next day. . . ."

"Hmmm." Jackson surveyed the bush. He leaned in toward her, reaching past her shoulder to a perfect round berry she had missed. While she inhaled the smell of his skin, he pulled the berry away easily, leaving its naked white stump behind.

"Shouldn't you be working?" she asked him.

"I am. Sort of. Had to bring one of the horses in for shoeing. I'm waiting around until she's ready to go. Have a list for the store as well, so I guess I'll stop in there and see your friend."

Christina resumed her picking, skin prickling under her dress. She found herself looking at the raspberries closely. The longer they hung on the bush, the more tender they grew, until they practically fell open, flattened out in your hand when you took them away. She had never really noticed before, the little frightened white hairs poking out between all their goose bumps.

"Speaking of the store . . . noticed you having a nice cozy chat with Mr. Dream Peddler the other day, didn't I? Sitting outside on the bench, the two of you, like old friends."

For the first time ever, Christina found herself silently agreeing with Cora's complaint that the town was too small. "If you say so."

"What would a sweet girl like yourself be doing mixing with him?"

"Nothing. He asked me to sit down. It would have been rude to go on past."

"I see. You a customer of his or something? I wouldn't have pictured it."

"You don't know anything about me."

Jackson edged closer to her, pretending to feel inside the bush, and she felt the hair rise all along her arms, like the little white hairs on the raspberries. "Come to think of it, maybe you're right. Maybe I don't know. Maybe you've been going to him regular all this time, since the day he first got to town, and buying up crazy wild dreams."

Christina didn't like this. Her skin wanted him near her, but her mind pushed at him, helpless.

"Hey, Christina? Have I ever been in any of your dreams?"

"No," Christina said truthfully.

"That's too bad," he said.

"I guess you'd better go on and get your list at the store, then. Maybe Cora would like to see you."

"You trying to get rid of me so quickly?"

Christina straightened her back, but she didn't answer.

"I'm surprised. I thought maybe you liked me."

"What made you think that?"

"A little bird told me."

Christina hoped he would think it was the heat, this flush creeping up her neck. "I guess I don't dislike you."

He slipped one hand into his pocket. In the other he still held the berry he'd taken, between his thumb and forefinger. The air around them shimmered with cricket song steaming off the grass.

"So maybe you'd invite me to try the cobbler when it's ready? I can be over after suppertime."

Christina's heart hammered like it was begging to be let out of a dark closet. This was happening. She'd always thought if she ever had a chance with Jackson, a sign that he wanted her, she'd have felt differently. Shivery, happy, not just dreading and sick. He stood close to her but looked away. He looked to the side, at the road, at the distance beyond.

"Open your mouth," he said.

She surprised herself by obeying, as if his voice tugged invisible lines that twitched her body to move.

He lifted the berry to her lips and pressed it gently into her with his thumb. When she closed her mouth, the berry broke on her tongue. He looked into her eyes then, but it seemed to her he was looking a question when she was expecting an answer. He leaned in quickly, past the looking into feeling, to feel her, and when she realized his movement would turn into a kiss, she backed away. She put a hand up and swallowed, as if she hadn't quite gotten the berry down.

"What's the matter with you?" he asked her.

She shook her head. "Nothing."

"Cora let me."

"She did not."

He laughed. "You take everything so seriously."

She couldn't tell if he meant she took kissing too seriously or the things he said. She turned back to her bushes, pushing their spindles apart, looking for the berries that hid from her. She plucked them out busily, as if they were beetles harming the plant. She was aware of Jackson still standing at her shoulder. Even though she felt certain she had just ruined everything, she was still content to be near him, humid air lapping at the narrow space between their bodies. Every time his arm shifted, the hair on her own did as well.

He spoke. "Can I just ask you something?"

"I guess."

"Did she tell me the truth?"

"What truth?"

"When Cora said you cared for me . . . Was she only teasing?"

Christina kept her eyes on her work. If she looked up, she knew she would lie. To the leaves only, to the basket, could she tell the truth.

"Don't you know just about all the girls in town like you? I thought that's what you wanted."

Jackson touched her arm lightly. "It must mean something, if you do. If . . . all of them. It must mean something." She felt his lips brush her forehead, absentminded now, the opposite of his intent in leaning toward her a moment before.

"Must go back and check on the horse," he said, and left her.

She spent the rest of the afternoon making up the cobbler and puzzling over what he'd said. After all the raspberries she'd eaten, their seeds stuck in her teeth. In the pockets of bone, she felt them, and she ground her jaw in an effort to work them loose. Her mother told her to stop it; she looked like a cow with its cud. She set the cobbler out to cool on the windowsill and said nothing to her parents of the possibility Jackson might come to call, but she checked her hair in the mirror after drying the supper dishes and sat out on the porch alone. She fanned her skirt around her on the seat, and with her tongue she felt over all the seeds still in her mouth. The scent of the raspberries cooling nudged her now and again, but Jackson never came.

★ ★ ★

The store bell tittered at Rose Whiting and her cracked brown bare feet pressing over the floorboards. The sawdust lifted with her first steps and left two empty footprints behind her.

Cora smiled tightly at Rose, glanced down and away

again, looking for something at the long counter to fiddle with. Rose's summer feet always made Cora queasy, and now she felt it even more. Even though she should have been used to it, when none of the children wore boots this time of year either. Their feet blackened day by day, Saturday-night scrubbings with a brush did little to clean them, and under their Sunday church boots and stockings their raw, tingling skin was still stained. When Cora was a little girl, her mother had made her wear her boots all year. Bare feet were countrified and uncouth. Cora remembered her playmates taunting her, saying she was a heavy foot, and when she couldn't run as fast as they, she was jealous. Until nighttime came and she took off her boots and felt the soft-underbelly whiteness of her own clean feet, slipped in between her nice clean sheets.

But Mrs. Whiting was not a child. As each foot swung out from the folds of Rose's long dress, Cora could glimpse it black-toed, sometimes bleeding, jumping as if in a wasted hope that it might escape its cruel mistress. In summer Cora wished she could avoid Mrs. Whiting altogether, wished someone else could be minding the store. If she looked at Rose's face, she faltered under the gaze of her strange flecked brown eyes, but to look down would mean the assault of those charred-looking feet.

She settled for somewhere in the middle, the waist region of Rose Whiting's dress. "May I help you with something?"

"Two pounds of sugar, please? And one of coffee."

Cora turned to reach for her paper bags and heaved a sigh as if the movement had wrung the air out of her. One at a time, she punched them open.

"Are you all right?"

"Yes. What? What do you mean?"

Rose smiled. "You sound like the weight of the world is

on your shoulders. But a carefree young lady like you couldn't have any problems, now, could you?"

Cora looked up from the task into Rose's eyes and felt herself all on display, clear as the new ribbons laid out in their case, the half rounds of penny candy in the transparent jars. She couldn't forget those rumors, those silly ideas about Mrs. Whiting and how she always understood, or guessed.

"No, that's right," she said. "I have no problems, of course not. I didn't realize I made a sound!"

"A sigh." Rose smiled again. "Just a sigh."

"I have a crick in my neck, from bending over the accounts. That must be it."

Rose watched as she hefted the lid off the sugar barrel, put her hand in for the scoop. While Cora was busy filling the bigger bag with sugar, the store went empty. Two little children who had no money for candy looked shyly over at Rose and, when she stuck out her tongue at them, made for the door. A lone woman who'd been fingering fabric decided against buying any and left.

When Cora was done weighing the sugar, she went to the coffee with the smaller bag and started over. The shiny, dark coffee beans blinked at the brightness when she lifted the lid. As she brought the full bag of coffee over to the scale, Rose spoke again.

"You're not well."

"I'm just fine," said Cora.

"I heard you had caught a bug, that stomach flu going around. Did Sam ever look at you?"

Cora's pale face briefly flushed. "No, it wasn't anything so serious as that. I just took some water and . . . some rest."

"So you're better now."

"Of course. I'm back at work, as you see."

Rose put her quiet hand over Cora's busy one and stilled

it. "But you don't feel well." She ran her thumb firmly up the inside of Cora's arm, to her elbow, and the girl's eyes closed like a cat's. She kneaded Cora's hand a little before she released it back to its work, and when Cora realized her hand was free, her eyes opened and she looked at Rose as if she'd never seen her before.

"You need a breath of air. Help me take these parcels outside."

Cora obeyed, squinting into the light as if she hadn't left the store in a long time.

"Sam's going to come around for me in the automobile. Sit down here with me on the bench and keep me company until he gets here."

Cora set the bag of coffee on the boards beside Rose but remained standing. "I should go back inside," she said, fingers worrying the front of her dress. She glanced in through the dark window. "I should be minding the store."

"Everyone left," Rose reminded her. "Sit here with me and rest yourself. All that standing, in your condition, it isn't good for the baby."

Cora stared down at her, waiting for anger to rush up her throat and out her open mouth. But there was something in Rose's face, the blank way she gazed at the distant fields, that deflected anger. Rose felt sorry for the fields, Cora could see that in her eyes, sorry for the beautiful way they waved at the town and how soon they would be cut down.

Cora moved to the other side of her and sat, deflating as the air held in her chest pushed out, then straining to breathe in against her stays. She didn't have any anger inside her, she realized, only this leaden heaviness that pulled her down next to the town witch.

"I never thought Evie would tell anyone," she said finally. "I know you're her mother. . . . Still, she promised me."

Rose's head came around quickly, as if pushed by some unseen hand. "She promised you? How long ago was this?"

"I don't remember. The time seems so long. It doesn't matter."

"My dear, she never said a word. I guessed. It's not natural, a girl your age to look so tired." She contemplated the view across the road. "What did Evie say to you?"

"Nothing. I . . . She won't help me."

"I don't see how there's any way she can help you. You must get married, that's all. It's the only thing to do. You must tell your parents and be married as soon as possible. Evie should have told you the same."

Cora shook her head. "I won't be married."

Rose's voice turned flinty, like she was digging for words down in the earth and could only turn up the sharp ones. "You will. You don't have to tell me how you've got yourself in this condition, but it will only end up one way now." She held a foot out in front of her and studied it for a moment before letting it swing back. "If you're thinking it may resolve itself, hoping . . . You'll soon be past the time when that's likely to happen. The longer you wait, the faster this baby will come following your wedding. I know your parents . . . well, you wouldn't want to bring shame on your family, and maybe it's too late to avoid the talk. But then there's Sam, I can enlist him. You could hide away after the birth, and he'll send word around about your resting in your last months. As far as the town need know, you can stay pregnant until the proper time. . . . You understand what I'm saying?"

Cora's face was worried, pinched in a manner that seemed to deny Rose's words entry. "Why would you help me?" she asked.

"I'd help anyone in this town, anyone I could, with anything I have."

Cora turned her head. "But why? Would they do the same for you? You see how people laugh at you, you must know they whisper about you. People who don't even know you." She held her hands turned up in her lap and looked at them. "I don't really know you. Why would you help me?"

Rose put her hand on Cora's arm again. "It doesn't matter what people say about me. I'd help because it's the right thing to do."

Cora looked into her eyes. "But don't you think I'm bad?"

"No. No, I don't think you're bad."

Cora thought about that. "Anyway, you don't understand me. I can't marry the father."

Rose's eyes narrowed, then widened. "Are you trying to tell me . . . Is he already married?"

Cora made no answer.

"I've heard some of the gossip about you and Mr. Owens. I admit, if he has done this, I've been mistaken about him. I thought . . . I wouldn't have been surprised to learn he was married before, is still married . . . but this. This beats all. I did think there was a limit to . . . and Evie . . ."

Cora began to wake to what Rose was saying, and her head started to shake with it. "No, no, you misunderstand," she said. "Robert—Mr. Owens . . . Oh, he can't be married, is he already married? Where is his wife, then? It's not him, I never said it was him, you can't think that. He loves me, he would never—" She clamped a hand over her mouth.

"I see," Rose said softly. "I made a mistake. I see."

Cora stood. She touched the back of her hand to one eye, to see it came away dry. "I don't want to talk about this anymore."

She moved toward the door just as it swung open and Toby peered out. "There you are," he said. "You can't just leave the counter like that. Dad would be mad."

"There's no one in there right now. I wasn't feeling well. I just came outside for some air."

Toby's slow grin began to rise across his mouth. "Out here? In the air like a hot, wet blanket?"

Rose stood, calling his attention to her. "It was my idea, Tobias. I suggested she come outside."

Toby colored.

"I need a walk," Cora said.

"What about—"

"Just go inside and mind the store for me, Toby."

When Toby was gone, Rose opened her mouth to speak, but she was interrupted by Sam gaily honking his Klaxon, churning up the dust around his wheels.

★ ★ ★

He saw Evie's lips moving but couldn't hear her words. He imagined the things she might tell him, about her cake that fell yesterday or the new litter of barn cats born into the hay-smelling dusk, one floury line of light wriggling over them as they nudged their mother for milk. How she watched George at work through her kitchen window, the perfect music of his movements as he shucked corn along the rows. Even though Robert had never farmed, he thought he understood it, the putting into the land and later harvesting. Only because you surrendered to it everything, all your muscled hope, did it yield you anything, the beaded pours of grain and the dark wrinkled vegetables, the bend of the wheat fields up against the tall, straight flutter of the corn. Maybe she would tell him what it felt like to see him coming. That now she wanted him to put dreams inside her, like small scraped parts of himself.

"I need to talk with you."

She looked so serious he dropped the smile, like something he'd just realized was too hot to hold. Reached across and pulled out her hand to place the vial within it, just because he wanted to touch her. She didn't seem to notice the touch, put her prize in the pocket of her dress absentmindedly, as though she were thinking of something else entirely.

"What's wrong?" he asked, and since she was not really paying attention to him, he kept hold of her free hand.

"I had a visit from Cora Jenkins."

He studied her. "I didn't know she was a friend."

"She isn't."

He let go of her hand and waited.

"What I tell you is going to be . . . in the strictest confidence."

"All right."

"She came to me because she's pregnant." She looked for his reaction, waiting for it to ripple across his features, but he kept his face still.

"I see."

"I think she only came to me because . . . because she thought I might be willing to take the baby. She hoped we could hide her somehow, pretend it was my pregnancy, and then . . . The whole idea was crazy. I told her it was impossible, that she should marry the father. But she kept insisting she couldn't marry him, and she said the strangest thing. That she only wanted to prove to him she was a woman."

This time her words hit. She watched his face change. "What did you tell her?"

"I said no."

He looked away. "Did she make you think it was me?"

"She wouldn't say who it was."

"That's not what I asked."

Evie bit her lip.

"I'm not the father."

"Of course not. I didn't think you were."

"Tell me," he said. "You said no right away to Cora's proposal. Why did you do that?"

"Because it would be wrong. It would be a lie. And it's not my child."

"Does that really matter? If Cora doesn't want it, if you could help her . . . would it be so terrible? Think about that." He reached out and pulled a stray curl from her face. "You could have a baby again."

"I have thought about it. But it wouldn't be mine and George's. It wouldn't be the same. Babies should be with their mothers."

"Are you sure that's the reason?"

"What do you mean?"

"Maybe you're afraid."

"I don't feel afraid. It's just that I don't feel . . . anything."

Robert sighed. "Is this how you plan to go on? Feeling nothing? Drinking my potion and walking around half asleep?" Evie was backing away as he spoke, each footstep taken as if to bring him into focus, as if she'd been too close to see him clearly. "How can you live like this?"

Evie made a choked sound, almost like stifled laughter. "You're one to talk, aren't you? How many years have you been running from your own life? Don't tell me you're not afraid. No one needs the stuff you sell. But instead of going back home, you just press on, town after town, taking advantage of all the people foolish enough to think you could sell them something real. You."

Robert held up his hand. "I have always stood by my products. I offer—"

"Oh, I know, I remember. A money-back guarantee." Now she made the start of a laugh, but it veered off hysterical. "What a shame we can't get these for everything in life, isn't it? Motherhood. Friendships. Dissatisfied? That's no problem. We have a guarantee for that. Your wife could have had one for you."

Robert spoke quietly. "There is no way to give back whatever my wife lost by choosing me."

He could feel that his calm infuriated her. And she honed her next words, trying to make them sharp enough to pierce it. "I don't understand you. There must be something wrong with a person who lives like you. So you were a drunk. So you made a mistake. That gives you no right to just leave. Your little girl. Every day you don't go back, you leave her again. You're a coward."

"Many of us are cowards, I think. But most of us don't ever recognize what it is we fear."

Evie's hand twitched at her side. "I don't know who you think you are . . . to come here and talk to me about my fears? About my feelings? The man who lives a few months in this town, a half year in that one . . . and never anywhere long enough for real feelings, friendships, or love. You'd rather be the stranger. But you still think you can sit in judgment on me."

Robert took a step forward into her space. He saw her brace herself, but he kept his voice low. "If you think I've never stayed anywhere long enough to have feelings . . . never stayed anywhere long enough to love . . . then you are mistaken."

They stared at each other. Then Evie turned on her heel and walked away, marching through the tall grass.

She got herself home, went through the kitchen into her pantry, and took down what she had been keeping in an old brown vanilla bottle. She went out again and wound through the woods to the bay. Standing stiff at the edge, she heaved the bottle as far as she could out into its quivering deep.

When she reached home again, George was already there, and he asked her where she had been.

"I walked down to the bay," she told him.

"There aren't any answers there."

"But I needed to go."

He held out his arms to her, and she went into them. "Come back to me, Evie."

"I'm trying," she said.

Chapter 24

Evie was known in town for her bumbleberry pie, and she was bringing one in to the county fair to enter the pie contest. The finished pie had come out of her oven perfectly golden and burnished with an egg-white wash. She'd baked up the scraps of crust as well so she could sample them, and she was pleased. George hitched the cart, and they rode early into town with June and Harold, the mare's head testing the day before them and her tail twitching the flies. George's best pig squealed and grunted in the back, while Evie's pie sat silent under its dish towel in her lap.

Evie had been wondering and worrying over Cora every day. She hadn't told George about their meeting. She didn't want him to start thinking about raising Cora's child—what if he wanted to say yes and Evie couldn't do it? She convinced herself it wasn't her secret to tell. And as she was already keeping too many of her own, this one slipped in so easily among them that she never noticed. She knew, though, that Cora would soon begin to show. Staying silent Evie could do, but she was not smart enough to think of anything more.

Part of her was tracing the future along like a riverbank, if she should say yes to Cora and take the baby as her own.

She wished she had refused because she was selfless, or honest, or righteous, but she knew that Robert had understood the truth—she was only afraid. To heal its wound, some part of her heart had closed over itself and would not open again. She hadn't even been aware of its happening until Cora had come to her, and then when she searched within herself, she found the mass of twisted, unyielding scar.

From time to time, George reached over as he used to do, to take her hand or rest one of his in her lap, but each time he did, the pie was there and Evie's hands busy holding it.

At the fairgrounds the Dawsons were tugged away from one another, as different neighbors greeted them and pointed out their finest work. The pies and preserves and cakes were displayed in rows, while the fat, bristly pigs and clean, spongy sheep wandered in their pens, poking their noses at the edge of freedom and then backing away. Inside barns the quilters had hung their Garden Gates and Drunkard's Paths, waiting for the judges who would pull up their corners, searching for untrimmed loose threads.

As well as the offerings for judgment and prizes were all the wonders for sale: lemonade and taffy apples; popcorn and sausages; animals, leather goods, and guns. George went to examine the horses while Evie carried their picnic basket and searched for a quiet place in the shade to unpack the lunch. Coming through the crowd, she saw her parents and waved them over.

"How are the flowers this year?" she asked her mother. Rose always participated in the flower-arranging contest with blooms from her garden.

"Beautiful. Mine are not behaving for me, but the table is lovely. We'll walk over and see them after we eat."

"Where's Dad going?" After pecking Evie on the cheek,

he had ambled away, and the crowd had already closed over him.

"Off to watch the shooting exhibitions, I expect. He always must comment on that, even though he could never hit the broad side of a barn himself."

Evie smiled. Her father had a long history of prizeless duck-hunting excursions. The one time he'd brought home a dead, flopping duck for them, he admitted, with a big laugh, that he had surprised a fox who'd already killed the thing, dropped it in confusion, and run from him.

Evie inhaled the annual smells of the fair, the hot corn oil and the tang of cider steaming. Inside her an unfamiliar hunger bubbled into being. She had been eating only to silence her stomach, while the flavors of things on her tongue were no good, like paper wrappings of food chewing down to hard pulp. Now she found herself eating bread and butter and crunching fried chicken, as if she'd spent the summer fighting a cold and just found she could taste again.

"You've brought an appetite with you," Rose observed.

"I guess I have."

"Good."

A group of small children went by, some of them slurping on candied apples while those without watched enviously. One of them pointed at Rose, and right away the whispers shuffled out of them, a sound like rubbing palms trying to start a fire. Obligingly Rose raised her arm very slowly and pointed her finger, out toward each of them in turn, as if planting a curse inside their chests. They squealed and scattered.

"Why do you do that?" Evie asked her. "Why do you play along?"

Rose smiled. "They're only children. They want to think

they've had a brush with danger, but they know they haven't, not really. They know it better than their parents."

She wiped her fingers, greasy from the chicken pieces, vigorously on a cloth napkin.

"I never set out to be the town witch, you know. It never crossed my mind. The things that seem so bizarre to other people were always natural to me."

She studied the sheen on her hands for a moment, then wiped them some more, then looked up at Evie. "I'm sorry if it was hard for you when you were growing up."

Evie shrugged. "I never cared," she said.

Rose sighed. "Then you are a lot like me."

Evie watched the children lining up for their potato-sack race, laughing as they struggled to pull the sacks up around themselves. Her own son was missing, but somehow the line of children still looked full.

★ ★ ★

Christina emerged from the quilt show and stood for a minute, letting her eyes adjust to the light. Her mother's quilt displayed well, and they hoped it would be pinned with a ribbon. She took in the fair, the long tables of harvest, the little children toddling away from picnics under the trees.

There was Cora coming down one aisle, unaware of her best friend watching. A little girl inside Christina's heart wanted to rush over, push her friend down in the dirt, pull at her hair, and rip off her fancy lace collar. She knew that Cora had told Jackson who liked him; it couldn't have been anyone else. She listened to the man in the dunk tank calling insults to passersby, trying to get them to buy a chance at sinking him. She wished she could trade places with him and yell out at Cora, crazy things like how ugly and dirty she was. And then she thought Cora had probably been trying to help, the way she always did, and Cora seemed sad, touching things here and there on the tables; Cora looked lost.

Christina began to move closer when she saw Jackson come up behind her friend, and Cora turn to him, and the two of them talking hot words no one else could hear. Jackson leaned into Cora the way he had for raspberries, and Christina closed her eyes. When she opened them, Rolf was sauntering toward her from the hitching post, and she let him come closer and closer until he was blocking the rest of the fair from her view.

"I thought I could buy you a lemonade," he said.

She let him take her elbow and lead her away. They wandered between the stalls, and Rolf bought a candy apple, despite her insistence she didn't want it.

"How could anybody say no to a candy apple?" he asked.

Christina had to admit it was pretty, as red and shining as a Christmas-tree kugel. She held it awkwardly, trying to pinch only the end of the stick so her hand wouldn't melt the candy.

As they walked away from the crowd and into the short grass, she took a lick from time to time, so as not to hurt Rolf's feelings.

The constant popping of the shooting competition made conversation difficult, but Rolf was determined.

"Seems like Jackson might be sweet on your friend," he began.

"It looks that way, doesn't it?"

"And does she like him?"

Christina twirled the apple. She could feel her cheeks warming to match it. "I'm not sure. But I don't think so."

"And what about you? Do you still like him?"

Christina didn't answer. It didn't matter what she felt about Jackson. But if she said no, it would be a lie.

"I don't want to be a bother to you," Rolf said. "So maybe I should just say my piece and be done with it."

She looked up at him.

"I know I might not be your first choice. But I think I could make you happy. We have a good farm, and it will pass to me when my father grows old. I have plans for the place, and I know how to put money aside. I would always take care of you. There'd be plenty of everything for you to cook with, and we could build our own house. We could even order one of those new Modern Homes from the Sears catalog. You can buy ribbons and lace for all your dresses and things—"

"I make my own lace," she told him.

"Oh. Well, that's even better." He smiled at her.

Christina looked into the mirrored red surface of the apple like it might be a gazing ball. She was searching for pictures of the life she might have with Rolf, how she might sew matching curtains for all the new windows, and bake the week's bread and pies on Monday mornings, and wait for him on fine days with her mending out on the porch. Their children might have his freckles.

"Anyhow," he went on, touching her silence, "I thought maybe we could spend more time together and get to know each other. I wanted to tell you . . . I know I'm not popular like Jackson, or handsome . . . but I do believe I could love you better than he could." He looked sideways at her.

"Maybe you could come around tomorrow, after supper," she said. "If you like."

Rolf took her hand. He looked down. "You're really not going to eat that, are you?"

She noticed he took longer than necessary to work the apple out of her grasp. She still avoided looking directly at him while they walked on. Instead she listened, to the crackling sound of the glassy apple breaking as he bit into it.

★ ★ ★

Jackson spotted Cora idling at a long table, looking down at the knitted shawls, sweaters, and baby blankets for sale. She walked along, fingering the soft, bumpy wool. She picked up a pink blanket dotted with white intarsia sheep. They waggled across its expanse when she shook it out.

"This is so sweet for a little girl," she said, half to herself.

He sidled over. "Hello, darling."

Cora edged away from him. "I'm not your darling."

"I just want to talk to you."

"Well, I don't want to talk to you."

She moved swiftly down the aisle, turning the corner at the end of the table. Jackson was faster, and he took hold of her arm.

"Please let me go."

"I just want to say one thing." He lowered his voice. "Look, I know that wasn't right. I know it, see? And I'm sorry about it. That's all I wanted to say. I'm not some kind of . . . I didn't mean for it to be like that."

Cora yanked her arm uselessly. "But it *was* like that. And I don't want to talk. Now, let go of me."

"Not till I've finished. You know we both agreed. You said yes. I just—"

Cora was looking down at the lumps of wool, trying to hide the tear wending its bright way down her cheek. "You wouldn't let me change my mind."

"I said I was sorry, didn't I? I don't know how to make you understand. . . . Once we got to that point and it was happening, I had to go through with it. I had to."

"I don't care," she said. He let go of her arm, and she rubbed it as if he'd hurt her. "Can't you please just leave me alone now?"

"You don't need to be like that."

She walked away from him, and he followed her.

"You can't just go around hating me. That's not fair."

She didn't answer. A dense crowd of people was moving past, and she couldn't break through. Instead she was forced back against him.

"Going to look for your dream peddler, then?" he sneered. "Does he have a booth set up around here somewhere? Next to the fortune-teller and the tent of curiosities?"

"Why would you dislike him?" she challenged.

"I just think he's a misfit, is all. Something's not right about him. You know little Ali McBryde? Can't be more than eight, right? Well, what would he be doing leading that boy down the street by the hand one day, no one else in sight? I don't think anyone else saw them, but I did, and I tell you it made me feel strange."

"I'm sure Ali was just buying a dream."

"Sure, maybe. But I don't know where he could have found the money. And even if he did, it don't seem fair, taking advantage of a little fellow like that. Something's not right with it."

"Well, it's not taking advantage if he gets the dream he asked for. And I saw Ali earlier, stuffing himself with a doughnut, and he looked right as rain to me."

"Sure. Sure he is, for now. But I wonder." He scanned the crowds, hands in his pockets. "You know, Ali's only a bit younger than Ben Dawson was when he disappeared. And wasn't that odd? Robert Owens just happening to come into town at the very same time?"

"Ben Dawson was drowned in the bay!" She wiped at her eyes, furious with herself for crying.

"It seems that way. But if a stranger did come into town and somehow got hold of a boy . . . well, cracking the ice on the bay and dropping him in would be a perfect way to make sure no one would ever know what happened. Bet he'd have thought the body would never be found."

They were walking by the fresh-made doughnut stand, where short braids of dough puffed in a kettle of melted lard over a fire. As Cora watched, the half-fried crullers began to twist, turning up golden backs. The smell of them went down into her belly and wallowed there, flipping over and over, and the heat of the day and the fire flushed into her and swayed her.

"Jackson Banks, that's a horrible thing to say. And it's just not funny."

"I'm not trying to be funny. Look at him there. Just look."

He gestured over her shoulder, and she turned to see the dream peddler amusing a group of little ones by pulling pennies from behind their ears. He held the coins up shining, and they all hopped back, whooping and clapping each time. Cora began to lean. It felt like the heat was pulling at her, tugging her away from the side of the table, when she knew she was too dizzy now to let go.

"I don't mean to shock you, now, Cora." Jackson's voice came low and prowling over her shoulder. "But there are some people in the world who are very different from us when it comes to these things. People who . . . aren't right." His lips were so close to her neck now she could feel his breath trying to nuzzle in under her hair. "Haven't you been wondering why he doesn't like you? How he can keep refusing you all this time?"

Cora felt the voice trying to find its way down over the front of her chest. No, it was crawling now inside her, following the coil of heat and finding the doughnut oil puddled deep in her stomach. Her faint pulled her forward into the ground, as the last thing she saw was the passing of an old, dirty copper from Robert's big hand into a small outstretched palm.

"Cora!"

Jackson picked her up out of the dirt and began to stagger with her toward the threadbare edges of the crowd. Seeing them approach, Robert stood and hurried toward them, arms extended as if he would help Jackson carry her.

"Stay away from her!" Jackson cried out, and people nearby turned to look as Robert backed away with his hands held open, beseeching the air. "Just stay away!"

He carried her from the fairgrounds and into the grass to lay her down. From her picnic spot, Evie saw what was happening, and she jumped up and ran. Ran to where she heard the gunshots of the demonstrators cracking the sealed heat open, searching for her father.

★ ★ ★

Sam Whiting held the salts under Cora's nose, and she opened her eyes to him.

"There," he said, laying his big hand across her forehead. It was damp with sweat but clammy and cool. "You've fainted—from the heat, I expect. Why don't we see if we can sit you up now. That's it. Have you had much to eat today?"

He motioned to Evie, who was standing by with a cup of lemonade. She gave it to him, and he held it up to Cora's mouth, as if he didn't trust her to hold it.

"I just felt so sick all of a sudden," she said after she drank.

"I got spots in my eyes, and then they all crawled in together and I was gone." She hung her head, looking as if she might start crying again.

"It's all right, little one, we'll just sit here until you've had your drink and are feeling better. The sugar will perk you up. Take as much as you can."

She shook her head slightly. Her hand went down to her abdomen, and Evie watched it settle there.

"I feel . . . I don't feel well. I'm not sure I can drink any more just now." She doubled over herself, and only the corners of her mouth wincing were visible.

"I need to go home, Dr. Whiting. Can you take me home? Something is . . . wrong with me."

"Let me get your parents. They'll want to take you."

She gripped his wrist with a strength he could not have imagined waiting latent in such a narrow arm.

"Please take me. I don't want to wait for them." She stared into his eyes. "I need your help."

He considered her and then turned to Rose. "Will you be all right if I take her in the motorcar? It'll be fastest and easier on her."

Rose waved her hand at them. "Of course. I'll go home with George and Evie. You can get me there."

He nodded and turned back to his patient, Rose forgotten. "Can you get up and walk, if you lean on me a little?"

"I think so."

He helped her up, and she held to him while they made their way back through the fair and out to the road. Evie watched Cora's back, under her father's arm, until she could find it no more through the shivering turmoil of the crowd. As Cora walked away, she left a staggered trail of blood drops in the dust, but they were scuffed and rubbed out by the fair-goers' footprints crisscrossing over the ground.

★ ★ ★

Rose and Evie had put together a light supper of stewed tomatoes and sandwiches made with the unfinished meats from the picnic. They sat with George at the table and waited for Sam to return. The days had begun to shorten again, as if they spent themselves faster now in making the Indian-summer heat. The falling light caught all the glass things on the table in its net, like flickers of fish, and held them still. Every window and door was open to lure in the breeze. It teased them from the distant treetops, and all evening they waited, but it never came down to them.

Sam walked in, hung his hat, and set his bag by the door.

"Ah, supper," he said. "I'm famished."

He went to wash up at the kitchen sink and leaned back to see his family through the dining-room doorway while he rubbed his hands together.

"Never had my chance to eat at the fair," he told them, "so the rest of those sandwiches are mine."

Evie tried to smile, but George and Rose did not bother.

"How is Cora?" Rose asked him once she had passed him the food and filled his glass with iced tea from the pitcher.

"She'll be all right, in time. But I've had to tell her parents she had a miscarriage."

Evie and Rose carefully copied George's surprise.

"My God," said George. He was the only one who spoke as they all sat there, allowing the news to settle.

"That's terrible," said Evie slowly. "Tom and Mary must be so upset."

"As you would imagine," he said. "But of course the problem has fixed itself, so to speak, just as they were being made aware of it. They all—Cora included, I think—understand that this is for the best." He speared a bite of tomato and chewed it thoughtfully. "She's been given a rare second chance. No one has to know, and her parents are angry, but I think they're very grateful that at least Cora can still be happy and have a good life. When she gets over the shock, she will see that."

Evie caught herself thinking they shouldn't be having this conversation in front of Ben, then remembered he wasn't there.

"Did she . . . say anything to you about who the father was?"

Sam washed down his food with a swig of tea, a habit that still made Rose wince.

"No," he said curtly. "She refused to tell me, but when I left, she was alone with her mother. I think Mary will be able to get it out of her."

"I hope so," said George. "Whoever it is needs to know what he's done, to take responsibility."

"Agreed," said Sam. "And his family needs to know, so they can decide what should be done with him."

"I'd make him see sense. Give him the hide of his life."

"Well, no one is going to go hiding anyone. I promised them secrecy, and they will have it, from all of us. Maybe in time Cora will be willing to speak up. But right now I think all she wants is to put it behind her."

"Poor Cora," said Rose. "What a burden for her to bear."

"Well, poor Cora will recover physically just fine. And she should not have been engaging in such behavior. She has disgraced herself."

"That might be so," said Rose. "But she is a young girl. And young girls sometimes don't know things."

"My money is on that dream-peddler character," said George. "That Robert Owens."

"You must be kidding," Evie said.

"Why not? They've been seen together everywhere—at the store, the dance. . . . He walks her around town all the time. Now she's pregnant. Cora's always been a flirt, but nothing ever came of it until that man showed up in town."

"I don't think so," Evie said. "He's so much older than she is. He looks at her the way a father would look at his daughter. I'm sure of it."

George waved his empty fork. "You've missed the point entirely. He *is* so much older. He could so easily take advantage. And all this dream hocus-pocus, he could be feeding her all kinds of nonsense. Giving her dreams. Making her like him."

"That's crazy!"

"I don't think so. Don't you remember, even way back at the dance, you were so aggravated with him for not returning the cups? And he was taking punch over to Cora, wasn't he?"

"Yes, but—"

"He could have put something in her drink. No one would ever have noticed."

"You're being ridiculous."

"It's what her parents think," said Sam.

Evie turned on him. "What? Why would they think that?"

"I guess she was seen after prayer meeting running away from him. . . . She was crying. She won't say what happened. Mary saw it with her own eyes, and Robert Owens looking very guilty at Cora while she ran off. I don't know if he gave her any dreams or not, but something happened there."

"Oh, my goodness. Well, I don't really know the man," Evie lied, "but I still think you're wrong. That's a serious accusation against him. It's so much more likely to just be some gangly boy who loves Cora, and the two of them got themselves into some trouble. That's all it is."

George shrugged. "Are we having some of that award-winning pie for dessert?" he asked.

Chapter 25

A rumor sifted up out of the ground and began to drift about the town. Like sand blown by a windstorm, its grains were driven in everywhere: in windowsills and doorways, in the cracks of the house walls and the soles of shoes, collecting in between blades of grass on the lawns. It went into seams and under fingernails, surfaced brown in the dishwater, was tossed into the garden with the waste and grew there again. It rustled in the pillowcases and the curtains and could not be swept out; it was tracked back into every house and settled in every family.

Robert Owens sat in Violet Burnley's parlor and waited, but no one came to see him. The trees outside began to preen their secret colors, the ones they had all summer long been hiding beneath the green. He walked down the road on some days and sat instead on the bench outside Jenkins's store, but no one spoke to him. Cora's father watched the back of his head through the front window and stared blackness at it, but he would not stoop to go out and tell him to leave. The glances of people as they walked by, even those who had to pass him to enter the store, flitted onto parts of him and slid away, as if he were a hill of mud.

"It's something to do with that fair day, it must be," he told Violet.

They were hunched over the late garden vegetables, searching out hidden squash and beets, digging up potatoes. He sat back on his heels in the dirt.

"The way Jackson Banks was hollering at me to stay away . . . people will think I did something to her."

Violet looked at him and then down, at the earthy clumps falling away from the purple skins of the beets she'd pulled.

"I was in town yesterday, for the first time since the fair," she said. "And more than one person made a point of coming to speak to me, because they worry for me, they say, with you living in my house."

Robert laughed. "Well, I haven't murdered you in your sleep yet, have I? And made off with the silver? Seems a bit late for that now."

Violet said nothing.

"So?" he prodded her. "Do they think I've been carrying on with Cora? That I've hurt her in some way?"

Violet looked down at her hands as if her words could be weighed within them.

"I hurt her feelings, Vi, nothing more," he insisted gently. "I can't imagine why, but she thinks she is in love with me. She wants to leave town with me when I go, and I can't let her do that. So I've made her hate me."

"I don't think Cora hates you. And anyhow she's been kept home sick. So it's not her who's been saying anything against you."

"The Reverend Arnold again?"

"I think it might have started with Jackson. He blamed himself for Cora's fainting spell, because he shocked her. With some things he said about you."

Robert dug hard into the ground with his spade, his

shoulder rolling and bucking under his shirt. "So what does he have to say?"

"Well, I don't even want to repeat it." Violet rubbed at the beets like she was trying to remove every trace of dirt before they went into her basket. "He says he thinks you aren't natural . . . with the children. That he saw you leading Ali McBryde away with you somewhere when you hadn't any business to. And of course that you . . . that you came into town that morning. When Benjamin Dawson went missing."

Robert's chest swelled. He wasn't sure if he could laugh at that, but the bubble of laughter was there, pressing painfully into his ribs like a big, friendly dog.

"So it's Jackson Banks, is it? Of all the people to try to run me out of town, I wouldn't have pegged him for it."

"Of course it's all nonsense, I know. . . ." Violet trailed off. Her words fell down into the furrows they were digging and seeded there. "But then you know there's his mother, Evelyn. You . . . you avoided her, when she came looking for you. You kept running away from her. . . ."

Robert glanced at her, but she was still staring down at the earth gathering under her gloves.

"I told you why," he said, surprised. "I thought she wanted dreams of him. I didn't want to take advantage of her."

Violet nodded.

"Yes, it's nonsense," he agreed. They dug on in silence, yanking the tough, resistant tubers out of the ground and banking them like sandbags before a storm.

★ ★ ★

Tom and Toby Jenkins spied Jackson as soon as they drew up to the house. He was chopping wood, and he'd taken off his shirt and draped it in the grass. Even so his bare arms and neck were oily with sweat.

Toby jumped down from the wagon and hitched their horses at the fence. Tom was just quick enough to stop him from rushing at his friend.

"Keep your head," Tom told him. "We're just here to talk. And you can't go off half-cocked at a man wielding an ax."

Jackson straightened as they approached, raising his empty hand and wiping his brow with the back of his forearm. "It's the Jenkins men," he said. He smiled uncertainly. "Glad to see you. I've been wanting to ask after Cora. She feeling better?"

"You don't even say her name," Toby growled.

"How's that?"

Tom kept a hand on Toby's arm. "You've got some explaining to do, son. Cora told her mother everything."

Jackson's eyes shifted. "What do you mean?"

"She was pregnant," Toby spit. "You understand? She didn't faint from the heat at the fair. She was losing a baby—your baby."

"I'm so disappointed in you, Jackson." Tom stepped forward, putting himself between the two younger men. "How could you do that? How could you use our Cora that way?"

Jackson let the ax slip out of his hand and bite the ground. "I never touched her."

"Liar!" Toby lunged at him, pushed at his chest so hard that Jackson staggered back and almost fell.

"Stop it!" His father went after him, pulling Toby away before his fist could swing out. "You're always too quick to jump in. You must listen. Take time to think. Then decide."

They turned back to Jackson, who was righting himself by touching one hand to the top of the chopping block. "I think I know what's going on," he said.

"Yeah," said Toby. "You're calling my sister a liar."

"I'm not. But I think we all could guess, if Cora was in

the family way, who is most likely to be the father." He waited to see the answer in their faces. "After all, it's not me who's been walking her home from church, is it? Not me dancing with her or mooning with her in the dark right outside the prayer meeting. Just think about it for a minute. If he's got her under some kind of spell, some kind of magic, wouldn't she say anything to protect him?"

They looked less certain now. The anger that tightened their bodies gave and slackened.

Jackson saw his chance and made his low voice smooth and soothing. "Toby, c'mon, you know me. We've always been friends. You have to know I wouldn't do something like this." He glanced quickly at Tom. "Not when you stop and think about it."

"We did think about it," said Tom. "We thought at first it must be him, but when Cora talked to her mother, she was so insistent . . . of course we believed her." He looked at Toby. "I guess we forgot all about the way she's been acting. . . ."

"Yes, the way she's been acting," echoed Jackson. "You just have to ask yourselves, who does she really love? It's not me. It's him."

★ ★ ★

Robert sat on Violet's porch, taking the air and cracking walnuts. He pried the broken shells open with his thumbs and worked out the meat in pieces, popping them into his mouth. There was a bowl down on the boards beside his chair to catch the shells and bits of dark skin, so he wouldn't leave a mess on the freshly swept porch.

He was still chewing bitter grease when he noticed a small figure wobble into the sunlight down the road. He didn't look up again until it was close enough to hear, and then the skipping sound of small shoes against dirt raised up his smile like a sail. To his surprise, Ali turned in at Violet's gate and made his way past her carefully tended rose borders. He took the porch steps one at a time, hopping up with both feet.

"You're back," said Robert.

"Yup. I got my hands on some more money, and I'd sure like to buy another dream."

"Oh, yes? Another nightmare? You enjoy that last one?"

"Sure. Sure I did." Ali shifted his feet. "But it's not for a nightmare this time. I want a dream where I'm playing in the big leagues." He held up the baseball he carried.

"I see."

"I got it all worked out. I'm the star player, best batter they've got, and it's bottom of the ninth, bases loaded."

"I think I understand." Robert smiled, studying him. Had the boy's parents not warned him to stay away? Or had he ignored their warning? "But I don't know if I can help you. There've been some . . . complaints, about me. Your parents wouldn't like it. And I'm about to close up shop here, see."

"Oh." Ali began to throw his ball up toward the porch ceiling, playing catch with himself. "That's okay." He was rapidly blinking his eyes.

Robert looked up and down the street, but there was no one about. "I tell you what," he said. "I suppose it couldn't hurt to do just one more. Make my wagon a little bit lighter, eh? You wait here. I'll bring it out for you in two shakes."

"I'm sorry you're leaving. It takes me so long to save up enough money. . . . I woulda bought more."

Robert smiled again. He left Ali still playing with his ball, bouncing it off the pillars of the porch.

Ali threw the ball and caught it. He stepped back a few paces and tried to spin around while the ball was still in the air. He missed, ran to grab it before it rolled off the edge of the porch and into the bushes. By the time he scrambled up, he could see someone passing by in the street, a tall figure carrying a sack over his shoulder.

"Hey," Jackson called to him. He'd caught sight of Ali up there on the porch and stopped in the street. "Hey, aren't you Barto's kid brother?"

"Yeah. So?"

Jackson grinned. "So nothing. Why you waiting around out here? Taking piano lessons with old Violet?"

"Nah."

Behind Ali the front door opened and Robert stepped outside.

"Oh, it's you," said Jackson. He turned in to Violet's yard and approached them. "I'm surprised you haven't gone."

"Not just yet," said Robert. He eyed Jackson's bag. "You going on a trip?"

"What do you think you're doing, messing around with Barto's little brother?"

"Not a thing. We're in the middle of a business transaction."

"Business, huh?" He looked up at Ali. "That true? You come here looking to buy a dream?"

Ali said nothing. He held the baseball tight in his hands.

Jackson set his bag down on the ground and climbed the porch steps. He hunkered down in front of the boy. "Don't you know how dangerous that can be, hanging around with a strange man? Taking his potions?" When Ali still didn't answer, Jackson stood up. "You'd better run on home now. And don't come back here again."

Ali looked to Robert, who nodded slightly. As the boy

passed him, Robert went to slip the dream vial into his hand, but Jackson noticed and snatched it away. He threw it into the garden, where it struck a stone and shattered, weeping into the grass.

"Do you think that was necessary?" Robert asked.

At first it didn't seem as if Jackson would bother to answer. They watched Ali head back down the road, the white ball lofting up into the sky like a tiny hope trying to take flight.

"He shouldn't be hanging around near you. I don't even know what you think you're still doing here."

Robert looked into his face. "It was you, wasn't it? You started that talk. You've got them all thinking I . . . can't be trusted."

"That's right. Because you can't. You don't have any scruples. Taking advantage even of little kids, taking their money like that."

"I never took money for something I couldn't give. Ali came back because the first dream he bought satisfied him. That's how it works."

Jackson shook his head. "I don't believe it. I took one of your so-called dreams, and it didn't work at all. Just wasted my money."

"I don't remember ever selling you anything."

"I got it from Toby. He's been selling those dreams you mix him, all along. Probably charges more than you for his trouble, makes himself a nice profit." He descended the steps and shouldered the bag he had dropped.

"I didn't realize."

Jackson laughed. "You must have thought Toby was one lonely sucker."

"I never thought that."

Now Jackson turned to look up at him. "The truth is, all

this dream selling is just a cheat. A cheap trick. This whole thing with Cora was your fault. I had to do it. The dream Toby gave me didn't even work."

Robert drew in his breath. "But, Jackson . . . you can't expect a dream to change who you are."

Jackson tilted his head back, veiling his eyes. "And why not? Why can't I?"

Chapter 26

There were no customers in Jenkins's store when Evie entered.

"Cora, do you know what you've done?"

Cora glanced up from the ledger, over which her lips had been moving in unuttered efforts of addition. "Why, what do you mean?"

She looked into Evie's eyes and was surprised to see their dismay—and something else that might have been anger, sitting in behind it like stones.

"All these awful things being said about Robert Owens, and he was never anything but kind to you. You know he wasn't."

Cora sniffed. "I wouldn't exactly say he was kind, Mrs. Dawson. He was very hurtful to me."

Evie threw out her hands in exasperation. "Hurtful to you? Hurtful? Hurtful would have been to drag you away from your family and into a nomad life with him, scraping your way from town to town. He's too decent for that. And so you thank him by helping that stupid Jackson Banks spread stories about him."

Cora was not to be cowed. "My parents already think he might have been the one . . . might have been the father. It's just easier this way. Don't you see? He will be leaving soon,

but the rest of us have to stay here. We have to face the judgment of everyone around us. And I can't bear that."

"But no one else understands why you really fainted at
the fair. Because of Jackson all they can talk about is Robert
Owens and the children. The day he came into town." She
swallowed. "It's my son, Cora. My beautiful son they're gossiping about." The girl looked away from her. "I know this
man. I've come to know him better than anyone else, and
there is absolutely no way he would ever harm a child."

Cora became thoughtful. "How do you know him? Why
do you know him better than anyone else?"

Evie backed a step away from the counter. "It doesn't
matter," she said.

Cora's eyes narrowed unhappily. "Oh, I see. I understand
it now. And the reason he never liked me, never even looked
at me . . ."

She lowered her eyes and tapped her pencil against the
ledger. It drummed there faintly, like rain beginning on
the roof.

"I didn't mean to help Jackson tell lies," she said finally.
"But we don't know they *are* lies, do we? How can you be so
sure? We don't know what the dream peddler might be ca-
pable of. He's a stranger."

Evie shook her head. "Not this."

The bell over the door awoke with a jangle, and Robert
Owens came in. He pulled his hat off and held it in front of
himself.

"Miss Jenkins, Mrs. Dawson," he greeted them.

The conversation they'd had stretched out between them
like a pull of taffy while they stared at him. The taffy thread
hung in the air and swagged heavily. Robert looked at Cora
sadly.

"You shouldn't be here," she said.

"I'm getting ready to leave town," he told her. "And I need to buy some things for my journey."

The door to the back room opened, and Tom came in.

"Stay away from my daughter!" He took four long, fast strides and landed his fist at the corner of Robert's mouth. Robert fell back against the far shelves, and he looked at Cora.

"What did you say to him?"

"You don't talk to her," said Tom, putting his body between Robert and the counter. "You aren't ever going to speak another word to her again. You are not going to look at her. You are going to turn around and leave this store."

As Robert began to obey, Tom muttered, "Jackson was right about you all along."

"So it's that again." Robert touched his face. "Poor Jackson," he said under his breath.

"I want you out of this town," said Tom. "And don't ever come back."

Evie followed Robert out of the store.

They stood in the street. Tenderly she took his hand away from his face and saw the blood creeping down from his lip.

"It wasn't me," he said. She reached into his chest pocket, pulled out his handkerchief, and pressed it to his mouth.

"I know it wasn't." He pulled the handkerchief down, and she searched his face. "But how can we ever prove you aren't responsible?"

For a while he stood turning the bloodstained cloth over in his hands, as if he were trying to figure out what it was.

"It doesn't matter," he told her. "Because I am."

★ ★ ★

Though he had known her for many months now, Robert had never been out to Evie's farmhouse. He had some vague

idea of where it was from Violet's description and walked
there for the first time to tell her good-bye.

George had taken a load of hay out to sell, and Evie was
in the kitchen canning. She had been canning all summer
since the berries had started ripening, and her fingertips were
always stained a claret color. Now the tomatoes were ready,
and she was canning them and making ketchup and pickles.
Steam hovered over her stove like a specter, but today she
hardly noticed it in the gluey heat. Evie didn't think you
could call what you did in this kind of air breathing. It simply
seeped into your weighted lungs and trickled back out again,
like a tide.

Through the back window, she saw him coming over the
fields. There wasn't time to wash or change, only for wiping
her hands on her apron and drawing the back of one across
her forehead without thinking, dragging the sweat. When
she stepped outdoors, it was with the feeling that something
painted inside her was weathering, flaking away. He was not
supposed to come to her home, ever. She had never told
George about him. Telling George would have meant hurting him, explaining about her own dreams.

She didn't know if George ever met Ben in his dreams.
Maybe if he did and woke to find him gone again, he'd become used to it. She could imagine George that way, suffering
the choked moment of waking for the sake of the dream that
came before. But she never asked him; they never spoke of it.
And for some reason she knew George hated Robert Owens,
even though he never said a bad word about him until Cora.
In fact, all he ever had to say of Robert was how he had tried
to help, tried to help find Benny and how that was a kind
thing, but even so she knew. And suddenly she realized it was
not for George's sake or the sake of the lie that she didn't like
seeing Robert coming across the fields. She was damp and

limp from the sweaty canning work and the heat, wearing her dirty apron. She didn't want him seeing her like this, and all at once she understood why George hated him. She almost laughed at how she hadn't seen it.

"Hello," he said when he reached the bottom of her porch steps. "I've come to say good-bye." And he stood sheepishly listening over what he had just said. She saw his cart with all his things waiting down by the road like a patient mule.

"I'm sorry you have to go," she told him.

Self-consciously she wiped at the back of her neck. She knew that the curls around her temples would be wild and wiry with drying sweat. She wished she would stop thinking about her looks, when this moment would be over so quickly.

"I always knew you would leave, we all understood that. But I'm sorry it's like this. I'm sorry . . . for Cora, for all of it. No one here will ever know you were a good man. How good you were to me. They'll only blame you."

"It doesn't matter. I told you once, it's always like this. This is the life I have chosen. If you remember me the way that you knew me, it's more than I deserve."

She looked out across the farms, the striping greens of fields that grew over and over again in the endless distance, the darker speckle of hungry animals grazing away the forever.

"Where will you go?"

"It doesn't matter. East. Maybe after this winter I'll go south, where it doesn't get so cold."

"Hard to imagine the cold coming again, isn't it? In this heat?"

He smiled at her, and she wondered how he could manage to crinkle the corners of his eyes like that and still look so unhappy.

"Oh!" he said, remembering something. He pulled his canvas bag off his shoulder and pulled out a large flask.

"I know you never wanted this much of it," he said, "but maybe if you could find somewhere to stash it . . . I was worried about . . . how you would manage, now. Without my medicine. I brought you some that should last a long while, if you want it."

She bit her lip. "It's very kind of you. But I'll learn to get by without it. I haven't dreamed in so long I think I've forgotten how. Maybe it would be better for me. To remember."

He nodded and put the flask back into the twilight of his bag.

"I have your book," she said. "I can run in and get it for you."

He shifted the strap of the bag back onto his shoulder. "Did you like it?"

She nodded shyly.

"Why don't you keep it, then. Or you can give it back to Violet. I borrowed it off her shelf."

He looked away, and she knew he'd been the one who dog-eared the page.

She came down to the bottom step so they were eye to eye. Telling herself it was silly to hesitate—it was not as if she had never touched him before—she reached down and picked up one of his hands with her pink-stained ones and held it.

"I need you to know . . . that I never believed them. I know you couldn't have hurt him. And if anyone asked me how I can know that, how I can be sure, I guess I wouldn't have an answer. It's just . . ." She shrugged. "I may as well not believe in God, if I don't believe in you."

He watched her eyes mirror over with tears. He would have liked to ask her to come with him, could hear himself asking it in his mind. She could leave behind this place where her only child had died. Leave behind this life and forget, the way people lost the last echoes of their dreams when they woke and let them slip, ebbing back toward night. He did not ask her out loud because he knew what the answer would be, but he thought it out clearly until she let go of his hand.

"It's all right," he told her. "I'll start again. I always start again."

She breathed in. "Tell me how you do that."

He put his arms around her and held on to her. While they stood there together, he hoped his breath might go all the way through her and come back into him, changed.

"No." He spoke quietly into her ear, so low it became her own voice keening inside her head. "Never, Evie. I don't want you to be like me."

Chapter 27

Softly Benjamin pulled the door closed behind him. Outside, the world was deepest blue, as he always imagined the bottom of the sea. The snow had grown a glass skin of ice in the night, and it cracked under his boots and sometimes gave way. Going through the woods to the bay was slow, and the little boy held his eyes on the moon as if his gaze would keep it from setting. The listless moon knew nothing of hurry; it lingered low, an impassive face, indifferent to Benjamin's progress. Small barbed branches held out by trees caught at the brown coat here and there but failed to hold him back. He emerged from the woods, and the moon was still, jeweling before him. He needed to go even closer. The snowcap dipped down and became the ice of the bay, but he didn't hesitate to walk out upon it as the moon drew him on. Farther out over the frozen tide he went, until even his own house had been swept away by the trees behind him. He stood in triumph, raising his hands into the cold.

The ice tore.

The moon looked on silently as the boy slipped down into a different blue and was gone. And lazily the moon became the sun, blazing the ice across the bay with a heatless light.

Chapter 28

For a few nights after she stopped taking Robert's medicine, Evie waited nervously for a dream. She expected Ben to visit her, and she wondered what age he would be. Sleep came back to her only slowly, like a friend she had wronged. At first she wasn't sure she could dream anymore, as she was waking in the mornings and not remembering anything from the night. Then, on the fourth night, she did have a dream, but it wasn't Ben who came.

Robert is once again standing in front of her, just outside her door as he had been to say good-bye, but also in the orchard where she remembers him. As soon as she takes his hand and walks out with him into the orchard trees, the house behind collapses soundlessly, and she knows without needing to turn and look that it has disappeared into a fold of time, like a castle of sand washed away. Hand in hand with Robert, she walks through the trees, and the apples gleam like polished stone, and some of them fall to the ground with a here-and-there thump. It is later in the season than when she last saw him, and the appled ground sends up a sweet rotting smell, and the chill of coming winter trots under the fitful breeze like a dog.

They emerge from the orchard at the edge of the water,

where autumn has been advancing. Robert helps her silently into a canoe and paddles her out on the bay, dipping his oar on both sides of the boat in turn while she sits, queenlike and idle. They float upon the still water for a long time, and Evie wants to ask him where they are going, but then she spies a long, shallow island coming into view, one she had not known was there. The island is glimmering yellow, covered in molting maple trees all standing in the reflecting pools of their own fallen leaves.

Robert beaches the canoe at an angle on the shore, and Evie wobbles, arms out at her sides, climbing over the seat until he takes her hand and helps her up onto the sand. The beach is stunted, chiseled from the grassy bank, and they climb up over the stones into the gold. It is colder here, and Evie has not dressed warmly enough, but Robert seems to feel nothing. His skin is smooth where hers is goosefleshed. Wondering what they are here to do, she sees her family, June and Harold, George, and her mother and father, pulling long fallen branches out of the woods and leaning them into a shelter, piling them quickly against the chill.

When George catches sight of her, he stops to wave, then puts his hand back to his work. She wonders, how did they know that her house disappeared? She wonders if all the other houses in town have collapsed, if anyone else is out here or only her loved ones. She turns to ask Robert her questions, but he is no longer beside her, and she spins around to where they left the boat. It's still there, wedged in the wet sand like the curved handle of the knife that carved out this beach. She looks back at the shelter builders, but no, he is not with them. On the surface of the bay, the sun scrapes up the little rippling waves, and in its distant tract of silver she discerns now a dark, round shape, floating along like a lost ball. And she recognizes Robert, that he's left them the boat and is swimming away.

The bay is wide, and she doesn't know if he can swim to the other shore or if he intends to drown. His head is swarmed by the fuzz of light, and then the light engulfs the air around it and it flickers out, disappears. She can't tell if it was only a trick of the blinding sun, or if he went under.

Chapter 29

Harvest time was past now, and the field was shorn of its beauty. When the air shimmered above it, this was like the haunting of the long, gold blanket of movement that had once been there. The leaves had not yet begun to turn, but they shook in the breeze, they quaked on the branches because the colder winds were coming, and they knew the time was approaching when they would lose their hold and fall.

Evie sat knitting a new sweater for George and thought about Robert as he drifted away from town, down the road and more roads, going farther away from them until he was no more than a speck, a mote of a memory tumbling out there in the rest of the world. She thought afterward that must have been the reason she saw it, that shadow, flickering in the distance at the farthest edge of the field. At first it was just a blankness wavering across the bottom of the trees, blotting out the trunks one at a time, skittering back and forth. Then she began to see more, arms lifting from the shadow's sides. She was watching it through her window handprint, flitting there in the spaces between the smudge fingers.

She set the soft, curly knitting aside and stood up to look. Many times before this, she had crouched and held her own hand up before the ghost one and come very close without touching it. She would marvel at its persistence, as if it lay no longer on the surface but had traveled inward like crazing, now part of the glass. She learned how grease on glass could stay, the lines of a palm could be perfectly marked there now and preserved, if he had not let his hand slip down the way he had.

This time she didn't think of these things, because she was looking beyond the handprint, watching the figure blink and dance along the edge of the trees. She stepped outside and walked down off the porch, crossing the field. The closer she came to the shadow, the faster it danced, and it was Peter Pan just on the other side of the veil, the other side of having a family. Then he turned his face toward her so he was looking over his skinny boy shoulder, as slight and twisting as a paper doll. And of course it was not Peter Pan, or a shadow, but her son. His smile was a beckoning for her to play with him, and so she did, picking up her skirts and running, too, running across the ground. She could see that Ben had no weight, and the light went almost through him as it would through a leaf held up to the sun, translucence glowing between the thicker veins. When their bodies had raced until there was no more, they tumbled onto the grass and let their chests heave up to the sky and fall, pumping the smell of the earth into themselves and out again, hard like laughter. It seemed such a short time until Ben stood up, brushed himself off while the chaff snowed down around her, and smiled at Evie his gap-toothed smile, then wandered off toward the woods.

She sat up quickly on one elbow, knowing she was not supposed to follow.

"Good-bye, Benny," she called. "Take care! Good-bye!"

He half turned over his shoulder and waved one hand carelessly, as he'd done so many times before. "Bye, Mummy."

And off he went to meet his boyish adventures in the forest.

Acknowledgments

Thank you to L. M. Montgomery, the author whose books accompanied me through adolescence and beyond. If I hadn't been so fascinated by her heroine, Emily Starr, and the mysterious manuscript she burned, this book would not exist.

Thank you to my wonderful agent, Bridget Smith, for pulling me out of your slush pile and changing everything. It took a long time to find you, but it was well worth the wait. Also, heartfelt thanks to my editor at Penguin, Shannon Kelly, whose insights and support helped me make this book better than I ever thought possible. And to all those at Penguin whose hard work brought *The Dream Peddler* to light, thank you.

I would also like to acknowledge Carrie A. Meyer, whose *Days on the Family Farm* became my primary source for information on early twentieth-century farm life in America, and Robert L. Van de Castle, whose *Our Dreaming Mind* taught me everything I needed to know about dreams throughout history.

In addition to the professionals, I've been lucky to have the support of many friends and family members. I'm so thankful to Patty Kline-Capaldo, Rae Theodore, and all the members of the Just Write group out in Collegeville, Pennsylvania. It vas just after I joined up with you that I started working in earnest to finish *The Dream Peddler,* and your companionship as readers and writers was invaluable to me. To everyone who generously read through early drafts for me, please know how much I appreciate you taking the time, and all your thoughtful comments.

To my mother, who has read this book more times than I can count, thank you for loving it in every incarnation. You have been my sounding board and cheering section every step of the way, and that has meant the world to me.

Thank you, Nate and Rachel, for being my young dreamers, now and forever the best things I have ever made. And Keith, I once joked with you that your support had provided me with "a room of my own." Thank you. This book is what came out of that room.

A PENGUIN READERS GUIDE TO

THE DREAM PEDDLER

Martine Fournier Watson

An Introduction to
The Dream Peddler

Traveling salesmen like Robert Owens have passed through Evie Dawson's town before, but none of them offered anything like what he has to sell: dreams, made to order, with satisfaction guaranteed. Soon after he arrives, the community is rocked by the disappearance of Evie's young son. The townspeople, shaken by tragedy and captivated by Robert's subversive magic, begin to experiment with his dreams. And Evie, devastated by her pain, turns to Robert for a comfort only he can sell her.

This story is about magic—the magic that Robert Owens captures in a bottle and sells to his customers, and the magic of the unexpected, of facing one's fears and unspoken desires head-on. But it's also about grief, and the different ways we have of reconciling the unspeakable things: the loss of a child, the dissolution of a family, the end of innocence. It's about a man who makes a living of escaping his own life and allowing others to do the same, and about how we reckon with the longings we keep secret. It's about who we are when we lose the things by which we define ourselves.

The Dream Peddler is a richly imagined, achingly heartfelt debut novel from writer Martine Fournier Watson that captivates from the first sentence with a bold, beautiful lyricism. Her prose dances, as delightful and unexpected as the mysterious salesman who wanders into a small town on the first page of chapter one and shakes an entire community out of its stupor.

A Conversation with
Martine Fournier Watson

The Dream Peddler *is your debut novel. What was the writing process like for a first-time author?*

I'm sure the process is different for everyone, but in my case the dominant feelings were of joy and discovery. I had written one terrible book in my twenties, just to see if I could buckle down long enough to produce a whole book, and I'd set that aside.

Almost fifteen years passed before I attempted another book project. Was I older and wiser? Perhaps. But I still approached writing with an optimistic belief that my experiments would magically turn into a coherent story. In other words, I'm a hopeless pantser.

I'm also not a particularly structured writer. At the time, I had just joined a writing group near our home in Pennsylvania, so I did have that weekly boost to look forward to and to keep me on track. For the most part, though, I just let the novel work its way through me in fits and starts, and in less than a year, it was done.

What inspired The Dream Peddler? *How did the idea come to you?*

I grew up on the stories of L. M. Montgomery, and have read and reread the adventures of her beloved Anne of Green Gables many times. But Montgomery's lesser-known heroine, Emily of New Moon, was really my favorite. So I hope dear old Lucy Maud will forgive me for stealing her idea.

Emily has plans to be a writer, and in the third installment of Montgomery's trilogy, reference is made to Emily's very first novel, a book called *A Seller of Dreams*. However, this book is never published. After a few rejections, Emily gives the book to a trusted friend to read, and because he is jealous of the book, he tells her it's not good enough. Heartbroken, Emily burns it.

For some reason, this destroyed book haunted my imagination. The reader is never given any insight as to what it may have been about, except that it was some kind of contemporary fairy tale. It was a book I always wanted to write myself, if only to satisfy my own curiosity about what shape such a story might take. I often wonder what Montgomery would have made of my efforts!

When you began writing the novel, did you always know how it was going to end? Were there any moments in the story that surprised you as you came to them?

I started my book with only a few characters and a vague idea of how it would end. As I went along I added more characters, and their desires really drove my plot. I was continually surprised by the people I invented and their choices. In the same way that I don't plot before I start writing, I also don't sit down and figure out who my characters are. Most of the fun for me comes from ing out more and more about them as I get deeper into the ook.

For example, I had no idea when I began that Jackson was gay. I created Jackson as Christina's first love interest, an interest that I believed would be misguided. As I painted him the kind of man I thought an inexperienced young woman might like—confident, funny, popular—I noticed his flirting was over the top. Outrageous, really, considering its frequency and scope. It didn't seem to have any particular target. His sexuality came to me in a flash of realization. It was the perfect explanation for his behavior—he was trying too hard. This realization served a second purpose, as well, because I did know from the outset that many of the townspeople would have to turn against Robert to drive him out. Robert being privy to Jackson's secret and Jackson's resultant panic also gave me the dream peddler's first enemy.

I didn't plan Cora's pregnancy, either. It simply grew out of her own feelings, her longing for romance, love, and adventure. I was taking a walk one day, thinking about my characters, and the question popped into my head: what if Cora became pregnant? I didn't even know who the father was yet, or that she would offer the baby to Evie. It's funny how these moments that are absolutely pivotal to the story were just a result of my musing and one thing leading to another.

You are a mother of two children yourself. How did your own experience with motherhood inform the writing of the mothers and mothers-to-be in the book—Evie, Rose, June, Cora?

This is definitely one reason why I don't think I could have written this book when I was younger. I read somewhere that authors often use their writing to explore what terrifies them, and I think there's no doubt I was doing that here. As soon as I had my son, I could imagine no worse fate than to lose him, and writing this book allowed me to explore that without actually experiencing it. Ben is nine years old in the book because that was my son's age when I began writing. In some ways I modeled him after my own children, but I gave him more independence because of his era and situation.

Beyond that, though, I found that writing motherhood is just like writing any other aspect of a character—they can't all be

reflections of my own beliefs and experiences. So that was fun, t
explore the ways that motherhood looks different for these
different characters: June being warm, affectionate, and
overbearing, for instance, while Rose is far more lenient and
absent-minded, though just as loving in her own way.

And of course, I didn't think about this until I considered this
question, but Evie and Cora also make quite a contrast in terms of
pregnancy—one trying unsuccessfully to conceive for so many
years, the other finding herself pregnant unexpectedly and under
disastrous circumstances. I honestly have no experience of either,
so there, too, all I could do was imagine.

*Robert is a mysterious character who deliberately keeps his own
background opaque for much of the novel. Was it difficult to write a
story in which one of the central characters has so many secrets?*

I think I might have been too inexperienced or unselfconscious
about that to find it difficult. Although I've always been an avid
reader, I was really flying blind in terms of novel craft. I was pretty
much learning about things like characterization, story structure,
and pacing as I went along. I think that over many years of
reading, I developed an instinct for the kind of details that help
bring a character to life for a reader, and the trick with Robert was
to give enough superficial details for the reader to have a strong
sense of him, while still holding back the substance of who he is.

In some ways Robert was different for me than the other
characters because I did know his backstory very soon after I
began writing. I was no more than a few chapters in when I
jumped ahead to write the scene where Robert describes to Evie
how he burned down his home. I wrote it in one sitting, one of
those rare times when a scene feels like it arrives fully formed, and
all I have to do is transcribe it. I hardly made any changes to that
dialogue, either, when it came time to edit. So that conversation
was like a touchstone for writing the rest of the book. I understood
why Robert had chosen to live a solitary, nomadic life, and I
allowed that to inform everything he does. My goal was for the
reader to either find him suspicious because of this, or, like Evie, to
trust him without really knowing why.

I also think it helped to have such a large cast of supporting
characters. Robert isn't in every scene, not even close. By letting

reader deep into the hearts of the other characters, I could end far more time exploring how Robert impacts their lives than the other way around.

What was your favorite part of writing this book? What was the most difficult part?

It's so hard to choose a favorite part—there are always certain scenes and characters that provide no end of pleasure, and I had many. Ali was definitely one of my favorite characters to write, and I'm glad his role was expanded a little as I tackled the major edits. I also truly loved writing the dream sequences. There was something about the immediacy of them, the freedom of exploration they allowed, that was really compelling to write. They were also an incredibly useful tool for exploring the subconscious minds of the characters.

The most difficult scene was actually the one I thought would be easiest. (I'd love to take a poll some time to find out how many other authors have experienced that!) I had a lot of trouble with the scene in which Ben's body is discovered. After torturing my characters for so long, I was anxious to get to it, and because it was momentous and important, I somehow thought the words would flow. What a surprise I got! I agonized over every detail, revisiting it so many times I lost count. Maybe this was because the scene bears such a heavy burden—I had to get it right.

Do you have many dreams yourself? Have you ever had a dream that was particularly meaningful or inspirational? How have your own experiences with dreams informed the dreams of your characters?

I think I must be one of the world's most content people, because my dreams tend to be utterly mundane. I dream that I'm shopping at the grocery store or putting on makeup. I do have a couple of recurring stress dreams. I did a lot of theatre when I was growing up, and if I'm worried about anything I'll dream that I have a role in a play and it's time to go on stage but I haven't learned the lines. Either that, or I'm responsible for getting someone, usually my mother, to a flight on time, but we're hopelessly behind and it's all my fault. Pretty typical stuff. Maybe that's partly why I had so much fun with the dreams in this book.

Many years ago, I had a nightmare about my son dying. He was still a baby, barely crawling, but I dreamed he somehow climbed out of an open window on the second story of our new house and fell to his death. In the dream, I looked out of the window and saw him on the ground below. To this day, I'm certain the anguish I felt was as keen as it would have been in real life, except I was lucky and woke up. I was soaked in tears. It's the only glimpse I've ever had into Evie's loss.

What message or feeling do you most hope readers take away from The Dream Peddler?

As far as feeling goes, I hope people take away a sense that their lives are full of magic. I set this book early in the twentieth century because it was a time when American farming was in its heyday, and when traveling peddlers selling mysterious potions and snake oil were fairly common. But it also happens to be right on the cusp of Freud and Jung and the advent of psychoanalysis, when dreaming would suddenly be demystified once and for all. No more divine inspiration, no more magic. One of the things I wanted this book to be was a return to a more mystical time, when people weren't certain where dreams originated and couldn't be as quick to dismiss them as we are. And in bringing magic to the town, Robert serves as a reminder of the magic that was always there.

I didn't intend to communicate any particular message, either, but realized after I had finished that certain moments in the book sit very close to my heart. When Robert puts his hand on Jackson's chest and tells him that all of life's adventures really take place there, that's me talking. I believe in that. Maybe because I've always been a sucker for good books, because my interior life and fantasies are so vivid and fulfilling, I've never really thought that it matters whether a person spends their time skydiving or lying in a hammock. Both experiences can be equally enriching.

QUESTIONS FOR DISCUSSION

1. Do you think Robert's magic is real, or only a con? How about what Robert himself believes? Does it matter?

2. What was your reaction to Cora offering her baby to Evie? Do you think it could have worked or made either of them happy? How did you feel when Evie refused? What do you think you would have done in her shoes?

3. Robert's character could be described as an archetypal wanderer or scapegoat. Does he remind you of any other fictional or historical outsiders who were treated as scapegoats? What about in your own experience? How does your understanding of that dynamic impact your reading of the book?

4. The role dreams can play in a person's life is central to this book. Have you ever had a dream that pointed you in a certain direction or revealed a truth you hadn't previously realized? Do you agree with Robert's claim that a dream can never tell us something we don't already know?

5. The dream peddler spends his life as an interloper, an outsider, because he never stays in one place. Yet some of the other characters seem like outsiders in a place they have lived their whole life. Which characters do you think experience this isolation? Is it always obvious? Which characters enjoy that status, and which don't?

6. It seems that much of what drives Robert's friendship with Evie is his desire to help her. How well do you think he fares with this? In what ways does he help or hinder her?

7. At the end of the book, Robert willingly shoulders the blame for Cora's pregnancy. Why do you suppose he does this? Would you agree that he is responsible in any way?

8. Robert is drawn to Evie immediately upon seeing her, and the relationship they form drives him to share more of himself and become more personally involved in the town than he has allowed himself in the past, something that you could say backfires on him. Why do you think he was so interested in Evie? Did their friendship change him? Will his role in the next town he visits be different as a result?